PRAISE FOR
SOON TO BE A MAJOR MOTION PICTURE

"A clever, zany page-turner." – *The Ottawa Citizen*

"Enjoyable and compelling. . . . a sort of urban fairy tale undercut by an obligatory dose of knowing irony."
– *The Globe and Mail*

"It is such a relief to read a book like *Soon To Be a Major Motion Picture*. . . . [It] succeeds on its execution, on the way it rolls apparently unconnected observations on, say, Anne Murray, into the goal of the plot; on the way it easily works in the author's generational preoccupations without the usual puerile fanfare; the way the author generally lets images, references, character insights lightly fall, leaving the reader to pick them up or not as they please."
– *The Toronto Star*

". . . it's not only awfully entertaining, it has immensely likable characters." – *Financial Post*

". . . an amusing novel. . . it's light and and frothy, but pretty well written and a fun read. And the best part is, you get to play Spot the Real-life Toronto TV Luminaries."
– *Montreal Gazette*

"Fast-paced and funny, never stupid or limp
– a thoroughly good patio read." – *Xtra!*

"Funny and accurate." – *FAB Toronto*

SOON TO BE A MAJOR MOTION PICTURE

A NOVEL BY WARREN DUNFORD

The Riverbank Press

Cover and text design: John Terauds

Canadian Cataloguing in Publication Data

Dunford, Warren, 1963-
    Soon to be a major motion picture

ISBN 1-896332-06-4

I. Title.

PS8557.U5388S66 1998   C813' .54   C97-932822-5
PR9199.3.D9868S66 1998

First published by
The Riverbank Press
308 Berkeley Street
Toronto, Ontario, Canada M5A 2X5

10 9 8 7 6 5 4 3
Printed and bound in Canada by Métrolitho

For Jack Corcoran,
who was always the most glamorous

So many people have been helpful and encouraging during the long process of writing this novel and bringing it to publication. Among them: Bruce Appleby, Debrann Barr, Attila Berki, Joanne Bigham, Rob Bowman, Daniel Brooks, Charlotte à Campo, Eve Cantor, Eliza Clark, Karen Cumming, Robert Daley, Lloyd Davis, Paula Devitt, Dino Dilio, Damon D'Oliveira, Lee Doran, The Duckworths, Larry Feinberg, John Firth, Stuart Fleming, Michael Gardner, Mark David Gerson, Andre Goh, Lori Greenberg, Martha Hale, Peter Kazaras, Elizabeth Kerr, Susan Kerr, Jeff Kirby, Mark Krayenhoff, Harry Lewis, Karen Lim, Adrienne Magnin, Lynn Harrison McLachlan, Jeff Morgan, Ira Mulasi, Janis Orenstein, Teresa Pagnutti, Suzanne Pope, Don Pyle, Susan Lynn Reynolds, Victoria Ridout, Susan Robertson, Brian E. Scott, Joey Shulman, Anya Seerveld, Pamela Sinha, Loreen Teoli, John Terauds, Shelley Town, Trudie Town, Liza Watson, Joan Williams — and my parents, Rita and Gerald Dunford. Thank you.

We knew that
if we were famous,
if we were glamorous,
we could say,
We are artists, and we would be.
We did and we are.
We are famous, glamorous artists.

— from General Idea's "Glamour" Manifesto (1975)

She's thirty-five minutes late and for the past hour I've been pacing the fifteen feet between my bathroom and the window, repeating like a mantra: "This place is so pathetic, this place is so pathetic."

She's going to take one look at my apartment and decide not to hire me. She'll never believe anybody this impoverished could possibly have any talent.

Normally I wouldn't allow a prospective employer to see where I live. I try to mislead them into thinking I'm already successful by meeting in the lobby of a luxury hotel. You might have to pay five dollars for a coffee, but it's a bargain when you consider how it inflates your image.

I stuck my head out the window to see if I could spot her arriving at the door downstairs. I looked back and forth, up and down Bloor Street. Block after block of three-storey buildings. Plain brick fronts with shops on the main floor and apartments up above.

I examined the people meandering along the sidewalk. This stretch of Bloor is all modern beatniks and health-food junkies, students and panhandlers. I couldn't see anybody who looked like a movie producer. Not that I'd know what a real one actually looks like.

Watching TV would really help right now. It's the only thing that can ever really calm me down. But I'm not giving in to my addiction. Instead, I'm playing the soundtrack from *The Gay Divorcée* with Fred Astaire and Ginger Rogers. I'm trying to create an atmosphere that's cheerful and relaxed, bright and sophisticated. But how sophisticated can you be when you live in a one-room apartment that's a two-storey climb above a Hungarian schnitzel house?

To prepare for this occasion, I cleaned frenetically for three hours – which is hard to fathom, considering that my entire living space is probably smaller than her walk-in closet. Even so, there's nothing I can do about the giant warps in the hardwood floor. And spraying Eternity cologne everywhere hasn't been able to overpower the smell of burnt cabbage and stale frying oil that constantly seeps into my bathroom from the restaurant downstairs. She's going to think I'm trying to cover a particularly pungent form of body odour.

To look my best, I meticulously ironed every wrinkle from my most flattering shirt – black and baggy enough to hide the fact that I have the physique of a praying mantis.

Anyway, I do find it soothing to sit here at the computer and type out my anxiety. When she arrives, she'll see I've been working. Like a real professional writer. Which I am, I have to keep reminding myself.

Maybe she'll be charmed by my bohemian lifestyle. She'll realize how desperately I need the $18,000. Which is practically my entire income from last year.

There's the phone.

She's calling to cancel.

It turned out to be my friend Ingrid Iversen.

I answered the phone with "Hello, Mitchell Draper speaking," which is how I always answer to give myself an air of professional credibility.

"Did you get the job?" (Ing and I call each other so often we've stopped bothering with hellos.)

"She's not even here yet."

"Do you want me to hang up or do you need some distraction?"

"Distract me, please. I'm terrible in situations like this. Any trace of self-worth just flies out the window."

"Once she reads your work, she'll probably give you the job right on the spot."

"I just can't afford to fuck up another opportunity. So hurry up and start distracting me. Has anything happened at the store?"

"Sidney Poitier came in," she said lightly.

"And I missed him," I said with exaggerated sorrow.

"I didn't want to call you in case she was there already."

"Did he ask about me? Did he say, 'Where's that tall skinny fellow with the sex appeal of a young Bruce Dern?'"

"We were too overwhelmed by passion. He asked me to marry him and then he took me in the back room and ravished me."

"Did you at least ask him his real name this time?"

"I couldn't!" she said. "I just clam up whenever I see him."

"Lust really does destroy communication."

This very handsome man started frequenting The Daily Grind a month ago. We don't know his true identity, but he looks just like Sidney Poitier in his prime.

"So what was he wearing?"

"Taupe linen blazer. Black mockneck. I think he'd just had a haircut. He was carrying *The Financial Post*."

"I bet he's rich. What did he order?"

"The usual. Skim-milk cappuccino with cinnamon. Pumpernickel bagel, no butter."

"He even has the perfect diet."

We don't know whether Sidney is straight or gay, but the mystery just gives us more room to fantasize. And we both need fantasies desperately. It's been six months since Ingrid's last date, and nine months since mine.

"The distraction's wearing off," I said. "What am I going to do about this meeting? What if she doesn't show up?"

"Can't you call and ask where she is?"

"She didn't give me her number. I looked her up in the phone book, but there's no listing under Carmen Denver."

"Maybe she's related to John Denver."

"Or Bob Denver from *Gilligan's Island*."

"Maybe she's being late on purpose. That's what you always hear about movie producers – they're always on some kind of power trip."

"Why do I even want to get into this business?"

"She'll love you, Mitchell. I have to go – a customer just came in. But you're going to be great."

And she hung up.

Well.

That was that.

I never thought I'd have time to type out the whole earth-shaking dialogue before she showed up.

She is now an hour and five minutes late.

I should just pretend not to be home.

But remember the $18,000.

She didn't mention the $18,000 figure herself, but when I described the job to my friend Ramir – who's an actor and the closest thing I know to a film business insider – he told me the official fee for the first draft of a screenplay is $36,000, but that as non-union writer, I should ask for half.

Actually this woman didn't tell me much of anything when she called yesterday.

I answered the phone with my standard "Hello, Mitchell Draper speaking," and I heard paper shuffling at the other end of the line.

A throaty streetwise voice said, "I'm looking for Mitchell Draper."

"This is him," I said, rolling my eyes, certain I was about to be offered a newspaper subscription.

"I found your name in the Toronto Screenwriters' Guide."

"Really?" I said, genuinely surprised.

It had been a whole year since I'd paid $75 for the synopsis of my screenplay to appear in that book. I'd figured the whole thing was a scam. I thought the book had never left the publisher's basement.

"I'm calling because I need a screenplay."

"The script that's in the guide is still available, if you're interested."

"No, I've got my own story. I just need a writer to flesh the whole thing out."

"Fleshing things out is my specialty," I said, realizing I sounded way too perky. This could be my Big Break. The road to Hollywood. On top of that, it meant money. Salvation from a return to office temping.

But I couldn't afford to sound too interested. I needed professional cool. "Of course, my schedule's impossible these days. But I might be able to manage. What kind of movie is it?"

"A thriller. Very dramatic, edge-of-your-seat. I can't go into details at the moment, but it'll be very controversial, very hot. I'm going into production in September. So I need somebody who can start right away."

"I might be able to rearrange a few other jobs."

That's when she said she wanted to meet at my apartment.

"The bar at the Intercontinental is always nice," I said.

"Privacy is important to me, Mitchell. It's better if we meet at your place."

"How about tea at the King Edward?"

Finally I was forced into admitting my address. She said her name was Carmen Denver and that she'd be here at three-thirty.

And now it's four-forty-five.

Of course, the biggest question is: Why would she call me in the first place? There are dozens of experienced screenwriters in Toronto. Practically everybody I meet is writing a screenplay.

But it really would be amazing if this worked out.

Two years ago I made the decision to quit my full-time job and focus entirely on my writing career. Now I work three-week stints as an office temp to make money, then I take two weeks off so I can write. Back and forth. At least until I get some kind of break.

There's actually a ton of TV and film work in Toronto. Lots of potential employment. Big-budget Hollywood movies, miniseries, cult TV shows for American cable stations. Plus the occasional Canadian art film. In fact, Toronto is the third-largest production centre in North America. Unfortunately, that also makes it the third-largest centre for wanna-be screenwriters.

Oh God, there's the door buzzer. She's here.

Please just don't let me screw this one up.

☆

She just left.

And, although I'm not quite sure why, I think it went okay.

As soon as I pressed the button to unlock the door downstairs, I rushed out onto the landing I share with the much bigger apartment in back. Rushing out on the landing is my technique for diverting people's attention while they climb the stairs, so they don't notice the wallpaper – metallic gold covered with red velvet cupids.

I called down the two flights in my friendliest fashion, "You must be Carmen!"

"Uh-huh," she huffed. Every footstep was a heavy clunk.

I could see her silhouette in the shadows. Her figure was wide and stocky. She was glancing from side to side, obviously wary of all the angels pointing arrows.

"Fun pattern, isn't it? It always reminds me of a seventies' hair salon. Some place with a name like Mister Tony's."

"Uh-huh."

"I'm Mitchell," I said, all hyper and cheerful. I reached out to shake her sweat-dampened palm.

"You should get a place with an elevator," she said.

"I'm still begging my landlord for hot water."

She didn't smile.

Her face was full and pale and she had serious, scrunched-down eyebrows. Rosie O'Donnell with a mass of curly dark hair. She was wearing an oversized black jacket and big gold hoop earrings. Maybe she was in her early forties, but she reminded me of one of those tough Italian teenagers you see coming out of Catholic private schools.

"I need something to drink," she said in her gravelly Brooklynesque voice.

"I've got a pot of coffee ready."

"It's too warm out for coffee. I feel like iced tea."

For a moment I stood frozen, terrified that I would lose this job because of a beverage.

"How about Diet Coke?"

"All right. But if this works out, Mitchell, I always have to have iced tea. From real tea bags, like they make in the States. You got that? Everybody in Canada uses a mix. It drives me crazy every time."

I nodded – I practically saluted – and started serving my potential dominatrix.

"Just have a seat over there," I said, pointing to the wing chair I'd found in someone's garbage and covered with a sheet of black canvas. Right in front of the chair, on my Fabulous Fifties coffee table, I'd strategically placed my screenplay and some other samples of my writing.

"Excuse the apartment," I called from the kitchen – which is actually just the nook in the corner with the fridge and the stove. "This place is only temporary. I don't like a lot of distractions when I'm writing."

"Is that you?"

She was staring at the giant painting above my couch – me floating in midair above my computer.

"My friend Ingrid painted it."

"Interesting." Did she intend that as a compliment?

I set down her Diet Coke, along with a plate of muffins and croissants from Ingrid's coffee shop.

"Did you have trouble finding the place?" This was my oblique, WASPy way of pointing out that she was an hour and a half late.

"I just looked for your street number," she said, implying that I must be stupid to ask such a self-evident question. She took a deep breath and wiped her forehead. "Actually I just came from a meeting with a casting director. Major prima donna. She kept going on and on, telling me how busy she is – fifteen projects on the go. I mean, the point is, do I want her to work on my movie or not?"

"I hear film production's really booming right now – with the Canadian dollar so low."

"L.A.'s still where it all happens," she advised me. "But this casting woman was a complete write-off. I'm looking for people with some vision."

With all her bravado, she reminded me of one of those stereotypical Hollywood bitch heroines from a Jackie Collins novel.

She picked up a croissant and tore it in half. Her hands were expensively manicured with dark red polish, but both of her thumbnails were chewed down and ragged.

I sat on the couch and took too large a gulp of Diet Coke. I choked, and the meeting officially began.

"So first of all, Mitchell, I want you to know that I *am* talking to other writers about this project. In fact, yesterday I met with a guy who was a total asshole. Totally full of himself. But you see that all the time in this business. I hope you're not like that."

"I barely have an ego left," I assured her, and then I kicked myself for sounding vulnerable. Change the subject. "Have you worked on a lot of movies before?"

"This is my first time as a producer, but I've worked in the industry for years. In L.A. mostly. And one thing I know is that the writing has to be top quality. If we get a good script, we'll get good actors."

I nodded in devout agreement.

"I've already been talking to some major directors – Penny Marshall, Quentin Tarantino. I'm looking at Jodie Foster, Julia Roberts, maybe Winona Ryder for the lead."

"Wow." Could all that be true?

"I saw that thing about the screenplay you wrote. What was the name again?"

"*Hell Hole*," I said, motioning to the copy on the table and once again feeling embarrassed at my choice of title. "That draft isn't totally up to date. I just started reworking it last week."

"I read the blurb about it and I thought you might have the right understanding for what I'm doing."

I tried to guess what that could mean. *Hell Hole* is a modern-day horror story about the insane landlord of a rundown apartment building. He takes gleeful pleasure in creatively killing any tenant who dares complain. The climax involves the hero pushing the landlord into a garbage incinerator, which results in the sponta- neous explosion of the entire city block.

It's not a reflection of my genuine artistic sensibilities. But I figured if I wrote something ultra-commercial, it might sell.

Apparently I'd miscalculated.

"You can take that copy if you want."

"I'll study it," she said.

"Well, maybe you shouldn't *study* it. I'm in the middle of making some big improvements." I remembered the rule that you should never criticize your own work. "So what's your story about?"

"That would have to remain confidential until we decide to work together. But it's got crime, murder – a love story thrown in to make it interesting."

"Romance always makes things interesting," I agreed moronically.

"This story's going to shake up a lot of people, Mitchell. We'll get major media coverage. So if you work on it, you're going to have to keep everything secret until the picture's released."

"Of course," I said, trying to memorize every word so I could repeat all this to Ingrid and Ramir.

"Frankly, that's why I'm talking to unknowns. I want somebody who's outside all the industry gossip. But I'm still looking for professional quality."

"Well, I've been a professional writer for –"

"This could be a really important opportunity, Mitchell. This is a chance to make a serious name for ourselves, get noticed by the big leagues. This project could put us both right up with the major players."

Despite the skepticism I was feeling, my stockpile of fantasies suddenly flashed in front of me. Sitting by a pool in Beverly Hills, chatting on the phone with my agent. Being photographed by Annie Leibowitz, interviewed by Barbara Walters.

"There's something you've got to understand, Mitchell," she said, leaning forward. "I know this is my first time producing – that throws people off guard and I like that. But I know what I want, and I always make it happen."

She was so fierce, I couldn't help but believe her.

"You're probably wondering about the money," she said.

I frowned disparagingly.

"It's private financing. The funding's all in place. You'll get a portion of your fee up front."

My head felt light. And just as I was about to ask exactly how much the fee might be, she came out with the classic job interview question.

"So tell me, Mitchell, why should I hire you?" She looked at me earnestly, searching my face for any glimmer of self-doubt. Then she took a big bite of croissant, flakes dropping onto her chin.

I turned my eyes away and started to blather.

"Well, I have a B.A. in English from the University of Toronto. I worked in corporate communications for three years. Which means I wrote catalogues for an office supply company. Twenty-word descriptions of Scotch tape and pencil sharpeners." Her eyes were glazing over. "Then two years ago I started doing some TV writing. I've written a couple of episodes of a kids' show – *The Big Blue Dog*, if you've heard of it." She was staring at the warps in the hardwood floor. "Ever since I saw *Sunset Boulevard*, I knew I wanted to be a screenwriter." She flicked croissant flakes off her lap. "I write really fast. And I'm really easy to work with."

She waved her hand back and forth as though she were erasing what I'd just said. "If I told you, 'Mitchell, your writing is shit. I hate it,' what would you do?"

My mind scurried for the right answer. "Well, I'm a professional, so I'd ask you to be more specific and I'd see if I could make some changes."

"But if you really thought it was great stuff and I just kept telling you it was shit, what would you do?"

"I'd see if we could change it some more, so we both liked it."

"It's shit, Mitchell. I hate it." She violently bit off another chunk of croissant. Crumbs cascaded onto my freshly cleaned floor. "What do you say?"

More than just making me nervous, she was getting on my nerves. Was this really the sort of person I wanted to work with?

"What do you say, Mitchell?" She was truly obnoxious.

I was stymied.

"Well?" she said.

What did she *want* me to say?

I leapt into the abyss.

"I – I guess you'd better find yourself another writer."

Say good-bye to another job.

But a big, winning smile grew on her face. "Good answer, good answer," she said, reminding me of a TV game show. "That's enough." She stood up. "But I want you to remember, Mitchell, I *am* talking to other writers."

I was bewildered by what had happened. Confused at what I'd said. Annoyed at the mess she'd made. But suddenly I felt happy that she liked me. Maybe we'd get along!

She picked up her big black bag and headed for the door.

"When are you going to be making your decision?"

"Monday. But you're high on my list."

She was already out on the landing.

I chased after. "Do you have a card – somewhere I can reach you?"

She was heading down the stairs.

"My production office isn't set up yet. But you've got a good attitude, Mitchell. I'll be in touch."

"What time of day do you think you'll be calling on Monday?" I tried to sound eager, not pleading.

But she was already out the door, yelling back at me: "*Ciao!*"

She said I was high on her list. That's good. Reason to hope.

But when I came back inside, I saw that she'd left my script – that precious, polished example of my talent – sitting among the crumbs on the coffee table.

WEDNESDAY, MAY 7

It's two a.m. and I have insomnia, so here I sit typing again.

I ended up drinking the entire pot of coffee that Carmen didn't touch and I've been jangling with the caffeine ever since. Of course I was already wound up enough, debating with myself whether or not she'll give me the job. And at the same time, wondering if the whole thing was some kind of *Candid Camera* hoax.

Then Ramir called and said he wanted to get together and discuss an idea for a new project. Normally I like to be in bed by a conservative ten o'clock, but since I was obviously going to be awake anyway, I decided to go.

Besides, Ramir can convince me to do anything.

So I set off walking eastward, on the half-hour pilgrimage to Church and Wellesley, Toronto's homosexual crossroads – the focal point of what is fondly referred to as the "gay ghetto." It's a ten-block cluster of highrises and brownstones, restaurants and food markets, bathhouses and sex-toy shops. Rainbow banners flap from every lamppost.

Heading down Church Street, I passed the regular gang of denim-clad men, cruising on the steps in front of the Second Cup. Every sip of coffee was a demonstration of sexual technique. Meanwhile, across the street in the window of Bar 501, a black drag queen was lip-synching to Gloria Estefan.

I crossed the street. Two women in Birkenstocks were holding hands as they argued about a paperback in the window of This Ain't The Rosedale Library, the neighbourhood bookstore. I heard one of them mention the death of the novel.

I checked my watch to make sure I wasn't too early. Ten-thirty precisely.

I'd made Ramir promise to arrive at Woody's punctually,

because he's always late and now that I've taken a vow of celibacy, I can't risk being left alone in a gay establishment.

I climbed the front stairs to the king of all bars, spread across the main floor of a massive nineteenth-century row house.

As soon as I stepped in the door, I made a high-speed circuit of the crowded premises. Woody's is a melting pot kind of bar, mixing everyone from lesbians to construction workers to angelic former choirboys. As I hunted, I maintained a concentrated searching expression to prevent myself from making eye contact and falling into an immediate infatuation – which is what I'm always inclined to do.

Of course, Ramir was nowhere to be found.

I tried to be inconspicuous. I stood by an exposed-brick wall, requisite bottle of beer in hand, and kept checking the door for Ramir.

The bar's mascot is a rhinoceros – chosen, I gather, for its prominent horn. There are rhinoceros heads everywhere.

Woody's also has TV, which can keep me content for hours. But they only show clips from vintage porn movies and it's dangerous to be seen watching too intently or people think you're desperate.

So there I stood, a self-conscious mess, my eyes shifting every ten seconds from the door to the TV screen, where two muscular gentlemen frolicked in the back of a moving van.

I nervously straightened the sleeves of my shirt and raked down my bush of hair. I felt even more tall and gangly than usual.

And then I saw the man of my dreams. Which is exactly what I was afraid would happen.

Over by the stairs. Sandy blond hair. Classic ears. The most perfect aquiline nose. He was wearing jeans and a blue-pinstripe shirt – which on a mere mortal would look nondescript, but on him, it had the casual grace of old money. This was the sort of man who's supposed to be sailing on a yacht or riding horses in a Ralph Lauren ad. He had the sensual elegance of Montgomery Clift.

One of my automatic infatuations happening again.

He was talking to a nondescript short fellow and smiling

beatifically. Just a sweet little turn at the corner of his lips proved that he was witty and intelligent and gentle and understanding.

He put his arm around his dull friend's shoulder. Maybe they were lovers? Or maybe it just showed that he took pity on the less fortunate, that he was warm and genuine, caring and supportive.

I tried to block him out of my mind.

Here is my psychosis: I am only attracted to men who match my fantasies of larger-than-life elegance and glamour. I immediately put them on pedestals – imagining a future of glittering dinner parties and international travel. And then as soon as something goes wrong, as soon as I inevitably realize that the guy is merely flesh and blood, I lose interest and try to escape. Which I always do very messily.

My last mess served as a kind of a wake-up call. His name was Adam. He was a real professional model – the happy-go-lucky, good-natured jock type – and he started talking to me out of the blue in the line-up at the Carlton Cineplex. Which was incredibly flattering.

So automatically I fell in love with him.

All very sexy. Very romantic. Fantasy come to life.

But somehow, it kept working out that whenever we went to a restaurant or to a movie, I always had to pay for everything. And it was beginning to dawn on me that perhaps I wasn't in the financial position to become a sugar daddy at the age of twenty-eight.

Then, nine months ago, on what turned out to be our last date, we went to a dance club and we had a lot to drink and then we came back to my place for sex. Adam was always a smooth talker and he took me by surprise, so to speak, without using a condom.

Actually I knew exactly what he was doing.

The next morning, when I was sober again and totally freaking out, Adam promised me he was HIV-negative. Even so, I told him I never wanted to see him again.

That little incident made me realize that maybe my infatuations are somewhat self-destructive. Unfortunately, making this realization hasn't led to a sudden burst of personal growth and maturity.

Since then, I've been trying not to get involved.

And there, standing across the bar, was Montgomery Clift.

I tried to distract myself by surveying the crowd. Not a sign of

Ramir. I noticed an older man with overly trendy eyewear. A mustachioed desk clerk I recognized from the Marriott. A guy in his early thirties with his head shaved bald. He was wearing a white T-shirt and a leather vest – sort of a rebel Yul Brynner.

I glanced back to Montgomery Clift. He was frowning at something his friend said, and when he frowned, he looked concerned and wise and compassionate.

And then he looked at me.

I raised my beer bottle to take a seductive macho slug. But somehow I managed to miss my mouth completely – pouring beer directly into my shirt pocket.

"Shit."

I twirled to face the wall, shaking my head at the stupid things I always manage to do.

"You want this?"

Yul Brynner was suddenly at my side, presenting a paper napkin.

"Thanks." I mopped at my chest. "You'd think I'd know how to drink by now."

I turned to see him up close. He was about five inches shorter than me. He had a friendly enough smile. Wide blue eyes. And a snake tattooed on the side of his scalp.

Over his shoulder I saw Montgomery Clift heading towards the door. I must have winced.

"You interested in him?" Yul asked.

"No, no," I said, like he'd made an accusation.

"Pretentious phony. Kind of guy who talks for an hour about how he went to Upper Canada College. As if it really made him a better person."

"I'm just meeting a friend," I said, smiling stiffly.

"Are you from out of town? I haven't seen you here before."

"I don't go to bars very often."

"I'm not too fond of them myself. Too much cigarette smoke. But it's the best place to meet people. Like I just met you. My name's Ben, by the way." He put out his hand for a shake.

"I'm Chad," I said.

"Well Chad, can I get you another beer?"

"I'm not staying long."

"That's too bad. I noticed you watching the video."

"I was just glancing at it."

He laughed. "Guys are always so funny about watching those videos." He motioned his beer towards the crowd. "I mean, this is a bar filled with gay men. Every one of us would prefer to be doing what they're doing on TV, right? But everybody stands around here like they don't want to meet anybody."

"Crazy, isn't it?"

"That's why I noticed you. You look sort of nervous."

"I'm not nervous. I'm just anxiously awaiting a friend."

"I didn't mean it as an insult," he said with a cocky grin. "It's a nice change."

At that very moment I saw Ramir rushing in – a ball of energy. Perfect timing, for once. "My friend's here. I have to go," I said. "Thanks again."

I rushed at Ramir, grabbing him by the arm and dragging him towards the exit – hoping that he might be mistaken for my boyfriend.

Behind me the bald guy cheerfully called, "Good to meet you, Chad!"

"What's going on?" Ramir asked, already laughing in anticipation of teasing me.

"I think I was about to be seduced."

"That guy you were talking to? He was cute."

"He's not exactly my type."

"Because he doesn't shop at the Gap?"

"He had a snake tattooed on his head."

"You really need to get over this slump, Mitch. A guy like that could open you up to a whole new world."

"I'll start begging men in leather masks to handcuff me to my pullout couch. Let's go to Fran's. I need rice pudding to stabilize."

We headed down the street, walking quickly to fight the spring coolness in the night air.

"Sorry I'm late," he said. "I got a big emotional phone call just as I was going out the door."

"Todd Trauma?" Ramir's been breaking up with him for two weeks.

"I got home tonight and he'd sung a five-minute Malaysian lullaby into my answering machine. Then he started crying."

"Pulling out all the stops."

"He told me a guy picked him up at Eaton's this afternoon. He was shopping for running shoes and this older man started talking to him."

"Let me smell your dirty sneakers, little boy."

"They had sex in the parking garage."

"So he's trying the old jealousy routine."

"It's not like I want to hurt him or anything. But when something's over, you should just let it go."

I wish I could have that attitude about men.

Ramir always has new lovers waiting in line. He's boyishly handsome with far too much sex appeal. He's one of those light-brown people of unidentifiable ethnic origin, and being an actor, he works it. Sometimes he'll pretend he's Spanish, sometimes Native, sometimes East Indian. He often gets bit parts as a Puerto Rican street thug in American cop shows they film here in Toronto.

He's actually from Trinidad, and he has the perfect exotic movie-star name: Ramir Martinez. But he moved to Canada when he was five years old and he's just as suburban as I am.

We met two years ago at a night-school course in film production at Ryerson. I'd enrolled in the class when I was in my first flurry of excitement about devoting myself totally to screenwriting.

From the first moment I talked to him, I thought Ramir was gorgeous and talented and charismatic. And we got along really well. By mutual arrangement, we ended up as partners on our final project – an artsy seven-minute ghost story we shot in Mount Pleasant Cemetery. The film got an A.

The night of our final class, we went back to his apartment and went to bed together. But the next time we went out Ramir said he didn't think it was a good idea to have sex with friends. So we carried on just as friends.

I've analyzed this situation frequently. Maybe it's because of my bruised ego. Maybe it's because he broke up with me before I had the chance to knock him off his pedestal. But the truth is, I've never really gotten over him. Not that he ever seems to notice.

"So don't hold back," he said, in his enthusiastic, adorable way, "tell me about your meeting with the big film producer."

"It was good, I think." I went over the details, leaving out mentions of Jodie Foster and Quentin Tarantino so it didn't sound *too* ludicrous. "It's the first film she's producing, so it might be terrible. But then again, it's *my* first movie, so who am I to judge?"

"I can ask a few people if they've heard of her."

"She's worked in L.A. mostly. So who knows? Maybe she's just another wanna-be."

"If she has the financing in place, that's a good sign. And if she wants to start shooting in September, she's got to make a decision pretty soon."

"It'd be an amazing opportunity. And of course, I could definitely use the money."

"I read an article in *Premiere* today about a woman who made a million dollars selling her first screenplay."

"I don't know whether Carmen has *that* much financing. Anyway, I'm not getting my hopes up." This was a blatant lie.

A million dollars.

That's the kind of carrot that keeps all of us aspiring writers slogging. Sometimes screenwriting just feels like a sleazy get-rich-quick scheme.

"You never can tell," Ramir said. "You might get lucky."

He told me a story about an actor friend who'd just landed a part opposite Stockard Channing in a movie that's shooting in town. Ramir always gives me the inside gossip about the film industry. It helps convince me that I'm an insider, too.

We finally arrived at Fran's diner. With its flashing lights and neon signs, it looks like a mini Broadway theatre. Inside it used to be 1940s' red leatherette, but ten years ago they ripped out the classic kitsch and brought in the pink-and-green tackiness of the 1980s. For some reason I still find it comforting.

My mother always brought me here when we came downtown to shop at Christmas. I always ordered the famous rice pudding. She always ordered the apple pie with Fran's exclusive apple-cin-namon syrup.

Following my personal tradition, I ordered warm rice pudding and a glass of milk. Ramir just asked for a pot of hot water because he always brings his own herbal tea bags. This quirk results from his job at Good Karma Natural Foods – where he works to ensure a stable income between roles.

"Ingrid told me you didn't call her today," I said in mock-accusatory tone.

He mock-flinched in reply. "I have to see her tomorrow – tell her about my plans."

"You'd better tell me first."

"Okay, if you're going to drag it out of me." Ramir gave me his trademark coy smile. No wonder everybody wants to drag him into bed. "You have to know some background first. I told you last week I was auditioning for a part. Nothing big. A lawyer on *Police Line-Up*."

"You got it?"

"Hold on. I'm building suspense. It became this huge controversy. Should they make the lawyer a person of colour? They even introduced me to Dominic Manno, the big producer."

"You talked to him?" I was sincerely impressed. "What was he like?"

"The most intimidating person I've ever met. He asked me a bunch of questions about what I want."

"*What you want.* What did you say?"

"I said I wanted the part. But in the end, they went with your typical white hunk. After my agent told me, I just got totally pissed off. I realized it's impossible. Mainstream TV has too many hang-ups about non-traditional casting."

"So you're going to produce your own all-ethnic cop show?" I suggested with a wacky tilt to my head.

"And all the bad guys will be white," he said, playing along. "So I just sat down and I analyzed what I really want. I mean, I love acting, but I don't want to be doing bit parts for the rest of my life."

"There are no small parts . . . ."

"Just big egos. Right. My parents have been on my case again."

"They want you to go back to school?"

"It's that whole immigrant philosophy – wanting me to get a

real job, become an electrician like my father. I mean, even *I* don't want to still be unpacking crates of organic Kraft Dinner by the time I turn thirty." He took a spoonful of my rice pudding. "I just have to give acting one final push. I know it sounds shallow, but when it comes right down to it, I want to be famous."

I nodded in understanding. "Sometimes I wonder if that's the main reason I want to be a writer."

"I know being famous doesn't make any difference to who you are and all that. But I still think it must be better than this."

"Do you think we're really shallow?"

"It's totally fucked up. But it's still what I want. I mean, no one's ever seen what I can do as an actor. Even *I* haven't. So I'm going to put on my own show."

"In a barn? With Mickey Rooney and Judy Garland?"

"If they're available. I just want to get people's attention. Invite a bunch of producers and casting directors. Show them I have a wider range than playing a gang member who gets shot in the head. I'm just going to do something small. A one-man show."

"It's a really good idea."

"I'm going to write the script myself," he said.

"That's great," I said. But my jaw tightened. I'm ashamed to admit that I felt a twang of territorialism. Writers can be very petty. "So what's it going to be about?"

He took a dramatic pause and sipped his linden-flower tea.

"Well, I've been trying to figure out what I really have to say – my own unique view of the world."

"Which is?"

"I'm a gay man. I'm a person of colour. I'm sort of a Buddhist. I mean, I'm a minority any way you look at it. So I'm going to talk about that. The frustration of being an outsider. And I've already got the title." Ramir squared his hands on the table to frame the word: "*Eruption.*"

"*Eruption,*" I repeated. "As in *Ejaculation?*"

"I hadn't thought about that, but I guess it works. I want something that's really in your face. And I've got a subtitle to explain it." He placed his hands down again. "*Eruption: Screams of the Oppressed.*"

"It sounds like a benefit for Amnesty International."

"I'm going to deal with some serious issues. I want to do something that makes a difference."

"That's good," I said with only a bit of doubt.

"And I've already figured out how it'll start. The stage is black. The audience is silent. And then out of nowhere I scream really loud."

"Erupting."

"Exactly. And just as I finish screaming, a spotlight comes up on me. And then I start my first monologue." He started reciting in a deep, serious voice: "'I am a brown man. Not a black man. Not a white man. But a man whose colour is blended somewhere in between.'"

I tried to phrase this delicately: "Don't you think people might like it better if it were a comedy?"

He laughed at my delicacy. "The whole thing's not going to be that heavy. There'll be some funny parts. I'll go through all these different characters, talking about their lives, explaining how they're oppressed. And in between each one I'll scream as sort of a transition device. The screaming'll tie the whole thing together."

"So it's sort of like performance art."

"That's too obscure. I want to make this accessible."

"While at the same time making you a star."

"You don't think it's a good idea."

"No, I think it's a good idea," I said slowly. "I just think it might be hard to do well."

"I can picture the whole thing in my head. I can probably write it in two days."

"Ramir, it's a lot easier to describe something than it is to actually write it."

"I know." Then he smiled with that sweet, seductive, hopeful smile he has. "That's why I need to tap all the talent I can find. I'm going to ask Ingrid to design the set and the poster. And I need you to help me with the script."

A wave of mixed feelings. The writing would be hard. But there was also the opportunity to spend more time with him.

"I'm going to be really busy if this screenplay job works out,"

I said.

"All I want is for you to read through it and make sure it all makes sense. It won't take long. Teamwork. It'll be fun."

"It's not that it wouldn't be fun." I shifted awkwardly in my seat – trying to appear difficult-to-convince.

Ramir grasped my wrist across the table. "Don't you ever wonder about all those famous people who were friends when they were just starting out. Rob Reiner and Billy Crystal. Danny DeVito and Michael Douglas. Dan Aykroyd and John Candy."

"Bette Midler and Barry Manilow," I said. "You can be Barry Manilow."

"But you know what I mean. Wouldn't it be incredible?"

I nodded. "We could look back at all this and laugh at how naïve we once were."

"This could be really good, Mitch. I mean, I'll just rent a small performance space at first. Once the show's successful, I can move it someplace bigger. And who says I can't take it to New York? It'd be perfect off-Broadway. Then you never know what could happen. The sky's the limit."

"The future's in the palm of your hand."

"Don't dream it, be it."

"Build your castles in the air."

"Even the longest journey begins with a single step."

We ran out of inspirational clichés.

"So are you going to help?" Ramir grinned at his own shamelessness.

Of course I said yes.

After we left Fran's, I offered to walk Ramir back to his apartment, but he said no, he was going to a bar on a fresh manhunt.

It's not surprising that I felt rather depressed.

He headed back to the gay ghetto and I walked home by myself.

I wondered if his show would be a disaster. But whatever Ramir does, it always seems to work out fine in the end.

In any case, he might have forgotten the whole idea by next week. Which is even more depressing in its own way.

And what if we are all just deluding ourselves that we have talent? What if I never do become a famous screenwriter?

I hope Carmen calls.

For a while I wondered what might have happened with Montgomery Clift. And even Yul Brynner.

It's probably for the best that I ran away.

It's been nine months since that episode with Adam, and six months since I went for my HIV test. I still haven't found the courage to go back to the clinic for the results. Just thinking about the whole thing I end up in a sweaty panic. And then I worry because sweating is one of the symptoms.

I shouldn't even be thinking about boyfriends.

Nothing is worse than getting morose at three in the morning.

I'll turn off my computer, climb into my sofa bed and pray for sleep.

THURSDAY, MAY 8

I spent the morning writing another porn story – my twelfth in six months.

This one is set in a swanky Connecticut golf and country club. My first-person narrator is a young caddie carrying the bag of a handsome college boy, who coincidentally bears a resemblance to Montgomery Clift. They share smouldering glances on the back nine and exchange double-entendres about gripping a putter. There's abundant soap lather in the shower, an empty massage room and, of course, condoms conveniently pulled from a shaving kit.

All of this builds to a highly dramatic climax.

It was really a thrill the day I got my first acceptance from *Blueboy* magazine in New York City. Positive reinforcement for my work, combined with the satisfying irony of a nice young man like myself being a published pornographer.

Since then I've been flooding the market – *Numbers*, *Inches*, *Advocate Men*. Each one earns me $150 American, which is nice, too.

I always use upper-crust settings and I publish under the provocatively prep school pseudonym of Chad Stiffman, in case someday I have a reputation to protect.

All in all, I consider it a benign way to handle my sexual urges.

I think the technical term is sublimation.

Anyway, after I'd wiped off my computer and placed the story in an envelope addressed to *In Touch* magazine in North Hollywood, I walked the block and a bit along Bloor Street to The Daily Grind.

A much-needed coffee break to re-energize.

By the modern Starbucks standard of coffee shops, the Grind leaves a lot to be desired. The place features a rustic motif. It's designed to look like a giant shipping crate with rough barnwood wainscotting on the walls. Burlap sacks are stapled to the serving counter which runs along the right side. It's tired-looking, I admit, but I find it homey. As a painter, however, Ingrid finds it frustrating to work in such a brown environment.

The main attraction of the place is the jumble of rickety tables outside where all the neighbourhood intellectuals come to bask in the sun and sip espresso. You see a lot of people hunched over notebooks, presumably at work on The Great Canadian Screenplay.

Personally I think it's pretentious to write in public.

This afternoon only three tables outside were occupied and all the tables inside were empty. The single customer in the shop was the enigmatic Frances Farmer, a local streetperson, perched on her usual stool by the front window. We've never heard Frances speak a single word. She has white hair – bobbed like a 1920s flapper – and an extensive wardrobe from Goodwill. Today she was wearing a bright orange pantsuit with matching eyeshadow.

When I stepped in the door, Ingrid rushed out from behind the counter and gave me a hug. "Thanks for coming. I'm so bored, I've been going crazy."

At the use of this apparently sensitive reference, Frances Farmer turned to give us a disapproving look.

"Business still quiet?"

"I think it's now officially dead."

"There's a big crowd across the street at the Future Bakery," I said, looking out the window.

"Sometimes it's hard not to take it personally. Do you want the usual?"

I nodded.

Ingrid stacked two complimentary Rice Krispie squares on a plate and poured a complimentary Mocha Java into the mug she'd magic-markered with my name. She brought it right to my table – a special honour, since there's a store policy that everything is self-serve.

"Did you notice Victor's new poster for Costa Rica?" Like an unenthusiastic spokesmodel on The Price is Right, Ing gestured to the array of posters on the back wall. "He's making a collage of countries that produce coffee beans."

"It looks like a discount travel agency."

"He always asks for input when he has those motivation sessions. He says he wants to make the place trendy – like all those coffee shops on TV."

"Life imitating sitcoms."

"And then he puts up ugly stuff like that. Sometimes I think he doesn't want business to get any better."

"He must use this place as a giant tax write-off," I said. "When you're rich, even being inept can be profitable."

"So how's work for you? Have you heard from Carmen?"

I shook my head. "She did say she wouldn't call until Monday, but I was hoping she'd realize I was such a hot property, she'd have to hire me before anyone else had the chance."

"Makes sense to me."

"I just wish I hadn't told anybody about it. Then I won't feel so stupid when she turns me down."

"I swear I'll never mention it again. But I have a good feeling about this one, Mitchell. Really."

Then a customer came in and Ingrid had to make him a chocolate cappuccino.

There's always a rush as soon as I arrive.

I resent this.

I shouldn't be so selfish, because Ingrid and I met right here at the store, just a few months after I moved into the neighbourhood. One Saturday afternoon I was procrastinating from writing, sitting at a table outside, reading a battered paperback copy of Jacqueline Susann's *The Love Machine*. Ingrid came out to pick up some empty cups and when she saw what I was reading, she immediately ran back inside and brought out her own vintage copy of *The Love Machine*.

Coincidence or fate? We had a passionate, ridiculous discussion about the overblown plot and the unbelievable characters. And we've been friends ever since.

Ing was steaming milk, making that soothing nasal gurgle with the Gaggia. And I noticed something different about her hair. Was it darker red?

It's always a puzzle to me why more men don't ask Ingrid out.

She's on public view behind the counter every day. She's pretty in an interesting bird-like sort of way. But she's always shy about her attributes. She wears baggy men's shirts like painters' smocks. Only occasionally can you catch an glimpse of her curvaceous figure being hugged by tight little T-shirts.

Ing sat down with me again.

"You put in more henna," I said.

She slapped her pile of curly auburn hair. "Is it too much? Do I look trashy?"

"You're gorgeous. Rita Hayworth."

"I went into a cosmetic frenzy last night. I nearly plucked out both my eyebrows. And I started a new painting. It's a close-up of little girl's face, staring into a giant bonfire in the forest. There's sort of a reflection of her face in the flames. Just a shadow – not so obvious that it's tacky."

Ingrid's paintings are always whimsical and mysterious. Big broad lines of colour that look like a confusing mass at first, but when you stare long enough, they clearly form a picture.

"I stayed up painting practically until dawn. Kinita opened this morning, so I didn't have to come in early."

"You sure were busy last night."

"Work, work, work. Keeps the mind occupied. I couldn't sleep anyway. I talked to Pierre." Her ex-husband.

"He finally called?"

"Collect. From Paris."

"What did he say?"

"He said he wants to be friends."

"And he called collect?"

"Honestly, Mitchell, I still daydream about him all the time. Isn't that disgusting? We always talked about moving to Paris together and now he's studying there. He's having a show next month. He said he'd send me an invitation."

"With airfare?"

"Not likely."

"Is he still with the same woman?"

"He didn't say anything directly. But when he mentioned going to the Musée d'Orsay, he said 'we'."

"*Oui.*"

I've never actually met Pierre. He and Ingrid had separated just before our *Love Machine* encounter. But from what I've gleaned, their love story is rather classically Jacqueline Susann in itself. Ingrid, an innocent young woman from the northern nickel-mining capital of Sudbury, voyaged to the big city of Toronto to attend art college. There she met Pierre, a sexy French-Canadian from Ottawa. Love at first sight. They married right after graduation. Everything was blissfully happy. Then Ingrid found out Pierre was carrying on an affair with a former professor (female). Divorce ensued. After which Pierre and the professor moved to Paris.

"I mean, we were only together for two years and it's been two years since we broke up. I keep telling myself I should be over him by now. I know it was the right thing to get divorced. But now it just feels like I got left behind."

For a moment we sat and watched as Frances Farmer blew kisses to her crowd of fans on the sidewalk.

Suddenly Ingrid jumped from the table, chipper as ever. "Victor! Hi!"

In strode The Daily Grind's owner, Victor Fellner, wearing a business suit. One of his daily surprise visits.

"Good afternoon to you both. Anyone call?"

Ing reached for a pink message pad by the cash register. "Your lawyer said that four o'clock is fine for the meeting."

"Perfect."

"Pinstripes and everything. Must be important."

"Could be, could be," he said ominously, hoping we'd read something impressive between the lines.

Aside from being a retail entrepreneur, Victor is a successful real-estate agent in the eastern suburbs. He's in his late forties and terminally pudgy, though he's always sucking in his gut. I'm sure he's had hair implants.

He inherited this store from his parents while he was going to university and one summer he ingeniously transformed it from a Hungarian deli into a coffee shop. He still keeps the title of man-ager, even though Ingrid handles all the day-to-day stuff.

Victor always says he's a self-made man, but personally I think he's a complete creation of Anthony Robbins.

"It feels low energy in here," he said.

"It's been quiet all afternoon."

"Have we hit our goal?"

"Not yet."

"What are we at?"

"Three hundred."

"Look at all the muffins sitting here. Why did we order so many muffins?"

"They're from that new supplier you wanted me to try. Nobody wants them. They look too dry."

"They do resemble wood chips," I offered.

Victor shook his head in disgust. "No one in this country cares about quality anymore. Can we send them back?"

"They were C.O.D."

"So we need to get busy and sell some muffins!"

Suddenly electrified with creative insight, Victor barrelled outside and came back in carrying the sandwich board.

Every day Ingrid adorns the chalkboard with a new squiggly-lined character consuming a different Daily Grind product. She calls them Human Beans because their heads are shaped like giant coffee beans. Her current masterpiece was a little green boy with orange hair like springs, sipping a bottle of fruit juice through a curlicue straw.

Victor took a damp cloth and rubbed him out.

I saw Ingrid frown in resignation.

"Mitch, you're the writer. What should we say? 'Fresh bran muffins? Healthy bran muffins?' What would get you in here?"

"'Free bran muffins'," I suggested.

"That's funny," Victor said, trying to laugh. He's always super-nice to me because he thinks I'm one of his best customers.

"Okay, we follow the standard sales approach. Be direct. Give the facts." Victor pressed into the blackboard with white chalk: HIGH FIBRE. LOW PRICE. 75¢ MUFFINS!

"Let's see what kind of results we get from this," he said, proudly carrying the board outside.

Ingrid grabbed a plastic fork from the counter and stuck it in the side of her head.

"He should just write CHEAP DRY PIECES OF SHIT," I whispered.

When Victor returned, he pointed outside to the patio. "Ingrid, somebody spilled some cappuccino out there. I didn't want to touch it, wearing my suit."

I lowered my head. It always feels weird to see Ing get ordered around. She went outside with a tray and a towel. I pretended to read an abandoned newspaper while Victor went to the cash register and fussed about.

A minute later he was storming out the door again. "I'll see you tomorrow. And make sure you remind people about those coffee mugs on sale."

Ingrid paused till he was out of sight, then rushed to look at his note.

"He took two hundred dollars. That's the only reason he came in. He treats this cash register like it's a bank machine."

"It's a good thing you don't have to do the bookkeeping."

"He's up to something, Mitchell. He's been meeting with his lawyer practically every day. I wonder if he's planning to sell the store. Or shut it down. Either way I should probably start looking for another job."

"You could apply across the street at the Future Bakery. He'd hate that."

"I don't even want to think about it. I took this job because it was easy, so I could concentrate on my painting."

"You've put up with him too long anyway. He treats you like you're brain-dead."

"I know."

"He's so condescending."

"I know."

"And he takes you for granted."

Ingrid stood up straight. "Contrary to what you may think, Mitchell Draper, I do not let Victor walk all over me. For example, these disgusting little muffins – they're going out to the squirrels. Victor's always telling us we have to believe in what we sell. And therefore, we won't need that tacky muffin sign either."

She marched the sandwich board back inside and sat down on

the floor beside my table. She spread out her collection of coloured chalk and began to create a new Human Bean.

For a while I just sat there and watched her draw.

"You really should take your work to some art galleries."

"This is just a doodle, Mitchell."

"You know what I mean. Your paintings."

"Just because I paint doesn't mean I have to show anybody. It's like writing a diary. It's private. I think it's important that people have hobbies."

"You can't compare your paintings to something like macramé."

"Macramé plant hangers are a beautiful expression of the human soul."

"So do you want to end up like Emily Dickinson?"

"Pardon?"

"Everybody realizing you're a genius after you're dead."

"It's probably easier. Then you don't let other people's judgements get in the way of your work."

"But you always like it when Ramir and I give you our opinions, tell you you're brilliant." She grinned – I'd caught her. "You're a sucker for compliments just like the rest of us."

"Okay, I paint for an audience of two. Pass me your napkin – I made a mistake."

I handed it to her and watched as she re-drew an eyebrow.

"You really wouldn't want to be famous?"

"Ramir's been talking to you, too, hasn't he?" she asked. "He came over to my apartment this morning for yoga and he asked me to work on the sets for his show. He's always so confident about things. You can't help but get inspired."

"You're changing the subject. Just because Ramir's putting on a show doesn't mean you can't, too."

She picked up a new colour of chalk. "You and Ramir have different ambitions than I do."

"But admit it, wouldn't you like it if everybody in the world loved your work? Ingrid Iversen's paintings hanging in the Museum of Modern Art right beside Cézanne and Picasso. Collectors from around the world fighting for your latest canvas. You could give up grinding coffee beans all day."

"I like working in retail."

"You could turn the Human Beans into a weekly sitcom. Like *The Simpsons* or *The Smurfs*. You'd be a millionaire."

"Are you trying to corrupt me with crass commercialism, Mitchell?"

"I thought you wanted some hot stud to corrupt you," I growled. "I wrote another porn story this morning. Can you tell?"

"Did you bring it? You promised you'd let me read your next one."

"I'm still too embarrassed."

"I don't know why. It can't be any racier than Judith Krantz. Anyway, I'm done." She stood up, clapping the chalk dust off her hands.

The sandwich board was now the frame for a purple female with bright red Medusa hair. The figure held a pastry in the palm of one hand, while in the other, she balanced the planet Earth on a single finger. The caption read: IVANA REALIZES THAT BY EATING A SINGLE DANISH SHE IS CHANGING THE WORLD.

"How Zen," I said.

Then, as if hypnotized by the power of advertising, Frances Farmer stepped to the counter, set a two-dollar coin on the cash register, and took a cherry danish from the basket.

Carmen didn't call.

WEDNESDAY, MAY 14

This morning I worked on *Hell Hole*, trying to emphasize the loving relationship between the happily married young heroes. I got this idea from a scrupulously detailed rejection letter I received last month from a New York script agent.

In fact, I have received twenty-six rejection letters on *Hell Hole*. A number of them have been very encouraging, telling me I have talent and should stick with it. But in the end, they all basically told me to fuck off.

Even so, I've invested such an incredible amount of time in *Hell Hole* and so much hope that it might advance my career and improve my financial health, that I keep coming back to it.

I know with utmost certainty that it's better than a lot of scripts that have actually been produced.

Sitting here at my desk (which doubles as my dining room table), I made a bunch of notes on new ways to portray our heroes' infinite passion amid the squalor of their tiny apartment. But I wasn't in a romantic mood.

For a while I polished a scene for my other screenplay – a totally non-commercial art film that I've been mulling over since university, but I've only been working on seriously for the past year. It's the sensitive story of a 16-year-old boy from a sterile suburban family who makes friends with his high-school English teacher, a fragile woman in her forties. She's very supportive and encouraging of his writing talents. And she's the first person to whom he reveals that he's gay.

The teacher takes him home for dinner one night and the boy meets her husband – a handsome, dynamic architect. Then the husband begins an affair with the boy behind the teacher's back.

Of course, she eventually finds out. Lots of gut-wrenching drama ensues.

Sometimes I wonder if the story's just too small and simple and dull. That's always the danger when you're trying to be artistic.

For a big climax, I've occasionally thought the boy might kill the husband. Or the wife might kill the husband. Or the wife might kill herself. But all that seems too crass. And too far from what really happened.

It's poignant and painful and, honestly, I think it's some of the best stuff I've ever written. But I don't want to show it to anybody.

Which isn't a very practical way to put bread on the table.

So, being practical, I phoned the producer of that kids' TV show I wrote for, *The Big Blue Dog*. She said she won't have any more work for me until September.

I put all my overstuffed file folders back in the freezer, where, I have been informed, they will be safe in case of fire.

I hope there's something worth saving.

FRIDAY, MAY 16

Due to imminent financial collapse, I went back one day early for my next three-week adventure in the glamorous world of office temping.

I called my agency at eight this morning and they sent me out on a job right away. I'm actually one of their favourite recruits, since I'm always blandly pleasant in office environments and I can type ninety-seven words a minute.

They told me it was an important emergency assignment at a prestigious legal firm in the business district. In a mad rush, I noosed on a necktie and took the subway down to King Street.

I love being surrounded by tall buildings, looking up and imagining floor after floor of ambitious executives in Hugo Boss suits influencing the fate of the nation with their every decision.

But the reality, as usual, was sadly disappointing.

I took the marble-clad elevator to the law firm's marble-clad reception area, with its stunning fiftieth-floor view of Lake Ontario.

But beyond the lobby, the office looked like every other place I've ever worked. The office manager – a woman who yawned perpetually and apologized for it – led me through a sea of powder-grey "workstations," formed entirely of moulded plastic. Padded half-walls rose up in every direction. Viewed from above, I'm sure the floor would look like a massive hedge maze.

My co-workers in such office settings rarely speak to me. They look at me with nervous curiosity or dismissive smiles. Rarely does anyone ask my name. Why learn something when you'll only have to forget it tomorrow?

The important emergency involved vast amounts of typing about a dead man. I was working for a tense, middle-aged lawyer who was preparing thirty precisely detailed letters regarding the estate of another tense, middle-aged lawyer who had recently succumbed to a heart attack. The living lawyer didn't seem to find this parallel ironic.

However, he did bear a certain resemblance to Gregory Peck in *To Kill a Mockingbird*. So I tried to concentrate on his positive qualities in order to find him more engaging as he droned on in dictation.

Back in my office cubicle, I would finish one of his dull letters, then reward myself with a call to my answering machine, checking for a message from Carmen. And then I'd smack myself for taking her seriously even for a minute.

The only message I got was from my mother, inviting me for dinner Sunday night at our family homestead in Willowdale – the flat northern subdivision that had made me imagine life in skyscrapers must be infinitely more stimulating.

Clearly that culture has damaged me enough.

I called her back and told her I was busy.

After lunch – teriyaki chicken amid the jostling crowds in the food court downstairs – I worked on another porn story, this one starring me and Gregory Peck. We were setting up for a presentation in the oak-panelled boardroom. I was kneeling down, plugging in the slide projector. He put his hand on my shoulder . . . .

When he suddenly called me into his office, I had to hold the note pad in front of my crotch.

The flatness of his monotone immediately deflated my interest.

The only thing that got me through the eight-hour workday was anticipating my dinner plans that evening.

Every two weeks, Ingrid, Ramir and I gather together in the Hungarian restaurant two floors down from my apartment.

The sign out front says Little Budapest, but everyone in the neighbourhood calls it the Little Buda. In fact, this entire section of Bloor Street from Bathurst to Spadina used to be Hungarian until squeegee kids and vegetarian university professors took it over.

The decor follows the longstanding Eastern European tradition of garishness, featuring yellow garden trellises strung with plastic grape vines. The tiny booths are upholstered with green vinyl.

I'm actually the one responsible for initiating our dinner custom. It started just after Ramir announced we were going to "just be friends," and since I'd just met Ingrid as well, I figured I'd invite her along to help loosen things up. And the chemistry sparked.

Over the past two years we've become a remarkably supportive little triangle. Ingrid pursuing the inner truth of art. Ramir passionate for the external glory of fame. And me, alternating regularly between the two aspirations – depending on the current condition of my ego.

As usual, I was the first one at the restaurant, commandeering our regular booth against the back wall. I was looking forward to bitching about the day with Ingrid before Ramir's chronically late arrival.

But Ingrid's eyes were dazed with excitement as she rushed towards me and took her seat. She held the edge of the table to steady herself.

"I got some bizarre news. You'll never guess. Victor is going to Florida."

"He was just there on vacation."

"No, Mitchell, he's *moving* there."

"Permanently?"

She nodded. "I never knew it before, but his wife's an American citizen. He's getting his real estate license down there and he's going to work for an office in Boca Raton. He took me out to lunch today and told me. That's what all his meetings have been about. He's leaving next Wednesday."

"Couldn't he give you more notice? How are you going to find another job?"

"He didn't fire me. That's the weirdest part. He wants me to manage the store."

"Full-time?"

"Forever."

"Is that a good thing?"

"I wasn't sure at first. But I've been thinking about it all afternoon and now I think it's perfect. Guaranteed stability, so I can paint with no distractions. No boss, no stress. Do you think I'm crazy?"

"I'm still amazed. Florida?"

"He's been planning it for months, he says, doing all the paperwork for immigration, selling their house."

"And he's never mentioned a word?"

She shook her head. "It's funny, because I remember after he came back from his holidays in January, he kept talking about how he wanted to move down south. I thought it was because he was sick of chipping ice off the sidewalk."

"Won't it mean you have to do a lot more work?"

"I'm pretty well the manager already. And this way I'll be able to delegate. I can give myself two days off in a row, maybe three, so I can paint nonstop. No morning shifts – I can work all night. And on top of my salary, I get 15 percent of the profits."

"Are there any profits?"

"Not much right now. But I think it might actually amount to something once I bring in better food and reorganize things."

"It sounds like a lot more responsibility, Ingrid."

"Maybe I'm being as insane as he is. But I feel really good about this, Mitchell. I'm flattered he asked me. And I'm excited. I haven't said that about a job since the summer I worked in the gift shop at the Sudbury nickel mine."

Magda the Waitress – an icon of old-world brusqueness – interrupted our conversation to confirm that we were ordering the usual: three authentic Hungarian raspberry sodas, two wiener schnitzels and one chicken schnitzel for Ramir.

"May I ask a selfish question?" I said to Ingrid. "If you're getting 15 percent of the profits, will you still give me free food?"

Ing cocked her head with bird-like delicacy to consider this. "You can pay me wholesale. Victor isn't leaving till Thursday, so we can stock you up before then."

"Florida," I said mistily. "No snow."

"I went to Fort Lauderdale once for March break with my sisters. We had a blast."

"*Where the Boys Are*. Remember Yvette Mimieux? She was Canadian."

"Québecoise. Can you imagine – walking on the beach whenever you want. Palm trees. My sisters took me to this place that had orange milk shakes."

"Of course, Florida *is* a complete cultural wasteland," I said. "Except for Miami Beach."

"All that art deco."

"All those male models."

"Victor and his family are staying in a luxury hotel right on the ocean until they find a house."

"Wealth is wasted on the wealthy," I said. "It's depressing."

A woman wearing a gaudy frilly dress walked by our table on her way to the washroom. "Look," I said, relying on our favourite game to distract me from my mood, "Barbara Stanwyck as she was in *Stella Dallas*."

Ingrid pointed to a booth where an older blonde woman was sitting with a slim Asian man. "There's Angie Dickinson sharing a beet salad with Bruce Lee."

"Don't look now, but that guy at the bar is Abraham Lincoln before he grew the beard."

"That could be Cyndi Lauper."

"And here comes the illegitimate son of Omar Sharif and Ricardo Montalban."

"Good evening, my beloved." It was Ramir, radiant in a white Indian cotton shirt. He leaned across the table, dramatically giving us both a kiss on the mouth.

"We were playing Spot the Celebrity," I said. "We thought you were Lena Horne."

"Give me a wig, honey, and I can play anything. I just came from an audition."

"Something big?"

"A continuing lead. Dominic Manno remembered me from that role I was up for two weeks ago."

"Dominic Manno remembered you." I was genuinely impressed.

"That really is a compliment," Ing said.

"It's for a brand new show called *Heroes in Blue*."

"And you'd be the star?"

"It's one of two leads." He smiled like a delighted little boy. "My character is this Puerto Rican guy from the ghetto whose younger brother got killed in a knife fight. So he decides to become a cop to help the other kids on the street. I know it's a cliché, but I think it's something I can work with."

"You could make him really sympathetic. You could steal the show."

"This could do major things for my career. Manno Productions is gigantic. They sell their shows all over the world."

"That's really wonderful news, Ramir," I said sincerely, but I have to admit that I felt envy rising up. "So you're not going to do *Eruption?*"

"I don't really need to anymore."

"You know, Ingrid's got some good news, too," I said.

"It's nothing by comparison," she said. She started telling him about Victor making her the manager, and Ramir leaned across the booth to give her a congratulatory kiss. Ing blushed girlishly. Even *she* can succumb to Ramir's charms. But her story of Victor was interrupted when Magda delivered the schnitzels.

We all performed the ritualistic squeezing of the lemon slice – anointing the huge flattened-out wafers of meat that spread off the sides of the plate.

Ramir turned his generous beam on me. "So has that movie producer called you yet?"

Ingrid jumped to my rescue. "He hasn't heard and we're not supposed to ask."

"I have officially stopped thinking about her," I announced. "I'm trying to accept my destiny as an office drudge."

"Listen, you should give me some samples of your writing. Maybe I can get you a job on the show."

"That'd be great," I said. I didn't mention that last year I'd sent Manno Productions some potential story ideas, hoping to be discovered. But I hadn't even received a form-letter rejection.

"So did they tell you who's the other lead?" I asked.

"They're keeping it a secret. But I think it's somebody big."

"It could be like *Starsky and Hutch* or *CHiPs*," Ing gushed.

"You could be the next Erik Estrada," I said, and Ramir spit a lemon seed at me.

"When would it start?"

"They told me to clear my calendar from the first of July. You won't believe the money. $15,000 a week."

Ingrid and I stopped chewing.

"That's incredible," I said.

"It's astounding," Ingrid said.

"I know. I can't believe it myself. As soon as everything gets signed, I'm quitting the Good Karma so I can take some time off before we start shooting. I'm just so excited, thinking about everything I want to do once I get some money in the bank. Buy a villa in Martinique, fly everybody down for a party. Maybe start my own production company, produce Mitch's scripts. Start a collection of Ing's paintings."

Personally I wasn't thrilled at the thought of taking Ramir's charity. But Ingrid seemed flattered. She said, "I could give you my paintings now. I've got so many of them."

"So what's Victor going to do in Florida?" Ramir asked. And Ingrid recounted more of her tale. But to my ear, 15 percent of a coffee shop's profits couldn't really compare to $15,000 a week.

They basked in each other's success.

"When are you going to know about the job for sure?" Ing asked.

"Maybe next week. Anyway, Fred's taking me to a guesthouse up north tomorrow to get my mind off things."

"Who's Fred?"

"My new boyfriend," he said, lightly, provocatively.

"You have another one already?" I think I sounded more disgusted than hurt.

"What about Todd?" asked Ing.

"*Gone with the Wind.*"

"I liked Todd," Ing said sadly.

"Where'd you find this one?"

"After we went to Fran's the other night, I stopped in at Byzantium."

"Your manhunt."

"Fred bought me a cranberry martini and the rest is history.

You'd like him. He's really handsome."

"They're all handsome," Ing said.

Based on my years of education by talk-show therapists, here is my psychoanalysis of Ramir: Through his multiple boyfriends and through his desire to be the object of adoration, he is seeking to find the unconditional love and acceptance that he does not receive from his conservative Catholic parents.

"So he's paying your way at this guesthouse?" I asked. "Is he rich?"

"Comfortable. He works for one of the banks downtown."

"Rich," Ingrid translated. "When do we get to meet him?"

"I invited him for dinner tonight, but he says he doesn't want to meet my friends until he's sure about things."

"Sure about *what*? He sounds like one of those clinging-vine parasite types."

"Mitch, you're being a bitch." Ramir loves to say that. "Fred is perfect for me right now. He's really interested in my career. He's really encouraging."

"Frederick of Hollywood. Maybe he's planning a palimony suit when you're a rich TV star. Remember Merv Griffin."

"I'm not worried. I just want to get this part. That's what really matters. The thing I hate is being left hanging like this."

I smiled with a dramatic stiff upper lip. "You'll get used to it."

Ingrid grabbed our hands. "You're both going to do really well. I know it."

I think I managed to sound upbeat for the rest of the evening – as Ingrid convinced herself about the wisdom of taking control of her life and Ramir went on about his imminent wealth and star power.

I marvelled to myself yet again at Ramir's good fortune with jobs and boyfriends. But I was also a tad smug. He probably wouldn't have been able to write a decent script for *Eruption* anyway.

But gloating wasn't very satisfying.

I really am happy for them.

Later, when I was alone upstairs in my apartment, I got obsessive again about the HIV test. I pressed my fingers against the lymph glands in my neck and under my arms. I was sure they felt swollen.

I brought out my secret stash of Cuervo Gold tequila, turned on the TV and drank myself into oblivion.

I spent a grey weekend hiding in my apartment. And then Monday I went back to work at the law firm.

Same thing Tuesday. Another day of mindless typing, living the Generation X stereotype of hopeless dead-end labour. Another night of coming home alone, collapsing on the couch.

There I lay last night, drinking away my sorrows, feeling a kinship with all the great, tormented writers of history. Except instead of sitting in Harry's Bar in Venice, I was watching *Entertainment Tonight* and being reminded that life isn't worth living unless you're famous.

The alcohol had slowed my brain down to a snail's pace. Therapeutic protection from more self-abuse.

Then, at exactly seven thirty-three, the telephone rang.

"Whaddayawant?" I slurred.

"Mitchell?"

Right away I knew it was her.

"Carmen!" I cried, as if she were my long-lost sister.

"Are you feeling okay?"

"Yes, no, I'm fine, I'm great," I said, straightening up. "I just – I thought you must have hired somebody else."

"My life's been pretty wild lately. Anyway, I'm just getting back on track and I decided you're my best option for the script."

"You're kidding."

"Don't say you're too busy."

"No, no, I'm just – this is just – I'm just so happy."

"Good, I'm glad. Listen, Mitchell, I need to get this whole project moving fast. So we need to meet tomorrow."

"That's perfect, sure. Any time is good."

"Your place at three o'clock."

"Three. Perfect. Fine. Sure. Thank you."

So here I sit, typing at my computer, awaiting her arrival just as I did on that momentous day two weeks ago. I feel stupid about having been so effusive on the telephone. But finally *something* in my life is working.

Last night I called Ingrid and I babbled on for an hour. Of course she said she wasn't surprised. (And this morning she donated six croissants for Carmen.) Then I phoned Ramir and he promised to bring over a bottle of Canadian champagne. (The casting director told him things still look positive, but now they're auditioning a few more people in New York and L.A.)

I stared at my chequebook and imagined the blissful relaxation that $18,000 would bring.

I couldn't help indulging in a few fantasies. My name gliding across the silver screen. Meeting with Jodie Foster to discuss the subtleties of her character's motivation. Mounting the stage of the Dorothy Chandler Pavilion, accepting the Academy Award for Best Original Screenplay.

This morning, right at nine, I called my temp agency and told them to put my file in the paper shredder. Yes, I'm burning a bridge, but I think it's important to commit myself fully to my new career.

BOLDNESS HAS GENIUS, POWER AND MAGIC IN IT, as Goethe promises in the quote that's magneted to my fridge. I sure hope he was right.

There's the door buzzer.

Let my real life begin.

It was *déjà vu*, standing outside my apartment door, watching Carmen huff to the top of the stairs.

"Why is it that real stairs are always harder than a Stairmaster?" she gasped. "I've never understood that."

I silently held out a glass of iced tea – brewed in my own gourmet kitchen.

"No, I'm off caffeine," she said. "I brought a bottle of Evian."

She dug into her bag, pulled out the bottle and took a belt.

I had the sense once again that I was witnessing a living, breathing Hollywood cliché.

She was wearing a loose black jacket and black pants, just like last time, though I could tell it was a different outfit. Her earrings were giant gold spirals.

"Everything's been going so totally right today, I can't believe it," she said.

"The movie's coming together?"

"At last. I just hired this incredible production person. She's worked on a bunch of David Cronenberg projects. Now we just need to get this screenplay into our hands and everything else can start moving."

"I'm all ready to go," I said. "I really have to thank you, Carmen. This is such an excellent opportunity."

"Just make sure you do an excellent job. The script needs to be so good we'll have all the actors clawing each others' eyes out to be in it. That way we don't have to pay them as much."

I laughed along with her. And decided that now may not be the best moment to ask about my salary.

"Would you like a croissant?"

"No croissants," she said. "But you could get me a knife and a plate. I brought a grapefruit. I just started going to this really amazing naturopath. He gives you a diet based on your blood type. I'm a Type A. No dairy. No wheat. And it feels like I'm eating grapefruit all day long."

"Grapefruit always give me canker sores."

"And that's not the end of it. This guy's making me do mud packs and herbal foot baths and high colonics."

"I've heard about those," I said, clenching. I didn't really want to hear more.

"They're not as weird as everybody says. You just lie there on a table with a blanket over you. But in the room next door, this woman brought in her two kids while she was having it done. Three- and four-year-olds. So these little kids are sitting on the floor, watching their mother's shit go by in a tube. Isn't that sick? Can you imagine those kids talking to their shrink someday?"

"I suppose they won't be anal-retentive."

"Anyway, the good thing is that I really feel like I'm getting my life on track." She started pacing the apartment, following my own exact route between the bathroom and the window. "This movie has got to be so incredible, Mitchell. I want people kissing our feet. Like I said, I've already got the story – the characters' names and all that. Frankly, I tried writing the thing myself, but I haven't got the patience."

"I'm an expert at patience," I said.

"This story is so hot, it's going to blow people right out of the water. And by the way, Mitchell, like I said, you've got to swear to keep all this confidential until we've got the final draft together and we're ready to go public."

"I won't tell a soul." (Excepting Ingrid and Ramir, of course.)

"My mother called me this morning from L.A. and I wouldn't even tell her what the story's about."

"Does she work in the movie business, too?"

"She used to be in make-up. But now all she does is try to screw up my life. So anyway, are you ready to get started?"

Carmen settled on the wing chair. I sat on the couch. I crossed my legs and rested my clipboard on my knee, feeling disturbingly like a temp about to take dictation.

"Okay." Like she was about to give me a priceless gift. "It's called *A Time for Revenge*."

"How trite and banal. It sounds like the title of a John Grisham novel."

No, I didn't really say that. But I did resolve to come up with a better title on my own. In any case, I wrote her suggestion at the top of the page and nodded deeply as if I thought it were magnificent.

She leaned towards me. "The main character is this beautiful young woman. Think Uma Thurman or Nicole Kidman. Her name is Pandora Tornametti. Let me spell it."

I carefully printed out this grandiose Harold Robbins-esque name, already wondering if she'd let me suggest something a bit less heavy-handed in the symbolism department. *What box of problems will Pandora open?* Using names that drip with meaning is a sure sign of an amateur who took Grade 10 English far too seriously.

"The whole thing takes place in New York, so it'll appeal to the American market. But we'll shoot in Toronto to save money." Toronto's fate in film is to serve as an anonymous stand-in for American cities. An ongoing insult to our civic pride.

"I hope you know Manhattan," she said.

"Like the back of my hand!" I've only been there twice, but I read *New York* magazine religiously.

"Okay, so Pandora is the daughter of this really rich business tycoon named Nick Tornametti. You really have to hate this guy. Maybe Robert de Niro, Al Pacino, Harvey Keitel. A real arrogant asshole type."

I repeated "arrogant asshole" as I scribbled it down in my own version of shorthand.

"Pandora's mother died when she was just a little kid. All the time she was growing up, she went to private schools, so she never really knew her father. Are you with me? So now she's got some big degree and she starts working for her father's real estate development company. But they agree to keep it secret that she's his daughter so she doesn't get special treatment. But the father is extra tough on her. Embarrasses her in front of people in the office, tells her that her work is lousy. Treats her like a piece of shit."

"Piece of shit," I said.

"And then she meets this guy at work and she falls in love with him."

"Who is he?"

"I don't know. Doesn't matter. But she falls in love with him and he tells her these rumours that her father has a really bad reputation in the business. That he's into money laundering, getting investors into fake companies, selling drugs – you get the idea."

"Sort of like *Mafia Princess*."

"Stay away from the Mafia stuff. Too cliché. Anyway, she also hears that, back in September '76, her father killed a lawyer who was going to turn him in on one of his shady investment deals. Money laundering on some shopping malls in Arizona."

Carmen took a break to sip her Evian, which gave me a chance to catch up.

"It's good so far, huh?"

"Very good."

"So anyway, Pandora gets curious and she starts to look into it herself. I want to have one of those scenes where she goes to the library and digs through the old newspaper microfilm to find information about the dead guy. And then, somewhere around the office, she finds some evidence that proves that her father *really did* do it."

"What kind of evidence?"

"That's up to you. Make something up. But the point is, now she knows her father is a murderer and she doesn't know whether to report him."

"Sort of like that Jessica Lange movie where she's a lawyer and she finds out that her father was a Nazi and she doesn't know whether she should defend him or not."

Carmen sat back sharply. "We want to make this an *original* screenplay, right Mitchell?"

Perhaps I should keep quiet with my comparisons.

"So then her father finds out that she has this secret evidence on him, and he tells her to shut up . . . *or else*."

"The turning point," I added, to show my understanding of story structure and to sound like a team player.

"But because Pandora's got such strong principles, she decides she has to turn him in. And when he finds out about it, he realizes that he's going to have to kill her to keep her quiet. Are you still with me? This is when we get to the big climax. I want something really spectacular. Like the two of them are having a fight over who's got the gun and then she points the gun at his head and shoots him."

"She blows her father's head off?"

"To show that she was actually stronger than him all along. She gets to show everybody how powerful she is. And that's the end!"

"Yes, hmm-mmm." I furiously scribbled down some more notes and tried to stall.

"So what do you think? It's fabulous, huh? Isn't it fabulous?"

"It's a tired old plot with lots of holes, and at best it might make a TV movie-of-the-week starring Valerie Bertinelli."

No, I didn't say that.

But I mean, *this* was the story she thought was so hot and

controversial? My stomach felt sick. There was nothing I could do with this.

I managed to find a big smile. I said, "I like it. I really like it. I've got some great ideas already."

"Like what?"

"It's going to take some time to work them out."

I reminded myself that the very reason she'd hired me was to make the script good. She seemed to believe in the story so much, I didn't want to let her down. And on top of that, there was no way I could say no to my first real job as a professional screenwriter.

"I want this movie to be really great, Mitchell. Really suspenseful, dramatic, edge-of-your-seat kind of stuff. *Chinatown*. *Fatal Attraction*. *Basic Instinct*. Good wins over evil. When you're right, you come out on top – that kind of big important statement. You know what I mean? And the other thing is, we need to do this fast. We're going into production in September. So how soon can you give me a first draft?"

I remembered what all the screenplay books and seminars had taught me. "Shouldn't I should show you an outline first? A treatment? Just so you can see how I'm thinking of developing the story, before I start the actual writing."

"How long will that take?"

"A week?"

"As long as we finish the whole script by the end of June. That's about five weeks."

"That shouldn't be a problem."

Five weeks. During which time I'd have to work around the clock to turn an episode of *Murder, She Wrote* into *Citizen Kane*.

"Carmen, I was wondering if we could talk about money – just to get that out of the way." I'd already rehearsed my bargaining strategy with Ramir, just so I'd be prepared. I said, "I know the standard fee for the first draft of a feature is $36,000."

Carmen guffawed. Which rather effectively rattled my bargaining strategy.

"But since I'm not union," I said, "I was thinking about cutting it in half to $18,000."

"That's still funny, Mitchell. This is my first movie. This is *your* first movie. And contrary to what you seem to think, we don't have the world's biggest budget here. So be serious. Like I said, this is a chance to make a name for yourself. If things work out, we're going to the top together, right?"

"Right," I said hesitantly.

"A lot of important people are going to be reading this script, seeing your name on the cover. I'm helping you build a reputation, and that's worth a lot, isn't it?"

She waited for me to say yes. I said, "Yes."

"I need to get this project off the ground, Mitchell, so I can't be spending all my money right off the top. When we go into profits, I'll cut you in."

"So exactly how much would I get now?"

She pulled a plain white envelope out of her bag. "Just so you know I'm working in good faith, I'm giving you an advance. One thousand dollars."

Silently I screamed with joy.

I took the envelope and looked inside. A neat little pile of one-hundred dollar bills. I'd be able to cover my rent and pay part of my Visa balance. But outside I stayed skeptical. "I'd like to get a sense of the total."

"You've got a thousand now. I'll give you another thousand when you finish the first draft. And another thousand when you give me the final draft."

Three thousand dollars. Clearly she was taking advantage. But it's not as though I'm in the Writer's Guild and can fight her.

Still, play tough. Hard Hollywood bargaining.

"Carmen, I'm going to have to turn down some very lucrative jobs to make sure we get this done on time."

"Okay, I can give you another five hundred. Say next week, when you finish the treatment. See how nice I'm being?"

"Thank you."

"Listen, Mitchell, I'm late for another meeting. So let's say you'll have the treatment ready for me next Wednesday. Same time, same place."

She got up and headed for the door.

"Can I get your phone number?" I asked. "You know, in case

I have any questions – maybe bounce some ideas off you."

"Sure, I just had my new cards printed."

She dug around in her bag until she found her wallet. The plain white business card simply read DENVER PRODUCTIONS with a phone number. No address.

"I'd better get going. And like I said last time, I know what I like and what I don't like. And I really want to like this, Mitchell."

"You will. I know you will."

"Perfect. *Ciao* for now."

I always hate it when people say "*Ciao.*"

As she clumped down the stairs, I wondered what I'd gotten myself into. Of course I had no idea whether she'd like what I did. I was being pushed to work at unrealistic speed, taken advantage of financially.

But $3,500 for five weeks of work was still a lot better than office temping.

And it's an opportunity. A challenge. If I can make something of this script, I can build the foundation for my whole career.

And then I remembered the thousand dollars in my pocket.

I was rich!

I had to celebrate.

Worry about the work later.

So I rushed out of my apartment to tell Ingrid and Ramir in person. I'd just crossed Howland Avenue when I noticed a man standing on the other side of Bloor Street. Staring at me. An attractive man. Wearing a white shirt and a dark patterned necktie. Black wavy hair. Brooding eyes. Pouty lips.

He looked like a young Antonio Banderas – in his early Pedro Almodóvar period. He was leaning on his car – an expensive, small, black, shiny car – right in front of Book City.

I looked around to see if some supermodel in a mini-skirt might be standing nearby. But no, he was definitely looking at me.

I didn't know what to do. I kept walking towards Ingrid's store and his eyes kept following me. I looked back over my shoulder and he was still staring, brazen as could be.

So I tried the ancient gay pickup technique – one I've always been too shy to actually attempt. I stopped and looked in the

window of the Hungarian butcher shop – as if I were truly con-
templating buying a giant jar of pickled peppers. Tradition dictated
that Antonio should cross the street and look in the window
beside me. But nothing happened. He stayed on the other side of
the street.

Maybe he'd follow me into the Grind. I walked the rest of the
way down the block and just before I turned to go in the door, I
gave a seductive come-hither glance over my shoulder.

He wasn't moving.

I was just about to throw caution to the wind and cross the
street myself when he climbed into his car.

As soon as I stepped inside the shop, I pressed my nose to the
window, Ingrid asking "What are you doing?" behind my back.

"Look at that car," I commanded. "In that car is a man who is
in love with me."

"Him?" she pointed as he drove by. "He looks like Antonio
Banderas."

"That's exactly what I thought! Do you think he looked this
way?"

"I think he turned his head."

"I think so too. I have just fallen into a serious infatuation. Not
that I'll ever see him again."

"Maybe he'll come into the store. I'll call you if he does."

"But I've got even *more* good news!" I let her peek in the envelope with the one thousand dollars. "It's official. I got the job."

"That's fabulous!" Ing gave me a big wet kiss on the cheek.

"Carmen's got a few eccentricities, but I think we're going to
get along."

"You've finally made it, Mitchell. I'm so proud of you."

Ramir wasn't at the health food store when I stopped by – he
was out on an errand at their non-dairy dairy supplier – so I left
him a high-impact note: "Sizzling new screenwriter viewed as hot
commodity by rich, handsome stranger." That garnered two messages on my answering machine as he begged for details.

I wasn't available for calls.

I decided to re-enact a segment of *Lifestyles of the Rich and
Famous*. After all, I'd be getting another $500 from Carmen next

week, so I convinced myself that I could afford some shameless excess.

I took a cab eastward to the elegant designer-label stretch of Bloor Street (Toronto's film stand-in for Fifth Avenue) and went directly to Holt Renfrew (stunt double for Bergdorf-Goodman).

I browsed the men's boutiques and selected a Calvin Klein long-sleeve linen shirt in beige with tortoiseshell buttons. $250. I have never spent so much money on a single piece of clothing.

The guilt.

But I told myself I'd need it if I was to go out on a date with Antonio.

Next on my list was a special little celebration I'd been planning for years, in anticipation of this occasion.

I walked towards the Park Plaza Hotel, its classic gold-brick tower a beacon above Bloor. I rode the elevator to the eighteenth floor: the penthouse.

In the washroom beside the restaurant, I put on my new shirt, hoping the fold marks weren't too conspicuous. Then I stepped into the renowned rooftop bar. Glowing dark wood against rich green wallpaper. Overstuffed couches around a fireplace. Waiters in white vests and black bow ties.

From the forties to the seventies, this was the celebrated meeting place for the Canadian literati. Novelists, newspaper writers and publishers. On the wall in the corner there are little framed caricatures of Margaret Atwood, Mordecai Richler and other important writerly types.

This afternoon, the bar was sparsely populated, mostly with tourists in white windbreakers. Nowadays, apparently, the publishing industry has moved on to fresher, more down-to-earth haunts.

But nonetheless, I went out to the terrace, high atop downtown, and took a seat at a quaint wrought-iron table. The view is famous. The most spectacular angle on the city skyline, looking directly south at the CN Tower and all the skyscrapers of the business district. I tried to figure out which building I'd been working in – only yesterday! May I never set eyes on that tedious lawyer ever again.

I ordered a very dry Rob Roy – because I read someplace that

that's what all the old-time journalists always ordered – and I toasted myself and my future as a genuine professional screen-writer.

I breathed a sigh of contentment. The breeze brushing my cheek. The city at my feet.

In that moment, for the first time in months, I felt a taste of calm.

Even as I type these words, I am in the grip of writer's block.

The more I stare at my notes – and I've been staring at them constantly since I got home yesterday from the Park Plaza – the more I see the fatal flaws in Carmen's story. The whole thing is internal. It's all one character trying to figure out the mystery by herself – which, all the screenwriting books agree, just doesn't work. For a movie, everything has to be visual, everything has to be action. Pandora needs people to talk to. Dialogue to help explain the details of the crime she's uncovering. The movie needs a sub-plot, the theme of which might explore the greater social issues under examination.

Maybe this boyfriend she meets at the office can be a spy her father plants to test her loyalty. But why would her father do that? Maybe the man has infiltrated the company on behalf of a competitor and he spreads rumours about her boss being a murderer to destroy corporate morale.

What if he's a Russian spy? What if the guy is secretly having an affair with her father? What if Pandora is moonlighting as a hooker in an S&M bordello?

So with all these unanswerable questions, I just got stuck – certain that the movie is beyond help and inevitably a piece of shit.

How could Carmen call herself a serious film producer and be committed to such a lame, unoriginal story?

My mother called a few hours ago and even that was a welcome interruption.

She invited me for dinner again. I told her that I'm really busy because I just got this important job writing the screenplay for a feature film – the kind they show in movie theatres. She said she was pleased for me. Then she changed the subject and told me about their neighbours' new Ford Windstar minivan.

My parents don't have much concept of my career aspirations. They can't imagine that anyone ever really sits down and *writes* a movie – even though all they ever do is watch TV.

I don't know why they want me to come for dinner anyway. None of us ever says anything when I'm there.

After I hung up, I sat and watched TV myself, staring blankly at a rerun of *McMillan and Wife*.

Then it came to me that maybe the boyfriend could be an undercover cop, trying to find evidence on Nick Tornametti. And once he's infiltrated the company, he tells Pandora about the case to get her to help. But of course, he doesn't know that Nick Tornametti is actually her father.

It fits perfectly.

Ah, the wonders of the subconscious mind.

Ingrid called at five o'clock.

"Victor just left for Florida," she announced.

As soon as I heard Ingrid's voice, I deserted my desk and reclined on the couch, my cordless phone tucked between my shoulder and my ear.

"He dropped in with his family on their way out of town. They're only driving as far as Buffalo tonight."

"Did you cry when you said good-bye?"

"I did actually."

"You're kidding."

"The whole thing was pretty sad. Victor kept rambling on in that motivational talk – how this is 'a win-win situation for both of us' and now he's able to his 'live the Canadian dream' by moving to Florida. Then he gave me a hug and said to take good care of the place. We both sort of sniffled."

"Who ever thought Victor Fellner had a heart? Of course, with you in charge now, he'll probably make more money than ever."

"He made me sign a contract, you know. For one year."

"Indentured slavery."

"I'm trying to look on the bright side and see it as stability. It *is* sort of exciting, standing here in the shop and knowing I'm the one in control."

"While the cat's away . . . ."

"I can't change too much. He's coming back for a visit at the end of July. Just hold on a second."

I heard the phone rattle as she set it down on the counter. I pushed back my cuticles while I eavesdropped on her making change for a customer, then giving a cheery farewell.

She was back.

"So did you get a lot of work done on your screenplay?"

"I'm still struggling with the plot. They say you're supposed to be able to come up with a one-sentence synopsis – like in *TV Guide*. That's the sign of a well-formed story."

"Have you come up with one?"

" 'A beautiful young woman discovers that her father is a murderer, and when she decides to turn him in, he decides to kill her.' "

"A dysfunctional family. Very nineties."

"It sounds awful, doesn't it?"

"It just sounds dramatic – in the finest Sidney Sheldon tradition. So when do I get to read it?"

"I'm working on the outline first. But I really will want your opinion. And Ramir's."

"Have you heard from him today, by the way?"

"I left a message on his answering machine."

"He said he was going to come over to my place for yoga this morning, but he didn't show up. He wasn't at work either. Maybe he's playing hooky with Fred."

"Fred," I said with more disdain than I'd intended.

"Ramir wants us to meet him for dinner on the weekend."

"I don't know why he bothers to introduce us to his boyfriends when they're always gone in two weeks."

"He just doesn't take dating as seriously as we do."

"I think he does it just to make us jealous."

"It doesn't make *me* jealous."

"Are you trying to imply something, Ingrid?" I said, only slightly exaggerating my indignation.

"You know what I mean," she said, squirming.

"I'm not jealous about Ramir having boyfriends."

"I just understand what it's like," she said, "with me still being fixated on Pierre."

"I am not fixated on Ramir. You saw for yourself. Just yesterday I started a major romance with Antonio Banderas."

"You're right. I'm sorry," she said. But I could tell she was only humouring me. "I'd better get back to work." Conveniently escaping the subject. "You know my first decision as manager? Tomorrow I'm staying home and all I'm going to do is paint."

As soon as I hung up from Ingrid, I phoned Ramir. He answered in a soft, creaky voice that made me think he'd been asleep.

"I left a message for you," I said. "Why didn't you call me back?"

"Sorry."

"And Ingrid said you didn't show up for yoga this morning."

"I totally forgot," he said, now sounding more beat up than tired.

"What happened? What's the matter?"

No answer.

"Are you okay?"

"I didn't get the show."

"Oh, Ramir, I'm sorry."

"They're flying somebody up from Los Angeles. They were just stringing me along."

"They must have thought you were good, or they wouldn't have kept auditioning you."

"Yeah."

"You always say things turn out exactly the way they're supposed to. Something better'll come along."

"Right."

"You know it's only going to be another tacky American cop show."

"I just have to learn you can't count on anything in this business."

"Do you want me to come over? We can sit and talk."

"No, thanks. Fred's here."

"Oh," I said quickly.

Suddenly I felt angry. Betrayed. Felt stupid for thinking Ramir and I were having an intimate conversation when actually every word was being overheard by a complete stranger.

"I'll get over it," Ramir said. "I'll phone Ingrid and tell her I'm sorry about standing her up."

"Don't worry, I'll call her."

We said good-bye and I hung up.

I pictured Ramir with his rich new boyfriend, lying in bed together, all cuddled up and cozy. And I felt really jealous.

I stood in front of the bathroom mirror, examining my out-stretched tongue and wondering if the blanket of tiny white bumps on the surface means I have thrush. Or maybe those are just my taste buds.

FRIDAY, MAY 23

INTERIOR. THE DAILY GRIND. DAY.

INGRID and MITCHELL are standing by the back wall of the store. The floor is damp and there are buckets filled with sopped-up water. Soggy posters of coffee-producing countries have been ripped aside to reveal a giant hole in the plaster. The edges are brown, wet and rotten.

INGRID
Kinita called me this morning as soon as she saw it.

MITCHELL
So Victor put up the posters to hide the water stains.

INGRID
He must have known for months there was a leak. It's so typical of him. Covering up a problem and then having someone else fix it.

MITCHELL
It doesn't smell very appetizing. It reminds me of a compost heap.

INGRID
I'll grind some extra beans to hide it. The plumber should be here soon. And then I have to get somebody to fix the plaster. Of course, I'm supposed to be home painting today.

MITCHELL
Couldn't Kinita take care of it?

INGRID
She didn't know what to do. And besides, I am the manager.

MITCHELL
At least things can't get much worse than this.

INGRID

If Victor weren't still on the road, I'd call him right now and quit.

The door opens. MITCHELL and INGRID turn to see a short but cute PLUMBER in overalls.

MITCHELL

(for Ingrid's ear only) Maybe Victor did you a favour.

PLUMBER

You've got a leak?

INGRID

You're from Mike's Plumbing?

PLUMBER

(smiling shyly, shaking hands) I'm Mike.

INGRID

I'm Ingrid. I turned off the water at the water main downstairs. But the leak is right over there in the wall someplace. I guess that's pretty obvious.

PLUMBER

I'll check it out downstairs first.

As he descends, INGRID and MITCHELL look at each other with eyebrows raised.

MITCHELL

Very Robby Benson.

INGRID

Did you ever see *Ice Castles*?

MITCHELL

(deadpanning the love theme) "Please, don't let this feeling end . . . ."

INGRID

My sister had the record. I loved that song.

MITCHELL
So what are you waiting for? You've got one of those letters to *Playgirl* waiting to happen in your basement.

INGRID
I can't! What am I supposed to say?

MITCHELL
Ask him about his plumbing! The double-entendres are endless.

INGRID
Okay, I'll just ask him if he wants a coffee.

MITCHELL
(coaching, in ultra-sleazebag style) "Hey there, cutie, any-one ever mention you look like Robby Benson?"

INGRID
What if he's never heard of Robby Benson?

MITCHELL
If he doesn't know popular culture, you don't want him. Just go!

INGRID
(calming herself) Okay, it's no big deal. I'm just going to see if he needs anything.

MITCHELL
"Do you need me to hold your tool?" "Do you need me to empty that great big pipe?"

INGRID
Stop it, Mitchell!

INGRID descends into the basement, trying to keep a straight face.

MITCHELL
You have to tell me everything.

CUT TO:

INTERIOR. MITCHELL'S APARTMENT. DAY /
INTERIOR. THE DAILY GRIND. DAY.

MITCHELL is practicing writing screen dialogue when the phone
rings. Cut between MITCHELL and INGRID on their respective
telephones.

INGRID

Just call me a shameless hussy!

MITCHELL

(eagerly) What happened?

INGRID

I went downstairs –

MITCHELL

You *slinked* downstairs.

INGRID

I told him my uncle was a plumber. That I know the basics
about turning off the water, changing washers . . . .

MITCHELL

So you have common interests. Was he impressed?

INGRID

He said it was very unusual. And he asked me about
managing the store.

MITCHELL

He asked you a question! That means he grasps the
concept of communication.

INGRID

I told him that I paint as sort of a hobby. So we talked a
bit about Emily Carr and Georgia O'Keeffe. About the
new art show at Harbourfront.

MITCHELL

A plumber who goes to an art gallery?

                    INGRID
That's when he told me that his lover's a photographer.

                    MITCHELL
(a verbal wince) Oh.

                    INGRID
Isn't it funny how heterosexuals never use the word lover?

                    MITCHELL
Except for Doris Day and Rock Hudson in *Lover Come Back*.

                    INGRID
That sums it up.

                    MITCHELL
So maybe you'll have better luck with the guy who's fixing the plaster.

Writing all afternoon.

I came up with an idea for the evidence that proves Pandora's father is the killer. The murder weapon – yet to be determined – is hidden in an office vault that Pandora is ordered to clean out. That'll build in perfectly with all her degrading menial labour.

The writing's really going well. I finally feel like I'm getting behind the story. Like it's mine instead of Carmen's.

But I've still got to come up with a more tasteful way for Pandora to kill her father. I can't stomach the idea of her shooting him in the head. It's too violent. Passive murder is so much more ladylike. Poison's always best. But at the same time we need something visually exciting.

Last night I tried to call Carmen to tell her my ideas, but the number on her card turned out to be a pager, and she hasn't called me back yet.

I looked up Denver again in the telephone book and there were six listings – but none of them with Carmen or a C. Unless her film company is actually known as the Denver Drain Service.

Maybe Pandora could jam her father's head in the toilet.

Okay. Brainstorm sensibly.

They're in the real estate business.

Maybe the big climax should be on top of a skyscraper – one of the buildings their company has constructed. The two of them arrange to meet in private to talk things out. Outside, up on the roof. Maybe there's a fierce wind. No, a blazing orange sunset, its fiery reflection bouncing against the neighbouring glass office towers. It'll make a stunning shot on the big screen.

Father and daughter argue violently, waving their arms, stomping their feet. He slaps her across the face. She spits in his eye. Then, when things get really vicious, Pandora gives her dear old dad a push. And as he plummets to his death, screaming in terror, his flailing body can bounce against the windows, just like Jennifer Jones did in *The Towering Inferno*.

Pandora gets her revenge, but with no dirty mess on her hands.

And I get a spectacular finale that will be remembered as a breathtaking highlight in the history of film.

On the sidewalk in front of my apartment, there's a lamppost that's always plastered with posters for local bar bands and Homo Hops and meetings of lingering Marxist-Leninists.

But this morning when I stepped outside to buy *The Globe and Mail* I saw a fresh sheet of green paper with huge black letters:

RAMIR MARTINEZ

ERUPTION

I practically erupted myself.

And when I looked down the street, on all the lampposts and walls of buildings, there were identical posters, alternating in colour between phosphorescent green and iridescent yellow. They stretched along Bloor Street as far as the eye could see.

Of course, I ran right back up to my apartment and called him at work.

Ramir answered with, "You've got Good Karma" – the store's official scripted greeting.

"You're doing the show!"

"Did you see the poster?" he asked coyly.

"It's everywhere!"

"I just couldn't stand feeling sorry for myself anymore."

"So now you're erupting on the world stage. You must have been out all night putting them up."

"Just until two."

"You should have called me – I would have helped."

"Fred came with me." My jealousy swept back, but then Ramir redeemed himself. "I've got a break in ten minutes, why don't you come over to the store and I'll fill you in."

We crossed the street to the miniature park at the corner of Spadina and Bloor. Concrete surrounding an island of grass. We sat on a stone bench with a chessboard set in the centre.

"Fred and I put up five hundred posters. But considering how anal Toronto is, they'll probably all be cleaned off by sundown."

"Anal-retentiveness is next to godliness."

"So we'll just put up another round tomorrow. This poster's really just a teaser. I have to talk to Ingrid about doing the real one with all the ticket information and everything."

"She's really busy with the store right now."

"It won't take her long."

"You always say that, Ramir."

"But this time it's important. Remember when you'd see k.d. lang flyers on lampposts?"

"And look at her now."

"Exactly. I just want to get my name out there, so people notice."

"You're hard to miss at this point."

"Market saturation. You wouldn't believe everything I have to do this week. Find a theatre, set the dates, send out invitations to all the casting people and producers." With each point, he leap-frogged his forefinger across the squares of the chessboard.

"You can't make these things happen overnight, Ramir."

"I know what I'm doing. Remember I worked on that show with the theatre collective last summer."

"That was different. There were eight of you."

"I'll take care of it," he said with utmost confidence. "And I forgot to tell you, I'm going to make the whole show multimedia now – so I have to rent some AV equipment."

"How much is all this going to cost?"

"I've got $1,500."

"From where?"

"Various sources."

"Your parents?"

He nodded.

"How did you convince them?"

"My last-ditch effort at being an actor."

"They must be praying for you to flop."

"Well, if I don't get somewhere with this show, I might be better off in electrician school."

"It won't come to that."

"Anyway, it's an investment. And I'll make some of it back in ticket sales. That reminds me, I have to buy a roll of tickets."

"And don't forget you have to write the script."

"I'm working on it."

"Which means?"

"I decided to drop the subtitle."

"No more 'screaming oppressed'?"

"Killed them. I've made a few notes for the monologues. But I still need your help."

"I already feel like I'm spending my whole life writing this movie for Carmen."

"Have you written a part for me yet?"

"Don't press your luck."

"Listen Mitch, you can't work all the time. Why don't you come out with me and Fred tonight? Maybe you'll meet someone."

"I don't *want* to meet anybody. You know I'm trying to avoid dating."

"And I'm trying to do you a favour."

"Thanks, but I think I'll decline."

"Have you gone back to the clinic?"

I looked down at the chessboard. "No, I haven't. You'd know."

"You should just forget you ever went for the test, Mitch. You were negative before you dated that Adam guy. And if you were only unsafe that once . . . ."

"He promised me afterwards he was negative."

"So if *he'd* been tested, then you must be okay."

"He could have been lying. I don't know. It just preys on my mind."

He squeezed my knee. "That's why you need to go out and meet new people. Have a good time. That's all you can do."

I looked up into his brown eyes. Suddenly I felt really sad.

"I just get scared sometimes," I said. "Sometimes I wonder if I'm going to drop dead before I can ever accomplish anything . . . before I ever have a real relationship."

"You're writing the screenplay for a major motion picture, remember?"

"Yeah."

"And you've got lots of real relationships. You've got me," he said. "And Ingrid."

"Right." I reached down to the ground and picked up a twig. My plea for sympathy wasn't having its desired effect. "Remember when we were teenagers and we all thought the planet was going to end with a nuclear war? Life was so much simpler then."

A giant black squirrel galloped across the pavement, sat up on its haunches and stared at us, demanding food. We stared back. When the squirrel saw all I had was a stick, it ran off towards a tree.

"Listen Mitch, I know I'm not a real writer. I know I'm not good at finishing things. But I have to make this show happen. I think it could be good. I mean *really* good. I've got some great ideas already. I'm doing the rough draft – all the time-consuming stuff. I just need you to come over and make sure everything sounds right."

I looked up into his handsome, hopeful face. I wished he was hugging me.

"We'll have a good time," he promised. "I'll make eggplant curry. We'll open a bottle of wine. Get the creative juices flowing. I'll help you with your script. You can help me with mine."

"But it has to be after Wednesday – after I've finished the outline for Carmen."

"Thursday it is!" He slapped his hand on the chessboard. "Shit, I need to get back to work. Listen, Mitch, you'll probably live forever. Things are going to turn out great for both of us."

He gave my arm a quick squeeze and bounded across the street.

I sat there on the bench for a few more minutes. I stared at the board until my eyes blurred and the black and white squares became a kaleidoscope.

At five-thirty a.m., as I lay in peaceful slumber, the phone rang. All of a sudden my heart was racing and I grabbed for the receiver.

It was Ingrid. "I think I've done something really stupid. You have to come to the store right away."

I was dressed in thirty seconds. My brain was still half-asleep, which helped keep me focused on my goal. I stumbled along the sidewalk to the Grind. The sun was beginning to rise in a yellow glow through the corridor of tall buildings to the east.

Ingrid was waiting for me outside the store. She was frazzled, manic. She grabbed me in a desperate clutch. "Sorry I woke you up, but I've been holding off calling since three this morning. I've got all the coffee brewed and everything ready to open the store. But I don't know whether I should."

"Ingrid, what's the matter?"

"Nothing's the *matter*, exactly. I just want you to swear that you're going to be totally honest with me."

"What happened? What'd you do?"

Her face was pained. "You know the back wall. The one that had the leak."

"It burst again?"

"It's fine. The new plaster was all dry and I bought the brown paint to make it match the rest of the store. But last night, after the first few brushstrokes, something just came over me. I ran home and brought back all my own paints. And I did this."

She opened the door and I stepped inside.

There on the back wall – the first thing you see when you come into the shop – was a huge floor-to-ceiling mural. Bold swirls of colour. Browns and dark blues, golds and magenta. As I stared, the swirls coalesced into a perfectly clear scene. A female figure sitting at a café table, leaning forward, elbow bent. A coffee cup, a plate. Just a few strokes formed her face, creating an expression of dreamy anticipation. A whirl of steam from the coffee cup twirled above her head, transforming into a vision of a tango-dancing couple.

"Is it okay?" Ingrid asked, still in a panic.

I just stared.

"I need to know the truth, because I can still paint over it before any customers come."

"It's fabulous."

"Tell me the truth, Mitchell. This morning I made the guy who delivered the pastries just leave them at the front door. I didn't want him to see it."

"It's perfect, Ing. It's just what the store needs. You've always wanted to redecorate the place."

"But people are going to see it – people I don't know."

"They'll love it."

"But if they hate it, I'll be able to tell just from looking at their faces."

"They'll think you're a genius."

"You really think so?"

"Ing, if I were a psychotherapist, I'd say this was a major breakthrough. It's like your inner artist has fought its way out because now it's ready to be seen."

"What if my *outer* artist isn't ready yet?"

"Then tell them somebody else did it."

"I don't want to do that either."

"It's like you've always said, Ing. You paint for yourself. It doesn't matter what other people think. You didn't do it for them."

"Exactly! And now I've put myself out on public view. I don't know what came over me!" She picked up the can of brown paint. "I mean, I'm going to have to paint over it anyway when Victor comes back for his inspection in July."

"Even Victor will love it. It's a masterpiece. This turns the place into the Sistine Chapel of coffee shops. They'll have to preserve the building forever. Art lovers from around the world will flock to The Daily Grind to buy a pound of coffee."

At last she smiled. "It's not too embarrassing?"

"Ingrid, it's your best work ever."

She took a deep breath and looked at the mural more steadily. "The colours are good, I'll give myself that."

Then we heard the door open behind us. The first customer of the day. The first audience. We turned breathlessly.

It was Frances Farmer.

She was wrapped in an oversized trench coat and in a nervous rush, as though a limousine were waiting outside to whisk her to the Paramount back lot.

She put her coins on the counter as usual, selected a small foam coffee cup and poured her customary Irish Cream decaf. She picked a banana-bran muffin out of the basket and set it on a plate.

She didn't seem to notice us, or anything anything else, for that matter.

She carried her breakfast to her favourite stool by the window.

Then, all at once, she turned to the mural. She stared at it intensely, almost furiously, as though she was angry at its intrusion into the familiar surroundings of The Daily Grind.

Just as abruptly she turned back to her own world. She arranged her cup and plate on the counter, just as in the painting, then placed one elbow strategically in front of her. She sat there perfectly still, as if she'd been Ingrid's model.

TUESDAY, MAY 27

This morning I realized that Pandora can't kill her father, even if it's only with a ladylike push. She wouldn't be sympathetic enough as a character. Nobody wants their heroine to be a cold-blooded murderess. The audience's innate sense of morality would be offended. People would leave the theatre feeling annoyed and dissatisfied.

So the ending is still unresolved.

This whole thing is so frustrating – all the unknowns.

What if Pandora's father falls off the building accidentally?

I worked until three a.m., preparing for today's meeting with Carmen. After I'd finished fine-tuning the fifteen-page treatment, I printed it out and took it to the 24-hour Kinko's down the street for photocopying onto the best quality bond.

And once I got home, I realized that Pandora's father can't die at the end of the movie – even by accident. It would go against everything they taught me about dramatic structure in my screenwriting seminars. The father and daughter have to come to some kind of satisfying resolution. That's the only way the audience will feel a satisfying resolution as well.

So I had to rework the last page of the treatment and take it back to Kinko's so the paper would match.

I was a zombie. I set my alarm and turned off the ringer on my phone. I slept restlessly, tormented by dreams of Carmen slapping my face, screaming, "It's shit and I hate it! It's shit and I hate it!"

Carmen arrived in person at quarter to four, laden with shopping bags from Cole-Haan, Tiffany and Hermès. She was wearing her trademark black ensemble, and judging from her scowl, she was in a black mood as well.

She had dark circles under her eyes and, for the first time, I noticed hard little crow's feet fanning out at her temples.

I tried to be sunny and upbeat. I said, "How are things?"

She said, "Things are shit."

"Can I get you some Evian?"

"I don't want anything. I'm having a bad day. A bad week. I can't stay long. I have another meeting. This place needs air conditioning."

"The fan's on and I've got the window open."

"Maybe I do need some water after all." I rushed to pour her a glass. She followed me to the kitchen nook. "Remember that production person I was telling you about?"

"The one who works for David Cronenberg?"

"The bitch dropped out. She said she can't work on the movie. Which is exactly what I don't need to hear at this point. She was going to be my right hand. And the casting person I finally decided on – she quit, too. Both in the same morning."

"That's weird."

"It's more than weird."

"Do they know each other?"

"Conspiracy theories have crossed my mind, believe me. Now all my planning is back to square one."

"It can't be that bad."

"It is." Her voice cracked.

She grimaced and looked as though she were about to cry. She covered her eyes with her hand.

I didn't know what to do. I figured it was unprofessional to give her a supportive hug.

She sniffled.

"Carmen, from what I've seen, if anyone can get things back on track, it's you."

She raised her head sharply and was back to her fierce self.

"Nobody's going to stop me, that's for sure. I'm just sick of everyone giving me such shit." She dropped her shopping bags, but held onto her purse. "I have to wash my face."

She went into the bathroom and closed the door. But considering the size of my apartment, I was still practically standing right beside her.

I didn't hear water in the sink. The toilet didn't flush. She was in the bathroom for a full five minutes and I didn't hear a single sound.

I sat down and waited – wondering what I would do if she slashed her wrists in there. And wondering if the whole movie was about to fall apart.

Then the door opened and Carmen emerged, looking perfectly normal.

"So this afternoon I went shopping to cheer myself up." She picked up the orange Hermès bag and ripped apart the tissue paper to reveal a fold of rich charcoal grey fabric. "It's a cashmere shawl for when it gets cold on airplanes. Feel it."

I felt it. The softest, most luxurious fabric I have ever touched. "It's beautiful," I said worshipfully.

The bill had fallen to the floor. I bent to pick it up. And of course I eyed the price: $1,895. More than half of what she was paying me to write a whole screenplay. For an airplane blanket. And she'd told me she was on a tight budget.

"Yeah, it's okay," she said and shoved the shawl in the bag. Then she took her place on the wing chair.

"Do you mind if I smoke?"

"Whatever you want."

"I need an ashtray."

"Oh, right." I went to the kitchen cupboard.

"Anyway, Mitchell, after a morning like I've had, I'm counting on you to show me something fabulous."

"Well, *I* really like what I've done," I said, and I sat down too. "I was thinking I'd let you read everything over first, and then we can discuss it."

"Frankly, Mitchell, I'm not in a reading mood. Why don't you just sum it up?"

I was thrown. She didn't want to admire my hours of exhausting labour?

"I'm not that good at telling stories out loud," I said. "I'm much better on paper."

"Pitching a story is part of the movie business, Mitchell. I just want you to give me the gist." She blew smoke in my face.

"Okay. Well. Then, I'd like to explain a bit about screenplay structure first – the three acts and the plot points – and show you how I've applied it to the story."

"No lectures, please. I have to be out of here by four-fifteen."

Thrown again.

"Maybe you can take your copy of the treatment home then, and when you have more time, you can go over everything."

"Sure, whatever."

"Okay, then. Well. First of all, one thing I've been wondering about is the title. I was thinking about a variation like maybe

Revenge at Last, Revenge is Sweet, but my personal fave is *Sins of the Father.*"

"The title stays. *A Time for Revenge.* It's had good feedback in L.A."

"Just an idea. Nothing more than that." I was practically shaking as I felt my confidence collapse. "Of course all this is just a rough draft. I can still change anything you want. It's all up in the air."

"I know that, Mitchell. And I know what I'm looking for."

"Well, I don't know where to start."

"How about at the beginning? We're sitting in a movie theatre. Bag of popcorn in one hand, giant drink on the floor. The lights go down. Then what?"

I inhaled and prepared myself for performance.

"Okay, the first thing you see – even before the credits – is a terrible brutal murder. Really fast cuts, sort of confusing. A guy stepping out the front door of his house. A metal bar coming down on his head. His body being stuffed into an old steamer trunk. The trunk being filled with cement."

"Good. Interesting."

"Then the trunk is dumped off the Brooklyn Bridge. Later we'll realize that this was a flashback scene and the murderer was actually Pandora's father, Nick Tornametti. I've called the victim Victor Felcher."

"No, no," she said. (I panicked. Did she know Ingrid's boss? Would she tell him I'd bastardized his name?)

"I forgot to tell you," she said. "The guy he killed has to be called Vogel. Aaron Vogel."

"A minor compromise," I said, scribbling down a note with only minor disappointment.

"Another thing," Carmen said, pointing to my note pad, as if ordering me to write this down, "I'd prefer it if he was knifed in the back."

"Sure. Knifed. That's fine. I like knifings better actually. More visual." I made another note and carried on. "Now we meet Pandora." I had intended suggesting we change the character's name to something more traditionally heroine-esque, like Kate or Jessica, but at this point, I couldn't cope with any more rejection.

So I carried on with the plot:

"It's the first day of Pandora's new job at her father's development company. As you suggested, she keeps it secret that she's the boss's daughter. And I've come up with this idea that she becomes friends with another woman at the office – a dumb but sincere secretary who can't stop yawning. Just a little character quirk. Anyway, this woman is an important character to add because she'll give Pandora somebody to talk to about her problems."

"Like in *Sleepless in Seattle*."

"Girlfriends at the office have a long movie tradition," I assured her. "She's the person who tells Pandora all the rumours that the company is into money laundering and general corruption."

"Good, good. You got that in."

"And I've developed the love interest a bit differently, too."

"I've been working on Johnny Depp and Tom Cruise."

"I thought it might be interesting if we didn't go with traditional casting. You know, give it an extra twist. Make him Latin American. Controversy about an interracial love story."

"Maybe Andy Garcia, Jimmy Smits. It's an idea."

(I'd mention Ramir later.)

"Anyway, she meets this guy who's also just started working for her father. I've called him Ricardo. Really handsome, sexy, a bit dangerous. They bump into each other getting into the elevator."

"And they don't like each other, right?"

"You got it. Hate at first sight. She knocks his arm and he spills coffee all over himself. He blames her, she blames him. Lots of sexual tension."

"Then we'll have some hot sex scene to get everybody steamed up."

"Hot sex scene," I wrote down – as if I hadn't thought of that myself. "And all along the way in these first scenes, we'll have Pandora's father embarrassing her in the office. She's supposed to be an executive assistant, but he keeps giving her stupid jobs – making her buy the toilet paper, go through all the old files to make sure they're in alphabetical order. Then he calls her into some big board meeting and in front of a bunch of people, he tells her she'll never amount to anything."

"Perfect. I want it really abusive."

"The first surprise twist happens about a half an hour in when Pandora comes into the office late at night and sees Ricardo going through a filing cabinet. He admits that he's actually an under-cover detective and he wants her to help him find proof that the owner of the company, Nick Tornametti, was involved in the murder of a lawyer named –" I checked my notes "Aaron Vogel. Because he doesn't know who she is."

"This is great. I can't believe you thought of all this."

My confidence was quickly rebuilding.

"Ricardo says that Aaron Vogel was going to expose the fact that her boss (her father) was involved in a big money-laundering scheme over some shopping malls in Arizona. Pandora gets really confused and angry. She tells him, 'If you don't get of here, I'll make sure you get fired.' But she doesn't tell her father, because now she wonders if what Ricardo said is true."

"Good. Good scene. I like that."

I was on a roll. I knew for certain that writing movies was my life's purpose.

"In the second act, Pandora tries to get back to normal at the office. She snubs Ricardo – even though he keeps calling her because he really loves her. But she can't get what he said off her mind. She has to find out for herself if it's true that her father is a murderer. One day when she's doing some menial job in the com-pany vault, she finds a . . . knife wrapped in a towel hidden at the back of a shelf. She gets suspicious. And that inspires her to go to the library to find out more about what happened to Aaron Vogel."

"Great! The library scene I wanted."

"The twist at the end of the second act is when she calls Ricardo and tells him she's got the evidence he needs. She still doesn't say that she's talking about her own father. But it turns out that her father has her phone tapped, so he hears everything she's telling Ricardo. Then her father phones and tells her to meet him at one of their buildings. He says he wants to give her more serious responsibilities. So we're leading up to the big climax and I've come up with a really great scene. They're out on the roof on the two zillionth floor of this office tower."

"Perfect!"

I must confess, I was glowing at this point.

"The father is planning to push her off if she doesn't shut up. And Pandora plans to push her father off because he's so evil. But we'll have this really touching moment where the father apologizes for treating her so inconsiderately in the office. They bond, they hug –"

"And she pushes him off the building!"

"Actually, Carmen, I'm worried about having her kill him. The point is, she *could* kill him, but she chooses *not* to, thus showing her ultimate strength. We then find out that Pandora told the undercover detective to meet her at the building. He arrives and the father gets arrested, while realizing the terrible error of his ways. The End."

"Mitchell, that is shit. You had me with you right up until the end. But the father has to get killed. He's a ruthless, arrogant asshole, remember? He deserves to die."

"I'm trying to make him more three-dimensional. So the audience can understand him."

"Forget three-dimensional. He doesn't have any doubts about ruining her life. Why would she worry about killing him?"

"Because she's our hero. We're supposed to relate to her. We don't want our hero killing her father. It's that whole patricide taboo thing. It's just – in poor taste."

"Mitchell, I'm putting my foot down – do you hear me? The father has to die."

"Okay, Carmen, I've got an idea. How about a compromise? Let's say they have their moment of bonding – I get my way. But then the boyfriend arrives and shoves her father off the building. He does a few back flips, then kersplat on the pavement."

"You heard me, Mitchell. You know what I want. Pandora does the pushing. The rest is fabulous. But I just looked at my watch and I have to get to my next meeting. So here's what I want you to do, Mitchell. I need a good chunk of the script to show the actors and get them interested. Write the whole beginning up to that scene where Pandora finds Ricardo in the office. And I'm giving you plenty of time – aren't I nice? I'm going to L.A., so you have two whole weeks."

I was calculating in my head. Up to the first turning point. That's twenty-seven pages according to my reference books. If I write four pages a day, that's one week to write the first draft. Then another week to rewrite the whole thing and polish it up. "I can get it done."

"Terrific. I have to tell you, Mitchell, it's a real relief to know at least one part of this movie is on track." She pulled a plain envelope from her purse. "Here's the next five hundred we agreed on. And I'll see you on Thursday the 12th, three o'clock again. I'll be doing some major power meetings in Los Angeles."

"Lunch with Steven Spielberg?" I asked, tongue in cheek.

"He's in Boston on a shoot," she said, matter-of-factly. "I have to admit, Mitchell, I was worried about you. But now you've got me believing. I think we've got a pretty amazing movie here. We're going to be a great team."

We shook hands.

I beamed.

She likes me. She really likes me.

She headed down the stairs, banging her load of bags against the red velvet walls.

"Bon voyage, Carmen," I called as she pushed her way out the door. "Have a great trip."

"*Ciao* for now."

I sighed with relief and smiled with satisfaction.

Then I realized I'd forgotten to tell her about Ramir. I rushed to my window to yell down to her.

And there on the other side of the street was Antonio Banderas. My heart jumped. He was looking right at my building – right at me.

Suddenly I had a vision of the balcony scene from *Romeo and Juliet*. This was too perfect. A second chance! I waved – as masculinely as possible – to make sure he knew it was me.

He didn't wave back.

Then I realized he wasn't looking at me. He was looking at something beneath my window. At Carmen, rushing along the sidewalk.

Antonio got into his flashy car and started driving slowly – as if he were following her.

I sank onto the couch in confusion. He wasn't interested in me after all. I'd been deluding myself once again. But why was he following Carmen?

Then it dawned on me. The first time I'd seen him was right after Carmen had left my apartment three weeks ago.

And just now, as I was sitting here typing this, I noticed that Carmen left her copy of the treatment on the table – exactly as she had the last time.

THURSDAY, MAY 29

Ramir and I were sitting on his futon, sipping licorice spice herbal tea. "Don't you think the whole situation is incredibly weird?"

"Maybe he's her bodyguard," Ramir suggested. "Or maybe he's her chauffeur and he follows her around until she gets tired of walking."

"But why would she need a bodyguard? She's not Whitney Houston or anybody. I'm actually worried about her."

"So call her."

"I've paged her ten times, but she never phones me back. She was in a really weird mood yesterday. I wonder if she knew Antonio was following her."

"What if he just started out chasing Carmen Miranda, and then when he saw you, he fell madly in love and now he's following you."

"Don't torment me, Ramir. I feel stupid enough already for even dwelling on something like this. I mean, she'll probably tell me he's just some magazine reporter doing a story on hot new movie producers."

"Exactly. It's probably something completely boring and ordinary."

"Like everything always is. But maybe she's really in trouble and –"

Then the phone rang.

This is what I hate about visiting Ramir's apartment. He spends most of the time talking to other people. In fact, today I'd warned him upon arrival that I could only spend two hours. And I did take note that instead of the lavish leisurely dinner I'd been promised, the event had turned into a meagre afternoon tea.

Ramir was chatting with one of his many connections in the

entertainment scene, getting advice on how to be featured in the theatre column of *Now* magazine.

I just sat there, playing with one of the amethyst crystals from his windowsill – remnants of the days when he was seriously into chakra-cleansing.

Ramir lives in a brownstone on Isabella Street, a quiet residential branch of the gay ghetto.

Even though Ramir always seems to have less money than me, he always manages to seem more glamorous. His apartment is just a small studio, but it's decorated like an exotic tent from the *Arabian Nights*. Midnight blue walls and gold-painted doors. The ceiling is draped with panels of blue and gold silk that he bought at a sari shop in Little India.

As I was staring up at the intricate patterns in the fabric, my hand slipped off the back edge of the futon and touched something soft. A lost sock? I pulled out a pair of white cotton briefs – which I immediately shoved in Ramir's face. I think that finally convinced him to hang up.

"And whose dainty undergarments are these?"

He grabbed them from me and jammed them in his front shirt pocket so they flopped out absurdly like a hanky.

"I can't remember," he said with artificial insouciance.

"I hope they're not Fred's. No self-respecting gay man wears Fruit of the Looms."

"He just has a conservative side."

"Everything you say about Mr. Flintstone makes him sound very dull. Saintly, but very dull."

"Fred's been really good to me. Actually he was the one who suggested I reconsider doing *Eruption*."

"Does this make him your eternal soulmate or something?"

"We can never know about eternity, my son," Ramir said with a thick East Indian accent. "Love exists only in the present moment."

"Ah, the burdens of a New Age sex god."

"I really like Fred a lot."

"You do?"

"Don't look so repulsed. You haven't even met him yet.

Actually, he's got a friend you might be interested in. We were thinking of inviting you both to an Art Fag party tomorrow night."

"You're trying to set me up?"

"Maybe."

"Oh my God. A double date. We can go to the malt shop and order sodas."

"Is that a yes?"

"No, I think it'd be too weird," I said.

"This guy's nice."

"What does he look like?"

"Nice."

"Stop, I'm getting turned on. Is he at least tall?"

"I don't remember."

"You obviously think Antonio has left me so desperate that I'll date anybody. Anyway, I have to focus all my energy on work right now."

"All work and no play, Mitch. You're letting all your sex appeal go to waste."

Then the phone rang again. Someone from the Poor Alex, the tiny experimental theatre just down the street from The Daily Grind. More negotiations.

I checked the ancient cedar cigar box where Ramir keeps his stash of marijuana. Recent shipment. Then I leafed through a vintage copy of *Vanity Fair*.

Finally he hung up. "It's all confirmed. The Poor Alex is dark for one week between shows. So *Eruption* opens Saturday, June 21st at eight p.m."

"That's in three weeks," I said, horrorstruck, but Ramir didn't seem to find the timing so scary.

"I got the space cheap. Nobody else would take it at such late notice. I've decided I'm going to make the opening night by invitation only – just for industry people. I can even do a Sunday matinée if I sell enough tickets."

"You can't possibly get everything done by then!"

"Think positive, Mitch. Of course I can. Now that I know the dates, Ingrid can do the poster. I can get all the publicity moving on Monday."

"Then you can write the script on Tuesday between three and three-fifteen."

"It'll get done. That's what we're working on now."

"Remember, you can only enjoy the pleasure of my company for another hour and ten minutes," I said – determined that he wasn't going to talk me into wasting my whole day while he gabbed on the phone.

"That reminds me. I've got a present for you."

"So now you're resorting to blatant bribery."

"Don't you want to know what it is?"

"Of course I do."

He dug under some newspapers and found a thick dog-eared script. He passed it to me as though he were being casual about it. "I found this at a director's office a few weeks ago," he said. "He gave it to me as a favour."

It was a copy of the shooting script from Martin Scorcese's *Taxi Driver*. A masterpiece of screenwriting by Paul Schrader.

"Oh my god. Where'd he get it?"

"Connections."

"This is going to be so amazing to read. I can't believe you found this. Thank you."

"See, I'm always looking out for you."

"But don't think this means I'm going to put up with any more phone calls."

"No more calls. We're getting to work." He sat beside me on the futon. "Like I said, the whole show is going to be multimedia now. I'll have a big TV in the middle of the stage. I'll do the different monologues, but in between I'm going to run scenes from the shows I've been in. Different characters, different accents."

"The male Meryl Streep."

"I went through all my material this morning." There was a mess of videotapes scattered around his VCR. "And I've got a great angle to make it all come together. I'm going to show all the stereotypical characters I've played on TV and then use the monologues to contrast them with realistic characters."

"That's actually a great idea."

"You're surprised?"

"Does this mean you're not screaming anymore?"

He nodded vigorously, Oh yes! "To break up the segments. For example, I'll show a clip from *Traders*, where I'm that stupid janitor in the office building. They made me play him like he could only speak broken English and I ended up sounding like an idiot. But in my monologue, I'll have him speak like a normal person with a Spanish accent, and he can talk about how much he hates all the stockbrokers. And then, before I show the next video, I'll scream."

"You could show that episode of *Due South* where you play a hardened criminal, then maybe do a monologue about how you're actually just a wholesome kid from the suburbs."

"Exactly."

"And the Mexican salsa commercial is hysterical."

"The Frito Bandito clone. And *Street Legal*. Maybe I can play clips from some of those Native-Canadian radio dramas I did for CBC."

"This could really work, Ramir." I was grinning I was so intrigued. "How much have you written so far?"

"I've got a couple of notes."

He meant that literally. He pulled out a single sheet of paper. "This is a monologue for that car thief I played in *Crime Wave*. I'd say, 'That night on TV, my buddy an' me, we were walkin' 'roun' downtown. Carlos is always tellin' me how much he hates bein' stuck in the city. He talks about the beach back home in Puerto Rico.' "

"I'd really emphasize the part about his past." At this point, I launched into an accent that was more Québecois than Puerto Rican: " 'Back in San Juan, every Saturday night, my buddies and me, we'd cruise the streets and pick up chicks.' Or whatever they do in San Juan."

"Good. Write that down." He pushed a pen and pad towards me. "A lot of it could be improvised."

Then – perfect timing – the phone rang. Ramir checked his caller ID.

"I have to take this."

It was Fred.

I wrote down the brilliant phrases I'd uttered and then I stalled – partially because I was listening to Ramir's conversation and partially because I hate the way I always end up writing everything when I'm only supposed to be helping. Whatever committee I join, I always end up being the secretary.

I scrawled another line about how "I stole the car because I needed to take Carlos' pregnant girlfrien' to the hospital." But I didn't want to turn some low-life car thief into a misunderstood Good Samaritan. And what do I know about being a Puerto Rican street kid anyway? Probably as much as Ramir.

I was having enough trouble with the characters in Carmen's script without getting stressed out over Ramir's too.

After five minutes of listening to him strategize with Fred, I was totally annoyed. Even though he had given me *Taxi Driver*.

Finally Ramir hung up. "Fred found a place that'll rent us a video monitor and all the audio equipment for a hundred dollars a day. But I have to get there before five to put down a deposit."

"So much for writing."

"I'm sorry."

"It's not *my* problem."

"Maybe we can get together again on the weekend. I have to work on my press release, too."

"We'll see if I have time," I said, trying to sound distant. I hoped he'd notice.

He kissed me on the cheek to make everything better. "You've really been a big help, Mitch. Just knowing you think it's a good idea means a lot."

I yanked the underwear out of Ramir's pocket.

"Don't forget to give Fred back his gotchies."

I walked him downstairs and he pedaled off on his bicycle.

I am making this pledge to myself: I will not help Ramir anymore with his script. I mean it. Let him find out for himself how hard it is to write something good. Let him humiliate himself in front of all those important people he's trying to impress.

But of course he'll probably pull it off brilliantly. He always does.

I wish I could be so sure of myself.

SATURDAY, MAY 31

For a break from working on the script, I went to The Daily Grind to visit Ingrid. But Kinita was behind the counter.

She greeted me with a sneering smile. "Mitchell, what a surprise."

"Is Ing in the back?"

She shook her head. "We ran out of brown sugar. She had to go to the Bloor Super Save."

Kinita works at the store part time. She has perfect Eurasian bone structure, accented by little gold rings pierced into her left nostril and left eyebrow. She was wearing a wide-necked black silk T-shirt that emphasized her arrogant elegance.

She moved towards the basket of Rice Krispie squares. "Can I get you something?"

"I'm fine, thanks," I said.

"Are you sure? No Rice Krispies?"

"Just had a big lunch."

Now although this little exchange was said with smiles on both our faces, I know that Kinita's snide welcome was to point out that I come to the store too often, and her offer to get me a Rice Krispie square was simply to point out that I wouldn't take one unless Ingrid gave it to me for free.

Kinita and I share a chemical dislike for each other based on the fact that each of us thinks the other is a total pretentious phony.

"I'll just sit outside until Ingrid comes back."

"Whatever." Kinita raised her beautiful chin to indicate that she wasn't yet finished with me. "So Ingrid tells me you're working on a screenplay."

I nodded confidently. "Big deadline in two weeks."

"I read someplace that the odds are like a million to one that a screenplay'll ever get produced."

"That's if you do a script on spec," I explained. (As if I hadn't abused myself with that statistic every day for the past two years.) "But you see, I've been *hired* to write this script. We start shooting in September."

"Is it like one of those typical Canadian films?"

I knew she was trying to set me up. "How do you mean 'typical'?"

"You know. Canadian movies always look sort of cheap."

"This one's very big budget," I fabricated. "They're bringing in a major cinematographer from Sweden."

"But isn't it funny how Canadian movies always turn out to be sort of boring? No plot. All the characters just sit around complaining and they never do anything."

"This is a thriller actually. Very exciting. Edge-of-your-seat. We're talking to Jodie Foster for the lead."

"Really?" she said, trying to sound disbelieving. But I could tell part of her was impressed.

While she was vulnerable, I pounced. "So is your band doing any more gigs?"

Kinita plays bass in a feminist jazz group called Nam Myoho. They only get hired for anti-fur rallies and pro-choice fundraisers.

"We're booked for a few dates in August."

"Ingrid told me about the El Mocambo. It sounded really intimate."

They had a show there two weeks ago and only seven people turned up.

"Sometimes the audience can just be a distraction," Kinita said. "I'm only in it for the music."

As an act of mercy, I altered my approach. "So is everybody telling you how much they love Ingrid's mural?"

"A couple of people have mentioned it."

"Nice mentions?"

"Frankly, I don't think most people have noticed it's there."

Just then Ingrid dawdled in. "Long line-up at the store," she said, sounding tired. She handed the plastic grocery bag to Kinita.

"Kinita was just telling me how much everybody loves your mural."

"Really?" Ing didn't seem to care.

She grabbed two bottles of Perrier from the cooler. "Come on, let's sit outside for a few minutes."

I gave Kinita a big smile as we exited.

Ing went to the back of the near-empty patio – a table under the shade of an umbrella.

"Are you feeling all right?" I asked.

"Just sort of blah. How are you?"

"Sort of blah, too. Although I think I just won a battle of pretension with Kinita," I said. "I wonder if you can pinpoint the exact moment in life when a person becomes bitter."

"She's been in a worse mood than usual lately. I think she wishes Victor had made *her* the manager."

"She's been sucking up to him long enough."

"Victor always tried to make us compete to increase sales. Maybe we'll get along better now that he's gone." She twirled a curl of hair. "So how's your script coming?"

"I'm not feeling very inspired today."

"I haven't touched any paint in four days. Managing the store is taking so much time."

"You'll get a rhythm going."

"Ramir's been on my case, bugging me to finish his poster. I said I'd do it last night, but I had to work. I'm just going to draw a Human Bean with a big screaming mouth. It'll probably only take five minutes. But I just can't concentrate."

"You've been really busy lately. You need some time to rest. When we're rich, we'll be able to fly away to the Canyon Ranch Spa. Maybe that's where Carmen is."

"Have you talked to her yet? Does she know the guy who was following her?"

"She never called me back. The thing I keep wondering about is what she was doing in my bathroom the other day without making any noise."

"There are lots of things a woman can do in the bathroom."

"Do I really want to know this?"

"She could have been putting on make-up . . . brushing her hair . . . ."

"Giving herself a colonic. Maybe she was taking pills. But she'd need to drink some water, so she would have turned on the tap."

"Maybe she had a bottle in her purse."

"I think she must be manic-depressive. She's not a very dependable type of person. I mean, it's not like I'm dealing with Disney or Time Warner or some big corporation. This whole movie project could fall apart at any minute."

"As long as you like what you're doing."

"It's hard. But it's satisfying, and she does keep paying me."

We heard a child having a tantrum on the sidewalk.

A three-year-old boy had dragged his mother to a stop in front of Ingrid's sandwich board. He was pointing in fascination, gawking at today's drawing of a green Martian Human Bean eating a bagel.

"You see," I said, "your art appeals to people of all ages."

Mother and child went inside the shop.

"I should go in and help," Ing said.

"Let Kinita handle it."

Ingrid took a thoughtful sip of Perrier. "Last night I went for dinner at my sister's. I played with her two kids. We sat around and watched *The Hunchback of Notre Dame* on video."

"The happy suburban family."

"When Pierre and I were married we always dreamed about that."

"I thought you dreamed about going to Paris and being painters."

"We dreamed about a lot of things," she said, sounding bittersweet. "Of course, now Pierre is actually *in* Paris."

"You could go too."

"I'm sick of dreaming. After dinner my sister's husband drove me back downtown. He offered to set me up with a guy from his office."

"What did you say?"

"I said sure. But the guy's away on a training course in Atlanta for a month, so it probably won't happen for a while."

"Then you can get married and become your sister's next-door neighbour in suburbia."

"Sometimes I think it'd be nice to have a life that followed a clear path. I'm so sick of struggling over everything, just so I can have time to paint. At this rate, who knows if I'll ever have any kids."

"You're only twenty-eight. It's not like your biological clock is going to break down any minute."

"At least with kids, you know you're doing something useful with your time."

"But you love painting. And like you said, as long as you enjoy what you're doing. . . ."

Suddenly there was Kinita, butting in. "Excuse the interruption, Ingrid," she said, intentionally baroque. "But there's a guy on the phone saying he needs a cheque. He wants to talk to the manager. I guess that means you."

Ingrid took a deep breath and rolled her eyes. "Power is so intoxicating."

I followed her inside.

Ing walked to the back of the store to go behind the counter. She looked at her richly coloured mural. "I don't know what I was so upset about the other morning." She wiped a fleck of lint off the painting's surface. "I'm getting so used to seeing it there it might as well be one of Victor's coffee posters."

Guilt, guilt, guilt.

I shouldn't have spent so much time talking with Ingrid and Ramir on the phone yesterday.

I shouldn't have gone to the Bloor Cinema last night, but they were showing a double bill of *Mildred Pierce* with Joan Crawford and *The Postman Always Rings Twice* with Lana Turner, and somehow I managed to convince myself that watching them was research.

I should have been sitting here typing for the last twenty-four hours.

THURSDAY, JUNE 5

I grabbed Ingrid's painting and set it on the shelf above the cream and sugar counter.

"Mitchell, give it back to me."

"Why don't we just leave it there until Mrs. Epstein comes?"

"I don't want anybody else to see it, that's why."

"It's not the first time anyone's ever put up art in a café. Everybody loves your mural. Why wouldn't they love this?"

Frances Farmer looked over at the canvas with nose-raised curiosity, but she showed no sign of approval or disapproval.

"Think of it as more personal growth," I told Ing. "You're sharing yourself with the world."

"I don't think I've grown at all. Last night I couldn't work on my new painting because I was too busy wondering if Mrs. Epstein was going to like this one."

"Don't take it so personally. Just tell yourself you're doing it for the money."

"She'll never pay $200. And I'm not doing it for the money. I'm doing it because she asked if I had a *green* one. Any serious artist would have been insulted by the question."

"She said she'd come in between two and three, right? So if she doesn't buy it, we can take it down."

"I don't want to worry about this stuff, Mitchell!" She pulled at her hair like a madwoman. "This is exactly the reason I hate showing people my work. I don't want to care what other people think."

At that moment, Sidney Poitier walked into the shop.

Ingrid shut up and we both smiled stupidly. He was wearing a simple white shirt and he looked positively regal.

"Hi, how are you?" Ing sounded like a silly schoolgirl.

"Unbelievably tired," Sidney said with a graceful Jamaican lilt. "A full day's work and it's not even noon."

To be elegant even when exhausted is evidence of true refinement.

"Skim-milk cappuccino with cinnamon on top?" Ing asked.

"You remembered! Perhaps I'll even try one of those nut squares today."

Ingrid set to frothing milk while I lurked beside her and hummed the tune from *To Sir With Love*. She blushed and glared at me.

"It's getting hot out there, isn't it?" Ing small-talked pathetically. "Supposed to be a great weekend, too."

But Sidney didn't answer. He was standing in front of Ingrid's new green painting. His eyes moved from the painting to the mural on the wall and back again as if he were being hypnotized by a pendulum.

"Are these by a local artist?"

"Nobody you'd know," Ing said quickly.

"They're really quite remarkable."

"They're hers," I said, pointing at her. "*She* did them."

Sidney looked at Ingrid as though he were seeing her for the first time. "I'm Geoffrey Abrams." He put out his hand. "A pleasure to meet you."

"I'm Ingrid Iversen."

"Mitchell Draper," I said, but it was clear that I didn't stand a chance.

"You never know what you'll find when you're not looking. I run a gallery in Yorkville." He smoothly pulled a leather case from his pant pocket and handed Ingrid a business card.

She practically gaped when she read it.

He pointed to the mural of the woman at the table. "You've caught so much expression in the face. And the atmosphere in the green one. Calm and controlled on the surface, but something mysterious brewing underneath."

"Thanks," Ing said, dumbstruck.

"It's very impressive work. Do you have a dealer?"

"No, no, it's just a hobby."

"You've never shown before?"

"She's been planning to show her stuff to some galleries," I said.

"So you have more work?"

"Her apartment's filled with it," I said.

"Are you her manager?" Was that comment intended snidely?

"I'm just a friend." After that he ignored me.

"You know, this style could fit in very well with a concept I've been experimenting with. This whole approach could be quite interesting. Let me think for a day or two. Perhaps I could come by your studio and see the rest of your work."

I raised my eyebrows at this blatant come-on.

"I'd be flattered."

"I'm flying out of town this evening, but perhaps we can get together sometime early next week."

"Any time you want."

"Phone my gallery on Monday and we'll make arrangements." He paused a moment and looked at the paintings again. "You have no idea what a delightful surprise this is. It's so hard to find interesting new artists. I've been searching high and low, but here you are."

"It's like *The Wizard of Oz*," I chirped. "You don't have to look any further than your own backyard."

He looked at me like I was insane.

Ingrid fastened a plastic lid on his cup. "This cappuccino's definitely on the house," she said. "Thanks so much. I'll call you next week."

I held my breath until he'd stepped out the door, then I grabbed Ingrid's arm.

"You have a date with Sidney Poitier!"

"Geoffrey Abrams," she said firmly. (It's always jarring to learn the real name of one of our mythical celebrities.) "And it's not a date. It's business."

"The way he looked at you was more than business. From now on I'm calling you Lulu."

"If he was interested in me like that, he would have done something by now."

"But now he knows you're a *grande artiste*. You have something in common. Something he wants. That makes you all the more bewitching."

She looked at me doubtfully. "Do you think?"

"Definitely."

"But I hope he really likes my work. Look at his card, Mitchell. He owns The Abrams Gallery. The one that had the Jackson Pollock show in January."

"You've just been discovered! Like Lana Turner in Schwab's drugstore."

Ing stood in front of the green painting. "He liked it." She took a deep breath and stared at it in silence. "It really is good, isn't it."

She lifted the canvas off the counter.

"What are you doing?" I asked, incredulous. "You should be proud of it."

"I'm going to tell Mrs. Epstein I forgot to bring it in. Geoffrey might want this one for a show."

"It didn't take much to get you singin' a different tune."

"When somebody who owns a gallery like his says he's interested in my work, I – I don't know, Mitchell! Maybe this'll be the only painting he likes. Now help me carry it to the back room."

She was talking down-to-earth common sense, but when I looked in her eyes I could see she was floating miles above the ground.

FRIDAY, JUNE 6

'll admit it right up front: I was trying to avoid writing. So I called Ramir at the Good Karma:

"Hey, Mitch, what's up?"

"Just thought I'd say hello. Wondering if it might be time for your break."

"We're really busy right now. I don't think I can take one."

"Isn't it amazing about Ingrid and the guy from the art gallery?

"It's great. Just a second. I have to get something for a customer."

I waited patiently. Even being put on hold felt like a satisfying time-waster.

"Sorry, Mitch. I'm back."

"Have you ever heard of Geoffrey Abrams?"

"Never. That's $4.99."

"What?"

"I was talking to a customer."

"I was just thinking, why don't you come over to my place for dinner? We can order chicken from Swiss Chalet."

"Actually Fred and I are going out tonight."

"Another big romantic evening?"

"We're shooting some video segments for the show."

"On location? Where are you going?"

"No, they're in the third aisle. Listen, Mitch, we're still having dinner on Sunday night at Ing's, right?"

"As far as I know."

"I'll tell you about everything then."

"Right, I should work tonight anyway. I'm really busy."

"That's great. I'm glad. Okay, bye for now."

We hung up. And now there's nothing else for me to do but go back to the script.

I hate writing.

SUNDAY, JUNE 8

In retrospect, the whole situation seems inevitable.

Dressed in our most fetching shorts and T-shirts (and sweating unattractively in the heat) Ingrid and I walked through Yorkville, the elegant retail enclave tucked beside the rich section of Bloor Street. Working-class Victorian row houses had been extravagantly converted into designer shops and art galleries. People at chic outdoor cafés wore big sunglasses and stared out impassively at passers-by.

It was hard not to feel intimidated as we traversed the maze of laneways and tree-lined streets.

"I just don't want to run into him," Ingrid said. "He'd probably think we were checking up on his business."

"That's exactly what we're doing."

"He'd think we were really tacky."

"I heard him say it myself. He's going to be out of town until next week. We can snoop all we want."

"Usually his gallery only shows artists who are really well-established."

"Soon you'll be established yourself. He wouldn't have said what he did if he wasn't genuinely interested. He must think you have a lot of potential."

We turned the corner onto Scollard Street.

"Here it is."

A granite boulder sat beside the front walk. Discreet engraved letters announced THE ABRAMS GALLERY. The front of the large red-brick house had been sliced open with an expansive plate-glass window. Stencilled in the corner was the title "Painters Eleven: Toronto Abstracts from 1953 to 1959".

We climbed the front steps and I pushed open the heavy all-glass door. White walls and bleached pine floors stretched before us.

A studious young woman with short blonde hair was sitting at a black table beside a white marble fireplace. She nodded to us as we entered.

Deafening silence.

We were the only visitors.

We stood in front of the first painting: a giant canvas covered with thick swoops of red and blue oil paint. Ingrid was more impressed than I was. But neither of us was in the mood for serious art appreciation. Our eyes flashed around the room.

"This is where all your paintings could be hanging," I whispered. "Imagine this place jam-packed on opening night."

"He could still say no, Mitchell."

"We could put a bar over there. And a table of finger foods."

"Shhh!"

"Your blue ones would look really good on that wall."

We paid appropriate respect to each of the paintings, but the splashes and blobs just weren't speaking to me.

"There are more upstairs," Ing said.

I shrugged my shoulders and followed.

The second floor was a labyrinth of smaller works. In one room, they were all dark single-colour prints of twisted nonsensical shapes.

"These are gorgeous," Ingrid said.

"I like them, I guess, but I don't really understand them."

"You don't have to understand them to appreciate them. That's the whole idea," Ing said. "Everything else in the world is abstract. So why not paintings?"

"I'm just being too literal."

"I think there are more over here."

Together Ing and I peeked around a corner and looked right into a tiny office where Sidney Poitier sat at an immaculate desk. He looked up from making notes.

"Ingrid!" Geoffrey immediately stood and came towards us with a warm smile. "How wonderful to see you again so soon!" He clasped her right hand in both of his. Then he shook my hand the ordinary way.

"I thought you said you were going out of town," Ing spluttered.

"I flew in this morning."

"Mitchell and I were just out doing some gallery hopping. We do it every Sunday. It's sort of a tradition. I really like this show."

"I like it too," I said.

"Tell me the truth. You've come to inspect my business. Do you approve?" He had a charming, teasing smile on his face.

"Oh, I've been here before. Lots of times. You always have the most interesting work," she said, and it was clear that she meant it – even though her cheeks were turning bright red. "I've always thought it would be wonderful to own my own art gallery."

"You know, I'm still very interested in seeing your work."

"You're still welcome to, if you really want."

"I have a brilliant idea. What are you doing right now?"

"Just out walking."

"What if I drive you back to your house for a look, spur of the moment?"

"It's fine with me."

He turned to me graciously. "Of course you'll come with us?"

I shook my head no. "I've seen Ingrid's paintings before. Not that they're not worth seeing again! It's just that – I've got some shopping I need to do. I'm running low on Lysol."

Geoffrey grabbed a ring of keys from his desk and the three of us started downstairs.

Ing caught my attention and pointedly said, "So Mitchell, I'll see you and Ramir for dinner at seven, right?"

I didn't want to cut into her date if it was really going well.

"It's okay if you want to cancel. Why don't you call me later if it's still good?"

"No, I'm expecting you for seven," she insisted, making sure that Geoffrey had heard as well. "I'll see you at my place, all right?"

There are some things about women that I just don't understand.

I stood there for a second on the sidewalk, watching Geoffrey and Ingrid walk down the laneway beside the gallery, Ing waving her hands excitedly as she talked.

What was I to do with myself? Go back home and write?

I decided to go window-shopping on Bloor Street instead.

☆

Ingrid took a sip of red wine. "Geoffrey says impromptu art shows are how he's making most of his sales right now."

The three of us were sweltering in Ingrid's kitchen. The hot day had turned into the muggiest night so far this year.

Ingrid lives on Shaw Street – about a twenty-minute walk west of the store – on the main floor of a narrow old house. Her neighbours are all friendly old Portuguese couples who like to plant statues of the Virgin Mary in their front gardens.

"So you're not going to be in his big fancy gallery?"

"He thinks holding it at the Grind will make it more interesting. It's going to be this Friday night, so make sure you can come."

"That soon?"

"It's part of his concept, doing it on short notice."

"I'll be the first one there," Ramir promised.

"This is incredible," I said, filling Ingrid's glass with more wine. We were all giddily on our way to inebriation. "I actually witnessed the discovery of a great new artist."

"It's really not going to be a big deal. He's only inviting a few clients."

Ing was grinding fresh linguine out of the pasta maker she'd received four years ago as a wedding present. A huge pot of water was on the boil. Ramir was tearing up organic radicchio from the Good Karma, preparing one of his complicated salad masterpieces. Since I have absolutely no culinary skills I was in charge of setting the table.

To avoid the heat indoors, we'd carried Ingrid's kitchen table out to her tiny backyard deck. I'd arranged a centrepiece of old Chianti bottles, drizzled traditionally with candle wax. I'd folded paper towels into airplanes to decorate each place setting.

"Geoffrey says people who collect new painters think galleries are too sterile. They want to go where the art scene is really happening."

"He thinks rich art collectors are going to like The Daily Grind?" Ramir asked.

"It's not *that* horrible."

"And remember," I interrupted, "you *have* to send an invitation to your ex-husband in Paris. Show Pierre he's not the only one who's making a name for himself."

"That is a truly malicious idea," she said, smiling in appreciation.

"Now tell us everything that happened. What did he say in the car?"

"Nothing important. I can't remember."

"You *have* to remember. What happened every second after you left me in front of the gallery?"

"She doesn't have to tell you anything!" Ramir scolded. He turned to Ingrid to complain. "He interrogates me like that all the time. I think it's sick."

"It's research!" I said. "I live my entire love life vicariously."

"*Nothing* happened with him," Ing said, holding down a smile.

"But you wanted it to, didn't you?"

"You like we Caribbean boys, dontcha?" Ramir taunted in a thick Jamaican accent.

"No seduction? No hot sex scene?"

"It was a business meeting, Mitchell. We talked."

"Where?"

"Well, after we left my place, he took me to a restaurant in Little Italy for a Campari and soda."

"That sounds pretty romantic."

"It really wasn't," she said, not convincingly. "He told me he bought a house around the corner from the store a couple of months ago. And he was in New York last night for a big party at the Museum of Modern Art."

"So what did he say about your paintings?" Ramir asked, already forgetting his sacred respect for Ingrid's privacy.

"He said he liked them."

"Adjectives! We want adjectives!"

"He said they were filled with 'inner turmoil'."

"Wow."

"He said they were 'involving', 'original' . . . 'passionate'."

" 'Passionate.' He definitely wants you."

"And he said it's the most mature work he's seen from a painter who's never shown before. He thinks I could build a long-term career."

"That's amazing, Ingrid."

"It's just so nice, because he really understands what I'm try-ing to do."

"He *understands* her!" Ramir repeated lasciviously.

"And just a week ago, she wouldn't show her paintings to her own mother!"

"She's been swept off her feet."

I swear Ing was blushing. "He picked out twelve paintings he wants me to hang in the store for next Friday. He said we should get together again this week to make more plans. We're going to have dinner."

"Dinner!"

"Make him take you someplace expensive."

"I don't care where we go. Once you get to know him, he's really sweet. He's totally charming."

"She's fallen for him."

"Totally."

"It's not like that at all!" She was practically writhing in embarrassment. But she tried to act sensible. "Ramir, can you test the pasta?"

He fished out a string of linguine from the pot and seduced her with a French accent. "You taste it, *ma chérie*. I don't care if you do have dinner with other men. You'll always belong to me."

Ingrid leaned her head back in ecstasy as Ramir taunted her tongue with the noodle. A grotesque parody of foreplay.

"*Lady and the Tramp*," I said.

"It still needs another couple of minutes," Ing said, wiping her chin. "So Ramir, what *do* you put in that salad dressing?"

They started in on recipes, which always immediately bores me, so I wandered into the living room to see if I could find some cooler air. My T-shirt was clinging to my chest.

The living room is Ingrid's painting studio, and there's not an inch of wall that isn't hung with her art. Dozens of canvases are stacked in the hallway. The piles are so deep that even I have to inhale to squeeze through. But, typical of Ing's timidity, the easel with her current *oeuvre* was covered with a paint-splattered white bedsheet.

I swayed to Edith Piaf singing "La vie en rose," sipped wine and perused Ingrid's bookshelves – my favourite snooping activity in anyone's home. Art books on Matisse and Seurat, Keith Haring and David Hockney. Her collection of Jackie Collins and Jacqueline Susann novels, including the fateful copy of *The Love Machine*.

"Somebody said they saw him at the baths," I heard Ramir say, which immediately enticed me back to the kitchen.

"Who?"

"That new player for the Blue Jays."

"You're kidding," I said. "Even I read the sports section when I saw his picture. He's got gigantic hands."

"Does *everyone* in the world have to be gay?" Ingrid wailed. Clearly the wine had had an effect on her, too.

"There are a few decent straight men left. You found Geoffrey."

"Every new movie star, you always say he's gay."

"We're just serious about claiming our own," Ramir explained. "When you're a member of a minority, you want to know you're in good company."

"But I think you're overcompensating."

"It's like Canadians know who all the famous Canadians are," I said. "Gay people know who all the famous gay people are."

Ingrid started the litany of famous Canadians: "Donald Sutherland, Alanis Morissette, Marshall McLuhan, Joni Mitchell."

Ramir listed the homosexuals: "Rock Hudson, Paul Lynde, Ellen DeGeneres, Martina Navratilova."

"Bryan Adams, Céline Dion."

"Elton John, Melissa Etheridge."

"k.d. lang."

"k.d. lang."

I added to the Canadians: "Keanu Reeves, Glenn Gould, Guy Lombardo, Alexander Graham Bell, Alex Trebek."

Ingrid continued the Canadians: "Mary Pickford, Leonard Cohen, Mike Myers, Jim Carey."

Ramir continued the homosexuals: "Alexander the Great, Socrates, Aristotle, Tennessee Williams, Truman Capote."

I added, "Oscar Wilde, Hans Christian Andersen, Tchaikovsky, Gore Vidal, Monty Clift."

"Monty Hall," Ramir countered, switching tacks.

"Liberace," Ingrid retorted.

"And of course," I jumped in, "the great artists Botticelli, da Vinci, Michelangelo and Mapplethorpe."

"All in all, you have to admit gay people win for quality," Ramir said.

"But Canadians haven't been around as long." Ing pointed to a cupboard above the fridge. "Can you get me the strainer for the pasta?"

Being the tallest one there, I rushed to the rescue.

"And speaking of famous gay Canadians," Ramir said, shaking his bottle of homemade salad dressing, "the printing shop said my poster'll be ready tomorrow."

"What's it look like?"

"There's a copy there on my desk," Ing said. "Just lift those papers."

There was Ramir as a Human Bean. Just his head. A big screaming mouth with ERUPTION planted in the middle of the tongue. Off to the side Ing had drawn a smoking volcano.

"That's hilarious."

"On pink paper with purple and green lettering. Really screaming colours."

Across the bottom ran the address of the Poor Alex and all the info on dates and tickets. The show opened in thirteen days.

"So how's the script coming?" I asked lightly.

"It's in development. I wrote the press release this afternoon."

"You wrote the press release before you finished the script?"

"You've sunk to an all-time low," Ing said.

"I have to send it out this week! If I wait any longer, nobody'll have time to give me any publicity."

"Don't they plan all those stories weeks in advance?"

"I have some contacts," he said mysteriously.

"Promiscuity pays off."

"So how did you describe the show?"

"I said it was 'funny' and 'moving' and 'a profound statement on society today.' "

"'Filled with inner turbulence', like Ing's paintings?"

"He said 'turmoil'!" Ing corrected.

"Let's hope it turns out that way when you write it."

"Now I know what to aim for. This afternoon I was strategizing with my agent. And tomorrow Fred and I are sending out the poster to every casting director and producer in the city. Even Dominic Manno, that asshole who didn't hire me."

"Fred's going to be awfully busy licking envelopes," Ing said.

"He might run out of saliva, and then what good will he be?"

"I'll bring him to Ing's show on Friday so you can meet him."

"I can hardly wait," I declared boozily, leaning on Ramir's shoulder. "And if you're wondering, I did some particularly fabulous writing today. I'm bringing new emotional realism and depth of character to the thriller genre."

"We always said you were a genius," Ing said, always sweet.

"*Mitch* always said he was a genius," said Ramir.

I ignored him and boasted onward. "It does feel exciting sometimes, writing something you know is really good."

"Making people laugh, making them cry."

"Lifting the human spirit."

"Giving a guy a raging hard-on."

Ingrid groaned. "Thank you, Ramir, for that uplifting sentiment."

Ramir shook himself loose from my weight. "When are you going to let me and Ingrid read some of your smut?"

"Never!"

"I can just buy a magazine myself, you know."

"I won't tell you which ones I'm in."

"We'll just look at the table of contents for any literary works by *Chad Stiffman*."

I laughed again at my ridiculous pen name.

Ramir grabbed me from behind and started playfully humping my rear.

"Did you ever write a story about that hot night we spent together?"

Through his shorts, I could feel his notoriously large appendage pressing against my ass.

"I can't even remember that night, the sex was so bad."

I pushed him away before it could look like I was enjoying it.

Ramir pinched my cheek. "What would your parents think if they knew their only son had become a sleazy gay pornographer?"

"You're the last person who should threaten blackmail."

Ingrid nodded. "We've got a ton of secrets on you."

"My parents know I'm queer. It's not a problem."

"Do they know about the Caligula party?" I said.

"They don't even know who Caligula is."

"Or that you slept with the superintendent of your building to get him to fix the radiator? And that you spent a night in jail in Puerto Vallarta."

Ingrid got into the spirit. "Then there was the time when you wore that ugly bridesmaids' dress to a Hallowe'en party."

"Those are our special private memories and you can only tell them to a reporter from *The National Enquirer*."

"It's funny, isn't it?" I said, turning philosophical. "I wonder what I would have thought when I graduated university if I knew that five years later my only published work would be gay pornography."

"Or that I'd be running a run-down little coffee shop."

"Or that I wouldn't be a movie star already in Hollywood."

"It's weird."

"It's depressing."

Naturally, Ramir recovered his confidence first. "I just have this feeling that we're all on the verge. All this talent and energy just waiting to burst out."

"I've had that feeling for years."

"But now things are actually starting to happen. You with your screenplay. Ingrid with Geoffrey. And despite what you may think, my show's going to be really good."

"It does feel like we've all got some momentum."

"In another ten years, who knows? I could be starring in a Francis Ford Coppola movie and winning my third Academy Award."

"I could be writing screenplays for Francis Ford Coppola."

"And I could be married again, having babies, painting all day."

"Anything's possible."

All of us were looking dreamily off in different directions. And the pasta pot overflowed, water sizzling onto the burner. "I think everything's ready," Ing said, practical again. We all jumped back to reality and set to work with the final preparations.

"Don't forget the salad tongs."

"And bring the corkscrew so we can open more wine."

"Shall we move out to the formal dining deck?"

"Dinner *al fresco*."

"Doesn't *fresco* mean 'cool'?"

It was still incredibly hot. There wasn't even a breeze to relieve the humidity.

Ingrid carried the pasta glistening with olive oil and pesto. Ramir carried a big wooden bowl filled with multi-coloured salad. I was in charge of the garlic bread, fresh from the oven. The aroma was intoxicating.

We all took our seats and I raised my wine glass. "Someday when we're famous, they're going to write our biographies and describe our fabulous dinner parties."

We clinked our glasses, and we watched the candlelight sparkling in each other's eyes and in the sweat on each other's foreheads.

A blissful smile spread across Ingrid's face. "We are definitely having a *moment*."

MONTAGE SEQUENCE.

Fast cuts to the theme from *Fame* – as sung by Irene Cara.

INTERIOR. INGRID'S STUDIO. NIGHT.

INGRID passionately daubs bright colours on a canvas.

EXTERIOR. THEATRE. DAY.

RAMIR proudly plasters his new poster beside the door of the Poor Alex Theatre.

EXTERIOR. BLOOR STREET. DAY.

The street is lined with Ramir's pink poster.

INTERIOR. MITCHELL'S APARTMENT. DAY.

MITCHELL alone, wearing a threadbare bathrobe, sits in front of his computer and stares dismally out the window.

INTERIOR. THE DAILY GRIND. DAY.

INGRID straightens a painting, then stands back to survey the collection of twelve that grace the wall.

INTERIOR. THEATRE. DAY.

RAMIR rehearses on a tiny stage, pacing and gesticulating.

INTERIOR. MITCHELL'S APARTMENT. DAY.

MITCHELL is collapsed on the couch, slurping from a large bottle of tequila and watching the home-shopping channel on TV.

INTERIOR. RESTAURANT. NIGHT.

INGRID sits across an elegant table from GEOFFREY ABRAMS, holding hands, laughing and talking.

INTERIOR. RAMIR'S SEX DEN. NIGHT.

RAMIR makes love with the mysterious FRED, shown only in silhouette, yet revealing a truly exceptional physique.

INTERIOR. MITCHELL'S APARTMENT. NIGHT.

MITCHELL sits alone, typing.

FADE TO BLACK.

This morning while I was out at Kinko's copying the script and then at the Good Karma picking up low-fat, wheat-free cookies for Carmen, I received a message from her on my answering machine:

"Mitchell, I'm still in L.A., so we have to move our meeting to tomorrow."

This of course pissed me off completely, because I'd just killed myself once again on her behalf, and tomorrow is the day of Ingrid's party and I'm supposed to be helping her all afternoon.

But Carmen continued:

"Instead of your place, let's meet at the Four Seasons. Make a reservation for one p.m. at the Studio Café."

After that, I was inclined to forgive her. The Studio Café is *the* restaurant for powerful business people and ladies who lunch. I've only been there once, treating myself to morning coffee and a fruit plate.

Besides, now I have extra time to work on the scenes of Pandora at work. I need to build more sexual tension between Pandora and Ricardo. And I can polish the red-hot consummation of their love.

This script is going to be so fucking good.

FRIDAY, JUNE 13

Even though I've loitered in the lobby of the Four Seasons dozens of times, I knew that this occasion would be special. Today I wasn't an encroacher, a wanna-be sneaking in to borrow their luxury. This time, I actually belonged.

I arrived at the hotel fifteen minutes early after a brief meander through Yorkville. Outside, a storm loomed. The air was hot and heavy. Inside, the atmosphere was perfectly climate-controlled.

Wearing my Calvin Klein shirt again, I sat in the tall striped-velvet armchair in the lobby and watched the doorway with all the wealthy hotel guests coming and going in their smoked-glass limos, oblivious to their surroundings. I wondered how they could take such opulence for granted.

I meditated on the lobby's giant floral display, the mirror-like marble and granite floor, the plush oval carpet – so deep you almost lose your balance.

After my intense two weeks of work, it was a wonderful reward to be in a world that was so calm and cool and orderly. And to-night would be wonderful too – attending Ingrid's art show.

I presumed Carmen would be late. But just before one o'clock, I took the elevator up to the Studio Café.

It's like an art gallery you eat in. White walls. Bold contemporary paintings. I'd read in a magazine article that the jewel-tone fabric for the tablecloths had been designed by Gianni Versace. White display cases divide the long narrow room into sections, each case filled with glass sculptures in candy-bright colours, sparkling and glowing.

I gave the maitre d' my name and he led me towards the back of the restaurant to a table for two by a tall slender window.

My waitress appeared immediately. Smart white shirt and a

black tie. I ordered an iced tea.

Then I did some serious people-watching. Ladies in wide-brimmed hats, executives with important wristwatches. So confident that it was my fault for not knowing who they were.

I pulled out a notepad from my briefcase and set the stack of screenplay pages on the table to show everyone that I was there on business. *Movie* business.

My mind drifted with happy thoughts about Carmen loving the script. Flying with her to Los Angeles for important meetings. Spending the day on the set, becoming best friends with Jodie Foster.

Suddenly a scowling Carmen burst through my reverie. She was carrying a briefcase and two Chanel shopping bags.

"This is the table they gave you?"

"Is something the matter?"

"You're supposed to be in the front section on one of the couches. The rest of the tables are shit. I should have made the reservation myself. But this'll do for today. I can't stay long."

She dropped her bags and stopped a passing waiter. "I need a vodka tonic."

She sat down and slumped, closed her eyes and took deep slow breaths. I wondered if she'd fallen asleep.

"How was Los Angeles?" I asked gently.

"Hell."

"I'm sorry."

"It's not your fault. My mother was more painful than usual."

"My mother gets on my nerves too sometimes."

"Trust me. You have no idea. This time she invited my ex-husband over for dinner. I haven't spoken to the guy in five years, he never pays my alimony, and she still wants us to get back together. Needless to say, it wasn't a fun evening. Plates were broken. Anyway, we'd better get to the script. I have another appointment at two."

"Before we get started, Carmen, there's one strange little thing I need to mention."

"Oh wonderful," she said cynically.

"It's probably nothing important. But the last time you came to my apartment, when you were leaving, I looked out the window and there was a man watching you."

Carmen's expression turned serious. "You're joking."

"He followed you down the street. I think he was there the first time you came over, too."

"What did he look like?"

"Maybe Spanish, maybe Italian. Not very tall. Pouty mouth. Boyish charm." I had to stop myself before my adjectives turned too lustful. "Actually he bore a strong resemblance to a young Antonio Banderas."

She grimaced and shook her head. "Doesn't this just top it off."

"You know him?"

"You didn't talk to him, did you?"

"No."

"Good." She took a large mouthful of vodka tonic. "I hate to mix my personal life and my business life, Mitchell, but I guess I have to fill you in. That guy's an ex-boyfriend of mine."

"Really?" A guy that gorgeous?

"We came up with the story for this movie together and now he's upset that I'm working on the project without him. You know how sensitive writers can be."

"He didn't *look* like a writer," I said. "He looked too – athletic."

"Maybe that explains why he was lousy at it. Listen, Mitchell, I'm sorry to get you involved in this. I talked with him last night and I think we finally got things settled. He won't bother you again. But don't speak to him if he ever does. Just send him back to me. And for your trouble, I want you to take this."

She pulled out her wallet and counted five one-hundred-dollar bills onto her bread plate.

"That's really not necessary," I said. I wondered if the people at other tables were watching, imagining I was a drug dealer or a gigolo.

But even though she was paying me, I still found it hard to believe that Antonio Banderas had been her boyfriend.

The waitress hovered.

"I don't have time to eat," Carmen said, shooing the woman away. "Anyway, I've got indigestion. Something I ate on the plane.

So Mitchell, let's see what you've done."

Clearly Carmen wasn't in the most creatively receptive of moods. But then, maybe she never was.

"Remember this is just a rough draft," I said, handing over my precious twenty-seven-page baby. "I hope you like what I've done."

"I hope so too."

She held the pages at arm's length and began to read.

I pulled out a copy of *Variety* and pretended to be engrossed. But my eyes were locked on her face, alert to any changes in expression.

In my head I chanted, "Please like it, please like it."

I finished my iced tea and began sucking on the ice cubes.

With every page, her eyebrows scrunched deeper and deeper.

It felt like forever waiting for her to finish – even though she managed to speed-read the material in ten minutes.

When she flipped over the final page, she said in a serious voice, "We've got a problem, Mitchell. A big problem."

For a moment I thought she was teasing. I chuckled to go along with her.

"I can't show anybody this," she said. "People would laugh in my face."

Beads of sweat were forming on her forehead. Her cheeks had turned red.

My stomach flipped.

"How you could do this to me?" Carmen said. She downed her vodka tonic and waved the empty glass at our waitress. "I promised to send this to Jodie Foster's agent by overnight courier. Do you know what I went through to even get them to take my call? I can't send them shit like this."

I tried to appear calm and in control, eager to please, as if I'd been waiting all week to hear how much she hated it. "Maybe you can tell me exactly what the problem is."

"The whole thing is the problem."

Vague criticisms are the scariest a writer can hear. "Can you be more specific?"

"It doesn't sound right."

" 'It doesn't sound right'?"

"It doesn't sound like a movie. The characters, they don't talk the right way. It's the dialogue. Look at this scene here."

She shuffled through the pages. A handful of paper fluttered loose and fell to the floor. Then she passed me the crumpled scene in question:

INTERIOR. TORNAMETTI CONSTRUCTION OFFICES. NIGHT.

It's 10 p.m. and PANDORA is walking through the darkened corridors of the office. She carries a large cardboard box filled with paper cups, milk cartons and packages of ground coffee.

As she turns the corner into the unlit file storage room, she sees a MYSTERIOUS FIGURE with a flashlight. PANDORA's eyes widen with fear as she silently watches. The MYSTERIOUS FIGURE is shadowy and unrecognizable – quickly flipping through folders in a file drawer.

PANDORA swallows her fear, gingerly sets the box on a shelf and flicks on the light switch.

RICARDO looks up with a short, surprised yelp.

                    PANDORA
    Ricardo?!

                    RICARDO
    Oh Pandora! It's just you!

They embrace in mutual relief, but PANDORA immediately breaks away.

                    PANDORA
    You scared me half to death! I practically tossed a week's
    worth of coffee supplies all over the floor.

>   RICARDO
> So now Tornametti's got you bringing in kitchen supplies?
> Let me help you put that stuff away.

>   PANDORA
> What are you doing here at this time of night anyway?

>   RICARDO
> Same thing as you. Staying on top of things.

>   PANDORA
> But what are you doing in the file room? You never come
> in here.

>   RICARDO
> I need to find out more about that slimy client, Victor
> Felcher.

RICARDO's flashlight rolls off the filing cabinet and clatters onto
the floor. Their jitteriness makes both of them jump.

>   PANDORA
> I gave you Victor Felcher's file this morning, remember?

>   RICARDO
> I just wondered if there was something you missed.

>   PANDORA
> I don't normally miss things. Besides, you told me you
> were having dinner with some old friends tonight.

>   RICARDO
> They cancelled at the last minute.

PANDORA examines the file drawer more closely.

>   PANDORA
> Ricardo, this isn't the F drawer. It's the V drawer. What's
> going on?

RICARDO looks at her meaningfully, soul searchingly.

> RICARDO
> We need to talk. Let's go sit down.

He puts his arm around her shoulders and leads her into the open office area. She sits in a steno chair, while he leans on a desk.

> RICARDO
> I've been going crazy over this, Pandora. I've been debating with myself for days whether I should get you involved. I just never expected to fall in love with anybody here. But I need your help.

> PANDORA
> What's wrong, Ricardo? Are you in trouble?

> RICARDO
> I work for the police, Pandora. I'm a cop. Undercover. I'm here doing an investigation of Nick Tornametti. And I need your help to find the evidence I need.

> PANDORA
> Ricardo, I don't understand.

> RICARDO
> I know you've got some sort of sick respect for him. But Nick Tornametti is a criminal and a murderer. Two years ago he killed a lawyer named Aaron Vogel.

> PANDORA
> (in shock at this revelation about her father) That's absurd, Ricardo. He may not be a saint, but that doesn't mean he's a murderer.

> RICARDO
> Everybody in the business knows the rumour. Everybody believes it's true. Vogel was planning to expose Nick's money-laundering schemes on a shopping mall in Arizona. But no one's been able to find proof. That's why I'm here.

> PANDORA
You think he's a cold-blooded killer?

> RICARDO
We know he is. We just need to find the evidence. Pandora, you rearranged all these files last week. If anyone knows what's in here, it's you.

> PANDORA
But why? Why would he do it?

> RICARDO
Vogel was investigating Tornametti's investments. He knew too much, so Tornametti killed him. It can't be that hard for you to believe, Pandora. Tornametti is the scum of the earth.

PANDORA looks at RICARDO long and hard, her heart breaking. There is no way he can understand her divided loyalty.

> RICARDO
All I want you to do is find some contract, any document that links the two of them.

> PANDORA
I can't help you, Ricardo. I'm sorry. I hate to say no. I wish I could explain.

> RICARDO
But why?

> PANDORA
Ricardo, if you don't get out of here right now, I'm going to have to tell Tornametti who you really are.

RICARDO looks at her in amazement. PANDORA sticks out her chin in defiance, but she can't look him in the eye. RICARDO slams the filing cabinet drawer shut – sadness and confusion in his eyes – and storms out of the office. PANDORA slumps down onto the desk and cries.

CUT TO:

INTERIOR. FOUR SEASONS HOTEL – STUDIO CAFÉ. DAY.

I handed the pages back to her.

"Honestly Carmen, I think it's one of the best scenes I've done."

"They're both crying at the end!"

"They're upset."

"They're wimps! And at the beginning, Ricardo 'yelps'. Can you imagine Clint Eastwood *yelping* because somebody turned on a light?"

"Maybe 'yelp' is the wrong word. It's more like – a startled grunt."

"Oh, a grunt is much better," she said sarcastically.

"That's what *I'd* do if somebody surprised me when I was looking through files I wasn't supposed to."

"And when he drops the flashlight he jumps. He looks like an idiot."

"I think it makes him more likable – sort of goofy."

"Right, Mitchell. Goofy is really sexy. There's supposed to be passion burning up the screen between these two. Look here. Ricardo says, 'I've been debating with myself for days.' He'd never not be sure about something. And Pandora says, 'I'm sorry, I'm scared, I don't understand'."

"She *doesn't* understand! She's confused and she's scared because she's just found out her lover isn't who she thinks he is. *I'd* be upset."

"That's exactly the problem! These people are supposed to be confident and ballsy. But they talk like *you*!"

I took a deep breath to steady myself. I prayed that people at other tables weren't listening.

"I'm just trying to make it sound real. Real people are plagued by self-doubt."

"Maybe the real people you know. If anybody in my life was that wimpy I'd shoot them to put them out of their misery."

Be calm, be rational.

"Listen, Carmen, I wrote it that way on purpose."

"That's supposed to make me like it better?"

"Just listen a second. I think we've got a really interesting plot here. But in most thrillers the characters are just stick figures doing brave, dumb things. Like walking into a building when you know there's a murderer inside. I want our characters to be realistic, to have realistic emotions."

"I want realistic emotions, too! But exciting ones – like anger and greed and lust. Bottom line, Mitchell, this isn't blockbuster movie dialogue. You have to give me better than this."

"Carmen, I can't help but remember that first conversation we had, when you told me that you respect somebody who stands up for what they believe in. And I really think this is a more interesting way to go."

"Okay, so I respect you. But you still fucked up. And in this particular situation, I'm the one with the money, so what I say goes. Do you get my point?"

"I guess I do."

"There! You just did it again – talking wishy-washy. Do you get my point, Mitchell?" With each syllable, she banged a dinner knife on the table, so hard that the glasses rattled.

"Definitely, Carmen," I said, hard and robotic, "I see exactly what you mean."

"This is really shitty, Mitchell, letting me down like this. I gave my word to important people about this script. Now I'm going to look like an idiot. Like some stupid amateur who can't keep her word."

"I know I'll be able to fix it."

"You'd better do more than fix it," she said, gathering up her bags to go. "I want all this stuff rewritten and I need the big climax scene too – the one on top of the building. I'll call you on Thursday and we'll set up another meeting. I just hope I can cover my ass with the people in L.A. Remember, Mitchell, I took a chance on you. Don't make me regret it."

She said "*Ciao*" and stormed out of the restaurant without leaving money for her drinks.

My face was hot. My ears were burning. I felt humiliated, embarrassed to be seen there among all those perfect, polished people. I knew everyone had overheard Carmen's condemnations. Knew I was a sham, a no-talent fake.

I gathered together the mess of pages and shoved them into

the ratty leather briefcase I've been using since university. I put down twenty-five dollars to pay for the iced tea and Carmen's drinks. I didn't wait for change.

I kept my head down, trying to be invisible as I left the hotel. It was pouring rain.

I didn't have an umbrella.

I took the subway all the way to Bathurst Street and walked back to my apartment so I wouldn't have to pass in front of The Daily Grind. I couldn't bear the thought of telling Ingrid what had happened. Admitting my incompetence. Especially on the day of her big opening.

I feel like such an imbecile. Because Carmen is right. My writing is sappy. The characters are bland and neurotic.

What was I thinking? I was trying to be profound and innovative, honest and realistic. I should have known all along that my version of reality would be too flat and unglamorous for a major motion picture.

Maybe the next draft will be shit too and Carmen will fire me. Make me pay back the money. I'll have to admit to everyone that the job hadn't worked out. That I have no future as a screenwriter.

I should just stop being wishy-washy, call the temp agency and beg them to take me back.

Now, in this cheery mood, I have to shower and prepare for Ingrid's opening night. Re-iron my wrinkled Calvin Klein shirt – which I'm already beginning to resent. I don't see why people think linen is such a wonderful fabric.

I have no idea how to fix the script.

I decided repression was the right way to handle things. I didn't want to ruin Ingrid's big night. So I decided I'd temporarily forget about my meeting with Carmen and pretend I still had hope and dignity.

And I knew going out would do me good – or at least distract me from jumping out the window.

To stabilize myself I finished the dregs of my tequila and watched the first hour of *The Barefoot Contessa*, starring Ava Gardner. Killing time was a priority. I couldn't bear to be one of the first people to arrive and be forced to have a lengthy conversation with some other loser – be forced to respond to that dreaded cocktail party question: "So what do you do?"

Picturing Ingrid standing there alone and vulnerable was my only motivation. Finally, at nine, I set out for the party. The air was finally cooler. The rain had stopped, but the pavement was still glistening.

As I walked towards the store, I tried to psych myself into confidence. I said to myself: "Tonight you're going to be charming and friendly and interesting. Enjoy yourself tonight. Be here now. Worry about the script tomorrow. Tomorrow is another day. The sun'll come out tomorrow."

I was so wrapped up in my inner monologue that I was startled by the crowd in front of The Daily Grind. A mass of smart-looking people spilling onto the sidewalk. A roar of voices, backed by Ingrid's favourite Parisian-esque accordion music.

This wasn't the normal casual neighbourhood clientele. These were glamorous, flamboyant people with money – out for a serious event. Bright-coloured linen jackets. Loose summer dresses strung with ethnic bangles and gold jewellery.

I'd expected a few blue-rinsed ladies huddled around a cheese tray. But the patio outside was jammed with people smoking and holding coffee cups instead of champagne glasses.

I squeezed through the doorway with a stream of excuse-me's. I couldn't spot a single familiar face. My private territory suddenly felt foreign. No sign of Ingrid or Ramir. I noticed Kinita behind the counter with two unknown women. Why were there strangers working at The Grind?

Small clusters of people were examining Ingrid's paintings – twelve of them spread across the wide expanse of the left wall. I heard people saying "lovely" and "wonderful." Over their shoulders, I surveyed the collection. An old woman flying through the night sky in a rocking chair. A child staring at his breakfast plate. A dog listening for rabbits in a wheat field. Three blue portraits, all showing the same young woman (Ingrid?), looking out the same window, but viewed from different angles. Familiar pictures that I'd admired in the quiet of Ingrid's apartment, now exposed to this babbling throng.

I was overwhelmed.

Where was Ingrid? Where was Geoffrey?

My sex radar was still working well enough to notice a cute blond guy with a brushcut – white T-shirt and chinos. On the short side maybe. He was chatting politely with two blue-haired matrons. (So I hadn't been totally wrong in my little-old-lady expectations.) And there was Frances Farmer, brooding in the corner in a peach-sequined evening gown dripping with spangles and bugle beads.

I felt a tug on my arm and there at last was Ingrid. Glowing with nervous energy.

"Can you believe this?"

"Ing, it's incredible! Who are all these people?"

"I have no idea!" We hugged in amazement.

"Do you like my outfit?" She smoothed her hands down the waist of a fitted black dress – a sleeveless silk shift. "Mint condition from a vintage shop in Kensington Market."

"*Very* Jackie Kennedy. You look gorgeous, Ing." Her dark red ringlets were pulled up in a stylized French twist. She poked at her hair self-consciously. But clearly she was pleased with her stylish transformation.

"This is all so strange. I feel so self-conscious. Everybody's whispering behind my back."

"At least they're saying nice things. I heard them! But where did all these people come from?"

"They're clients of Geoffrey's. His assistant's been on the phone all week. Geoffrey's introduced me to most of them. Architects. Interior designers. A couple of famous opera singers. I think I saw a guy who Ramir used to date. He's not here yet, by the way."

"No surprise in that." I pointed towards her paintings. "What are all those red dots on the wall?"

"Sold stickers – eight already!"

"Forgive me for being crass, but how much are you charging?"

"It's how much *Geoffrey's* charging. Twelve hundred."

"Each? And you were only going to ask for two hundred dollars!"

"Geoffrey gets 50 percent."

"Is that legal?"

"It's standard for galleries. And I wouldn't have made any of it without him. Thank God he's been here to get me through this. He told me one person bought three paintings – the three blue ones."

"Who was it?" I said, scanning the room for the most conspicuous wealth.

"He wouldn't tell me."

"Do you think Frances Farmer is secretly a millionairess?"

"Then she owes me for a lot of free coffees."

A man passed by and wordlessly did a thumbs-up signal in front of Ingrid's face.

Ing said, "Thanks," and the man continued on his way.

"It's so weird, the idea of selling my paintings. I'm actually going to miss them. Those blue ones are my favourites. I did them all in the same week after I'd signed the divorce papers from Pierre."

"Maybe you can arrange visitation rights."

Ing glanced quickly over her shoulder in another moment of paranoia. "So how was your meeting with Carmen?"

"I'll tell you about it tomorrow. I just hope Ramir gets here soon. Then I won't have to cling here to your side all night."

"Keep clinging. It's so nice to see a face from my real life. But I'd better check with Kinita on the coffee situation. I'm scared we'll run out." She leaned towards my ear, "I've got a bottle in the fridge in the back room for special guests. Keep it a secret. We don't want to get raided."

Ingrid pressed towards the counter.

Through a gap in the crowd, I noticed the blond brushcut guy heading out to the patio. All clean-cut and collegiate. Perfect material for one of my stories.

But I was still too fresh from my mistake with Antonio Banderas, still feeling tainted because of Carmen, still too hung up about the HIV test. I wasn't ready to deal with romance.

I turned to get in line for a coffee. Holding a cup would give me something to do with my hands.

While I waited at the counter, I could see Ingrid fussing with the CD player in the back room. And I overheard snippets of passing conversations: "You *must* tell me whether he's sleeping with her" . . . "Far better than your typical restaurant art" . . . "We'll be late for our reservation" . . . "Last month Abrams had us marching along concrete ramps in a parking garage."

When I got to the front of the line, Kinita was ready and eager to serve me. Her hair was gelled into total verticality and, for tonight's special festivities, her nose ring was connected to her earring by a gold charm bracelet. "Cappuccino, Mitchell? Don't worry, everything's on the house."

"Regular Mocha Java's fine," I said.

"Finished your screenplay yet?"

"I had lunch with the producer today. We're in the fine-tuning stage. How are things with your band?"

"Ing made me skip rehearsal tonight, so who knows?"

"Quite an amazing crowd, isn't it?"

"Amazingly obnoxious. Everybody reeking of self-importance."

"I was just thinking the same thing."

"This city is one big inferiority complex. Everybody pretending they're so sophisticated, trying to prove they're 'world-class'."

"Ing said there are a couple of famous opera singers here."

"Big fish in a little pond. I bet nobody in New York has ever heard of them."

"Weren't you going to move down there?"

"I changed my mind. New York's just a big theme park now."

"Nowhere left to escape," I said, and escaped.

I stood near the wall and focused on sipping my coffee. Occasionally I'd scan the room, using my old camouflage strategy of intently "looking for a friend," so I wouldn't appear too pathetic. No sign of the brushcut. Maybe he'd left. A mix of disappointment and relief.

Beside me were two forty-ish gay men, both with tiny round spectacles clamped to their noses. They were scrutinizing the girl-staring-into-bonfire painting that Ingrid had been working on just a few weeks ago.

"Marvelous how she's layered the paint to capture the depth of the flames."

"A brilliant colour technician."

One of them tapped on my shoulder. "Excuse me, but you're blocking our light."

So much for my infectious charm.

I had no idea that Ingrid strategically layered her paint for added depth or that anybody could be considered a technician of colour.

After a début night like this, she was obviously going to be a major success. Which made me think again about my disaster with Carmen. But I'd promised myself not to follow that train of thought.

For a good ten minutes I stood there, shifting my weight from foot to foot. I repeated to myself, "I do not look like an awkward goof. I do not look like an awkward goof."

After I'd finished my coffee, I kept sipping from the empty cup – just so I wouldn't have to let go of my prop. I wondered about pretending I'd left something at home so I could escape and come back later once Ramir was here to talk to.

Ingrid had disappeared. Maybe she was out on the patio. There was Geoffrey Abrams, schmoozing his clients. (He must be even more important than I'd fantasized.) He was wearing a severe black suit, which made him resemble a style-conscious funeral director, but even so, he was devastatingly handsome.

He'd always be Sidney Poitier to me.

I could say I'd forgotten my wallet. Or left the iron on. No one would miss me.

Where was Ramir?

I witnessed one of Geoffrey's peons pressing a little red dot on the wall. The half-blind gay men had purchased Ingrid's "Bonfire." I sneered at their self-satisfied glow. They'd just discovered a new artist. Weren't they something!

I crept downstairs to the washroom and locked myself in a stall. I sat on the toilet and re-read ancient graffiti until a gentleman knocked sharply on the door and asked, "Will you be coming out of there any time soon?"

I hate to think what he thought I was doing.

I had just come up the stairs, ready to scurry home and check if I'd left the shower dripping, when I caught the eyes of the cute blond guy. He was coming towards me, smiling as if we were old friends. Don't panic. This is a good thing. Be suave. Be debonair. Be Cary Grant.

He put his hand out for a shake. "Chad, it's great to see you."

The big smile. The forthright friendliness. Suddenly it came back to me.

"I've been hoping to run into you again at Woody's," he said. "But I remember you said you don't go to bars very often."

"I've been really busy lately." The punk Yul Brynner. Why hadn't I recognized him right away? "Your hair's grown in," I said, actually meaning that the snake tattoo on his scalp had been buried in blondness.

He rubbed his hand back over his head, obviously enjoying the feel of the bristles. "Yeah, I wanted a change. It's been over a month, I guess. My name's Ben, by the way, in case you don't remember. It's good to see you again. I like your shirt."

He was actually the first person to compliment it, or even notice it for that matter. "Calvin Klein," I name-dropped out of the side of my mouth.

"Ooo," he whispered back, raising his eyebrows in a satire of being impressed – which I actually thought was sort of cute.

Then he stroked the linen against my chest with the tips of his fingers. "Feels good."

Now I know that the whole reason I'd spent two hundred and fifty dollars on a shirt was to receive flattery. But this was more than I'd expected.

Stirrings of sexuality.

Panic.

"Do you like the paintings? My friend Ingrid Iversen is the artist. I'm helping out tonight. Actually I have to check something in back. I'll talk to you later."

I practically knocked a blue-haired lady out of the way as I rushed towards the back room. I dug among the milk cartons in the fridge until I found Ingrid's stash of Canadian Club and poured a shot into a stray mug.

What were the odds of Yul Brynner being here? Of me accidentally flirting with him? Hair really can work wonders.

It was ridiculous that I'd run away from him. I'd just been overwhelmed. Surprised. Out of practice. And now I was too embarrassed to face him again.

I really had to leave. I could pretend I was feeling ill. Which was fast becoming the truth.

Why wasn't Ramir here to protect me? Of course he'd think the whole situation was hilarious. I couldn't tell him about it.

I downed the rest of the whisky in my cup, then drank two mouthfuls straight from the bottle. I came back out into the crowd feeling light-headed. Booze on an empty stomach.

The first person I bumped into was Geoffrey.

"Mitchell, incredibly glad you could come." That genteel Jamaican accent always melts me. I latched onto him in order to avoid Ben.

"I had no idea the party would be this big," I said, more syrupy than I'd intended. The alcohol was acting fast.

"To be honest, Mitchell, tonight is rather on the small side. You and Ingrid should come to the next opening at the gallery."

"We'd love to. It'd be an honour."

"But I must say this evening is turning out exceptionally well. I haven't seen a new artist sell so quickly in quite some time."

"Maybe this'll finally convince her she has talent. She looks great, doesn't she?"

"Lovely. Sparkling. Forgive me, Mitchell, but I see an old friend." He turned to air-kiss a surgically enhanced *grande dame*. "Hilary, incredibly glad you could come."

I couldn't be peeved at his snub. He was working, after all. But he thought Ing was lovely and sparkling. She'd love to hear that.

And there was Ingrid being cornered by a tall, bony woman with an elegant swoop of hair and a gargantuan amethyst pendant. I sidled up to them. At least with Ingrid I knew I belonged.

The lady's voice was an excited sing-song. "You've caught a magical spiritual current. Blurring the outer edges. Bringing everything together. You've encapsulated the entire Buddhist philosophy right there on the canvas. Have you ever been to Nepal?"

Ingrid managed to utter, "N–," before the woman rushed on, "I've just returned from Katmandu. Filled with great lessons. Spiritual connectivity floating in the air."

Obviously there was nothing I could do to help, so I detached myself and edged away. I turned to go out to the patio, but when I got to the door, I saw Ben out there, chatting to the two snide art patrons.

I backtracked.

Ramir should be here any minute.

There was Geoffrey doing his sales pitch to a black woman wearing a traditional African turban. I drifted over to eavesdrop. "She's building on the sensitivity of the Impressionists, but as you can see, she cuts it with a contemporary edge. A darker palette. The visual play. You can see influences of the Group of Seven, van Gogh, Modigliani. And she's only twenty-eight. There's a major career ahead."

"Very special," the woman agreed, nodding solemnly. "Very special."

Very special.

Of course I knew it was all hype. I'd never heard Ingrid say anything about cutting van Gogh with Modigliani. But then I wondered if she really *was* putting all those influences into each of her paintings and I was just too much of a philistine to notice. I decided I'd ask her about it tomorrow.

"What I love," Geoffrey said, "is that all of her paintings have a hidden surprise." He talked as if they were boxes of Cracker Jack. "The more you look, the more you find." Like they were "Where's Waldo?" cartoons.

It all sounded like grandiose B.S. to me. But perhaps Geoffrey was actually being authentic and, because I'm so accustomed to *poseurs*, I was simply mislabelling it as pretension.

Ingrid materialized at my side. "Sorry about that. I would have introduced you, but she never stops talking. That was Mrs. Epstein – the woman who asked about the green one and started all this."

"Please forgive me, Ingrid, but at any moment I think I'm going to turn green with jealousy."

"Don't be ridiculous, Mitchell. There'll be an even bigger party when your movie comes out."

"We can all stand around the video-rental counter at Mac's Milk."

"Stop pretending you're humble." She stood on her tiptoes and looked at the counter. "The line-up for coffee just doesn't stop. Can you imagine if we were actually charging tonight? Sorry, I've got to go – Geoffrey just waved."

I watched Ingrid as she wound her way through the crowd to charm an elderly billionaire. Despite her nervousness, Ingrid seemed like a natural – perfectly poised and confident. Sparkling. She looked beautiful. The red in her hair was glowing. She touched Geoffrey's arm and laughed.

I couldn't take any more of it. I had to leave. I didn't belong here. Tomorrow, when I had a chance to tell Ing what had happened with Carmen, she'd understand.

Then Montgomery Clift walked in the door.

Montgomery Clift from that night weeks before at Woody's. He of the perfect nose and the air of quiet wealth.

A miracle.

It made perfect sense that he'd be a client of Geoffrey's.

There he was, parting the crowd the way Charlton Heston

had divided the Red Sea. Classically understated in another striped Oxford shirt, this one a soft pink.

I had learned my lesson. This time I wouldn't let him get away. My one gift from God on this miserable day.

I started to push towards him, hypnotized with happiness. It was like one of those soft-focus slow-motion TV commercials. Two lovers running towards each other through a field of daisies.

And right behind him was Ramir. "This place is packed! Ing must be ecstatic. Anyway, Mitch, finally you get to meet Fred."

Montgomery Clift turned his face towards me.

"Fred?" I said.

"Hi," he said, producing that gentle and intelligent smile I remembered so vividly, yet he seemed more interested in something over my shoulder.

"You're Fred?" I said again, the horrible implications beginning to dawn.

"Right."

The facts swirled through my memory. After Ramir and I left Fran's, Ramir had gone for a drink at Byzantium. And that's where he'd met Fred.

"Actually I think I've seen you around before," I said chummily, hoping our first encounter would come back to him and that he'd find me infinitely more enchanting than Ramir. "At Woody's – about a month ago."

"That's possible," he said, as though he was weary of people recognizing him. "Excuse us, but we really need coffee."

Ramir smirked back to me, "We've been busy. I'll talk to you in a minute."

Exhausted from all that hot sex.

The depth of the absurdity slammed into me. Yul Brynner and Montgomery Clift in the same evening.

This was just so typical.

I suddenly felt hot and light-headed. Stupid and self-conscious. All the people, all the noise. The blaring accordion music. I felt claustrophobic.

The same anxiety attack I'd felt at the restaurant with Carmen.

I rushed downstairs to the washroom and locked myself in the stall again. I'd just wait a few minutes, calm down, yes, calm down, and then I'd go home to bed.

It was all swirling.

Ramir with the man of my dreams.

Ingrid the toast of the art world.

Carmen saying my writing was shit. That my personality was wimpy and wishy-washy.

Then I remembered Ramir wanting to set me up with a friend of Fred's. What if it was that lumpy oaf who Fred had been talking to that night at Woody's? Was he all that Ramir thought I deserved?

I was furious. All the bile I'd been holding back since lunch rose up and I choked, tasting the whisky. I leaned over the toilet, but I couldn't throw up.

I let myself out of the stall and went to the sink. I looked in the mirror and saw how pathetic I was. Swollen eyes. Red face. I felt my anger grow hotter. At Ramir. At Carmen. At Ingrid. At myself.

Here I was, waiting for destiny, crying in a toilet.

I splashed my face with cold water and dried my tears with a coarse brown paper towel. I made a fierce face in the mirror and stomped up the stairs.

I barged through the party straight to Ben. I spoke so fast, my words collided. "Do you want to go someplace for a coffee?"

He set down the coffee he was drinking, said, "I'd love to," and took me by the hand, leading me through the noisy throng. (I prayed Ramir and Fred were watching.) Ben looked over his shoulder and smiled at me like a co-conspirator. Those wide blue eyes.

Out on the street, the booming background of the party evaporated. Silence by comparison. Cool fresh air. I stood still for a moment. Tried to feel my feet on the ground.

"Are you okay?" he asked. "Your eyes are all red."

"The smoke. I'll be fine."

"Where to?"

"You decide."

"The place across the street?"

"Great."

We dodged the Friday-night traffic. Teenagers cruising down-town in Dad's car. For a few moments we didn't have to talk. I took deep breaths to speed myself back to normal. I didn't want him to know I'd been crying.

The windows of the Future Bakery open like garage doors, sliding up across the ceiling. We grabbed an empty table right beside the sidewalk.

"So you really want another coffee?" he asked.

"Definitely. Black."

While Ben went up to the counter, I steadied myself. I gazed across the street at the party inside The Daily Grind and mar-velled at how I'd suddenly ended up over here. So close and yet so far. I caught a glimpse of Ingrid in the crowd. What would she and Ramir think?

Then Ben was back with two coffees and two cinnamon rolls.

"I've never set foot in this place before," I said. I sounded des-perately perky. "Ingrid would kill me if she knew I was giving business to the competition."

"She'll probably forgive you just this once."

"I guess she won't have such petty concerns now that she's a famous artist." I had to stop talking like some lobotomized Gidget.

But he chuckled. That was good.

"So how do you know her?" he asked.

"From the store. That's where we met. Two years ago. I just kept going in every day, hanging out. Now she's pretty well my best friend."

"She's really talented."

"That's what I keep telling her. But sometimes she has a hard time believing it." How saccharine. I sipped coffee to cover my inanity. I'd totally forgotten any dating skills.

"I'm always amazed when I see that kind of creativity." Ben said. "I had no idea what to expect."

"I didn't either. I haven't been to that many art shows. But it looked like most of the people buying were just boring and pre-tentious. Just showing off how much money they have."

"Some of them seemed okay."

"But it's great for Ingrid. It's sort of a real-life Cinderella story.

Two weeks ago, she was just happily working in a coffee shop. Well, maybe not happily."

"So what do you do? Are you a painter too?"

"No, no, I'm a writer. Sort of. For a while I worked in corporate communications. But now mostly I'm writing for film and TV and some other stuff."

"Interesting stuff?"

"Sometimes. But when I'm not making any money at that, I work as an office temp. Now that's *very* interesting. So what do you do?"

"I'm a bike courier."

"You're kidding!" I said with a hearty, isn't-that-fascinating grin and told myself I didn't have any right to feel superior. "When I work in offices, I always see a lot of bicycle couriers." I felt myself going Sandra Dee again. "Are there many gay bicycle couriers?"

"I'm sort of a renegade."

"I didn't think I'd ever spotted one."

"I like it. It's straightforward. None of the power games you get working in a big company."

"I wasn't very good at those either."

"I worked in computers for a while, but when you have a full-time job they think they own your whole life." He tilted his head like he was sizing me up. "So Chad, if you're a writer, you must be working on a novel or something on the side, right?"

"I have to tell you something stupid. My name isn't Chad. It's Mitchell. Mitchell Draper. I'm sorry, I was just being dumb that night at the bar."

"Mitchell, eh?" He stared at me like he was trying to fit this information into an equation.

"If you've lost all respect for me and you want to leave, I understand."

"No, actually you look more like a Mitchell than a Chad."

"Is that a good thing?"

"You must have figured out I like you."

I rolled my eyes.

"You're fun to embarrass. You blush every time."

"Wonderful."

"No, it's a good sign. That's what I noticed about you that night in the bar. You looked so uncomfortable. It means you're not all jaded and blasé."

"I've always wanted to be jaded and blasé."

He laughed.

"And besides, I wasn't *that* uncomfortable."

"I'm not saying you are *right now*. But if you're going to be nervous, I think you're better off showing it, rather than acting like some stuck-up snob."

"I suppose," I said, although in the past I've always attempted the snobbish approach.

"So what made you get so assertive all of a sudden tonight?"

That took me by surprise. "I don't know." But he was looking into my eyes so sincerely. "I just got tired of being my same old self."

"I know the feeling." He was still staring, smiling – those blue eyes – and there was a long moment of silence. Which I couldn't cope with, so right away I looked outside and said, "Look, there's Jimmy Durante," pointing at a streetperson with a swollen alcoholic nose.

Ben said, "What?" and turned around to look after him.

A woman with a giant Barbie smile. "And, I can't believe it, there's Vanna White!"

"What are you talking about?"

"It's a game. Spot the Celebrity. You see somebody and you say what famous person they look like. It's your turn."

Ben looked intently at the people passing by. Easily I spotted an Abbie Hoffman, a George Michael and an old lady who could have doubled for Quentin Crisp or Hermione Gingold.

"Not working?"

"I guess I'm too left-brained." He rubbed his hand across his bristly hair again, and this time as he raised his arm, I noticed the tender, firm roundness of his biceps.

"Ing and Ramir and I do it all the time. I guess it's sort of stupid." Our eyes locked again. "I like you a lot better with hair," I said, and I couldn't believe it had come out of my mouth.

He laughed. "So did I come on too strong at Woody's?"

"For someone like me who's not very jaded and blasé."

"I'm sorry. I'll try to take it easy."

"So what's your last name anyway?"

"Cosgrove. Ben Cosgrove."

He formally shook my hand across the table, as if we'd just met.

"And how old are you?" I asked.

"This must be the part of the date when we get all the statistics out of the way. I'm five-nine. One-hundred-and-sixty pounds. Non-smoker. Minimal body hair."

"You know, you sound sort of jaded yourself."

"A habit I'm trying to break."

"You still haven't told me how old you are."

"Thirty. You?"

"Twenty-eight."

"Ooo, a younger man."

"And where are you from?"

"Winnipeg. You?"

"Toronto."

"Really? I didn't think anyone was actually *from* here."

"I grew up in Willowdale actually."

"You don't *still* live there?"

"No."

"Good. So would it be too pushy if I asked if you live around *here*?"

"Actually my apartment's just in the next block, above the Little Buda." I pointed down the street. "You can come over if you want."

"For coffee?"

We left our half-full cups and walked along the sidewalk in silence, but my mind was racing. I shouldn't be doing this. Sex was too complicated. How could I escape?

"It's funny about your name and your being a courier," I said. "It's like that old Michael Jackson song. 'Ben, you're always running here and there.' That killer rat movie from 1972."

"I've heard enough rodent jokes to last a lifetime."

"I should just keep my trap shut."

Oh God, another stupid pun.

We got to my downstairs doorway. "Anyway, this is it."

I led him into the vestibule.

Taking note of the cupid wallpaper on the stairs, Ben said, "Reminds me of my Aunt Mabel's bathroom." Just the right response, but my heartbeat was still staccato as we climbed the two flights. I unlocked my door and we stepped inside.

"So this is my kitchen and living room and dining room and office."

"I like it."

"Someday I want to sleep in a room that doesn't have a fridge in it." I rushed to turn on some music. The soundtrack from *Twin Peaks*. Slow and hypnotic. Perfect date atmosphere.

"So where do *you* live?" I chirped, preventing any hypnotic effects.

"A warehouse around King and Bathurst."

"One of the ones they've renovated?"

"Not yet, thank God."

"It must be great."

"It can get pretty hot in my place, too."

"Sorry. It's like a sauna in here." I rushed to turn on the big fan by the window. "Sit down. Would you like some iced tea?"

"All this caffeine – you must want me awake for something."

I laughed nervously and fussed at the refrigerator.

Ben noticed Ingrid's painting of me, hanging above the couch. "That's you!"

I brought him his drink. I looked at the painted version of myself levitating above my computer. "It's called 'Mitchell in Midair'."

"I like it even better than some of the stuff she had up tonight."

"It was excruciating to pose for. She had me hold my arms up like Superman for hours on end." I demonstrated. Like an idiot.

"That could be worth a lot of money some day. She's very talented."

"She's lucky she met Geoffrey Abrams. He's a regular at the store and we always called him Sidney Poitier because he's so good looking."

"You really keep track of all your celebrities."

"Sometimes I'm like a game of Trivial Pursuit."

I went back to the kitchen to get my own iced tea, cursing

myself for sounding so ridiculous.

"So what are you working on?" he said, motioning to the computer and the piles of paper on my kitchen table/desk.

"Nothing. Everything. It's complicated. It's a script."

"For a movie?"

I nodded, drinking.

"What's it about?"

"Oh, it's sort of your typical B-movie romantic thriller. Right now it's mostly a disaster. I'm trying not to think about it."

"Sorry I asked." Suddenly he was standing right beside me again, grinning that sexy, provocative grin.

"I have to rewrite the whole thing this weekend."

"Is that a subtle way of saying I can't stay the night?"

I grinned back nervously. "Well, maybe I can do it on Sunday."

He set his glass down on the coffee table and he pressed a hand on each of my shoulders, as if to hold me still. And then he kissed me. Hard and insistent, but smooth and luxurious. The kind of kiss that makes your brain shut down.

"Maybe I can put it off till next Tuesday," I said, and I kissed him back, determined to make a good impression.

He smiled appreciatively, raised his eyebrows and whispered: "You're not so shy after all." Which was exactly the right thing for him to say.

He was about to kiss me again but I held him away. "Everything safe, okay?"

"Perfectly safe."

I squeezed the firm curves of his biceps, and pulled him against me, and before I begin writing a hot sex scene that might be more appropriate in a screenplay by Chad Stiffman, I will simply give the camera direction:

CUT TO THE ROTATING FAN.

I called Ingrid right after Ben left.

"Ten months, one week and three days."

"You had sex!"

"I guess this means I lost the celibacy contest."

"It was that blond guy, right?"

"You saw me talking to him?"

"I had my fingers crossed."

"You weren't mad I left?"

"I was happy! So do you like him?"

"Yeah."

"You're not convincing me."

"He's really nice. He's just really different from the guys I've dated before."

"How do you mean?"

"I mean, he's not intimidating, and usually for me intimidation and infatuation are inextricably linked. Anyway, enough about my rampant promiscuity. What happened after I left?"

"You'll never believe it, Mitchell. We sold all the paintings!"

"Of course I believe it."

"Everybody seemed to have a good time. They were all gone by eleven-thirty. Then Geoffrey helped me straighten things up and he drove me home."

"And then?"

"And then, nothing!"

"After you made him all that money? Not even a peck on the cheek?"

"I don't even think he's interested in me that way, Mitchell."

"He told me he thought you were 'lovely' and 'sparkling'."

"He did?"

"His exact words – both of them. He probably wants to keep a professional distance for now."

"I hate this dating thing, Mitchell."

"But now you're the queen of the art world. You'll have men falling at your feet."

"I don't want them on the floor."

"It makes them easier to kick around. So tell me the truth, what did you think of Fred?"

"He was handsome," she said with a note of uncertainty.

"But?"

"He didn't look me in the eyes. I never trust people who can't make eye contact."

"Good. You don't like him either."

Then Ramir:

"Remember that bald guy from Woody's?"

"There are lots of bald guys at Woody's."

"The one who came on to me. The one with the snake tattoo on his head."

"That was the same guy?"

"He's been searching the city for me ever since. So you see, you're not the only one who's a sexual magnet."

"If you'd taken my advice back then, think of all the fun you could have had in the meantime."

"I was waiting for his hair to grow in."

"Bald men have their advantages. But at least he got you out of your rut."

"Back in the saddle again."

"Did you talk about the Big A?"

"Sort of."

"Is he positive?"

"He didn't say. But he wore a condom, if that's what you're asking."

"Was it an extra-large condom?"

"A gentleman doesn't kiss and tell."

"So what did you think of Fred?"

"He looks like Montgomery Clift."

"But what did you think of him?"

"As long as you like him, that's what counts."

"You know, if I let you and Ingrid pick my dates, I'd be wearing a chastity belt, too. So are you seeing your bald guy again?"

"We made plans for Tuesday."

"Must be serious."

"Might be. Anyway, I need to get a good night's sleep and then work all day tomorrow. Carmen wants me to make the script more commercial."

"But she liked what you did?"

"She had a few suggestions. I want to give you and Ingrid the next draft on Monday so I can get your opinion."

"Maybe suggest some ways to make my part bigger."

"Actually I'm writing a scene where you're a waiter in a Mexican restaurant. You wear a sombrero and play maracas."

"Ay, yi, yi, yi," he said. "I'll be home all day Monday working on *my* script, so you can come over anytime."

SUNDAY, JUNE 15

I am now prepared to begin the Herculean task of doing a complete rewrite in a single day.

I have unplugged the TV and radio to avoid the temptation of distraction. And I've turned off the ringer on my phone. I'll let all calls go directly to my answering machine.

A pitcher of iced tea is chilling in the fridge, along with four Jamaican-style vegetable patties from the Good Karma to serve as lunch and dinner. A variety of junk foods, including potato chips, jujubes, a giant Kit Kat bar, peanut M&Ms and six Rice Krispie squares, are positioned around me for rapid access.

According to my plan, I will finish rewriting today, then I'll give the script to Ingrid and Ramir tomorrow and get their comments back on Tuesday, so I can incorporate their changes on Wednesday and give it to Carmen on Thursday. Perfect scheduling.

I can now see that Carmen was completely right.

My first draft was too neurotic. Too meek, static and self-conscious. I'd been writing the stereotypical Canadian film. How would I have ever faced Kinita?

Now I must pretend I am writing an old-fashioned Hollywood melodrama. Send the dialogue right over the top like a 1930s Bette Davis picture. Confident and brash with stormy emotions that ignite as easily as gasoline. Make the characters larger than life – the way I've always fantasized one should live.

Okay. I'm ready. My writing marathon starts (deep breath) now.

☆

Big Ben. Gentle Ben. Ben Cartwright. Ben Casey. Ben Gay.
Benjamin Franklin. Benjamin Moore. Benny and the Jets.
Benedict Arnold. Benedictine monks. Benedictine liqueur.
Sodium benzadril.

I only managed to write for half an hour before I got distracted
thinking about Ben.

I ended up writing half a porn story about a bike courier – I
skipped the introduction and just jumped to the juicy bits.

And then I started obsessing again about my test results.
Wondering what I would tell Ben if I turn out to be positive. It'd
be easier to just break up with him in advance. Considering my
dating history, that's probably what's going to happen anyway.

I'm just no good with real-life relationships.

And Ben's not exactly my ideal man. He's so decidedly unglamorous. And not very career-oriented. I've always dreamed
about dating a lawyer or a politician or a famous actor. A rich man
who could rescue me and take me away from all this.

I shouldn't be rambling. I must get back to work.

I have eaten all of my food supplies and it's only two o'clock.

Eight p.m.

I got to page fifteen of the section I'm rewriting and then
switched over to do the first draft of the climactic scene on top of
the building.

It's just not dramatically satisfying for Pandora and her father
to make up and live happily ever after. So I'll give Carmen exactly
what she wants. A screaming match, nasty threats, a big push
. . . and Nick Tornametti is pulp on the pavement.

Pandora can shed a few tears, embrace Ricardo and then, roll
credits.

No more procrastinating. I'm just going to settle in and get
this thing done.

I finished at four a.m. and collapsed into bed. I had a fitful sleep, dreaming of climbing stairs in an endless office tower with Carmen yelling "faster, faster" from somewhere on high.

I finally got up at ten and took a long shower, turning the water from womb-warm to ice-cold.

Almost half of the screenplay is now complete. The beginning and the end. Fifty-four pages. But there's still a sixty-page gap in the middle. Fleshing it out should be pretty straightforward at this point – if Carmen likes my new version. And I really have the feeling she will.

At Kinko's, I made two photocopies – one for Ingrid and one for Ramir. Then, when I was home again, I put the original in the freezer on top of my other half-finished writings. Cryogenically preserved for resuscitation when science is sufficiently advanced.

I slid each precious copy into an oversized envelope and then headed out to distribute them.

When I got to The Daily Grind I was taken aback. The patio was packed. Every table inside was occupied. At eleven-thirty in the morning on a weekday! This was unheard of.

I noticed two separate people reading Noam Chomsky.

Behind the counter stood an unfamiliar teenager with ultra-pale skin and long dyed-black hair. She chimed "Hi-eee" at me.

"Hi," I said quickly. "Is Ingrid here?"

"Ingrid? She's in back. Can I tell her who you are?"

I told her.

I must admit I was miffed at having to introduce myself in a store that I practically own through squatter's rights.

The girl ducked in and out of the back room. "She says to come on through."

There was Ingrid at her desk, surrounded by stacks of invoices and ledgers.

I whispered, "Is that Morticia Addams?"

"Her name is Madonna."

"You're kidding."

"How could I make that up? I just hired her."

"Oh my God. And her mother probably thought that name was a blessing."

Then Ing wordlessly held up a folded-open copy of *The Globe and Mail.* She pointed to the "Buzz" column – the Monday roundup of arts gossip. I read:

Grinding out fresh artwork

Yorkville gallery owner **Geoffrey Abrams** has come up with a new way to bring the art market out of the doldrums – taking art out of the art gallery. He's herded his legion of devoted collectors from a five-storey parking garage to a shopping centre food court to an abandoned slaughterhouse.

His latest opening was at the comparatively elegant Bloor West coffee shop, The Daily Grin. "Bold Impressionist" paintings by Abrams' latest find **Ingrid Iversen**, manager of the coffee shop, were being admired by daring society art aficionados, including **Hillary McCuaig**, **Edwina Janiszewski** and **Fenwick Green**.

Deemed "esoteric Tupperware parties" by one attendee, the events combine glittering guests with paintings by unknown artists. Sales of the artwork are reported to be brisk as Mr. Abrams works his mysterious magic once again.

"This is incredible. You're famous!"

"It says I'm unknown."

"That was before. Now you're a Bold Impressionist! You've started a whole new art movement."

"It's just a little mention, Mitchell."

"You're on the same page as a story about Oprah Winfrey, so

you must be equally important."

"I'll admit, it *is* sort of nice."

"Well, there's a major concession. I remember when you said you only wanted your birth and death announcements in the paper."

"You're not hiding your envy very well, Mitchell."

"How did this happen?"

"Geoffrey's P.R. connections. He called me this morning and told me to buy the paper and look in the arts section. And there I was. My stomach flipped over. I never expected anything like this."

"The publicity is obviously paying off. The store's packed."

"I don't know if that's the reason. Come out front. I have to check on Madonna." She scrunched her nose. "How am I ever going to say that with a straight face?"

"Maybe you can call her Donna. Or Maddie."

She led me back into the store.

"Kinita's working this afternoon so I can spend some time at home painting. Then tonight I'm coming back here with Geoffrey."

"Another late night?" I raised my eyebrows insinuatingly, but she ignored me.

"We're going to take down the paintings so he can deliver them to the people who bought them."

"It's going to look pretty empty in here."

"Then we're going to bring in twelve more. He says we're creating 'a retail environment for art'."

"And making more money. Dare I ask how much you're up to so far?"

"Well, there were twelve paintings. After Geoffrey's 50 percent, that makes $7,200." She grimaced with guilty glee.

"Ing!" I cried. "You're rich as well as famous. You could quit your job and paint full-time."

"I signed a contract with Victor for a year, remember? At least now I can finally pay off my student loan. But next time we go out for dinner, it's going to be somewhere a damn sight fancier than the Little Buda."

"Then you'll sell more paintings and you'll make even more money."

"Mitchell, I'm not doing it for the money. Besides, you're going to make a million dollars selling your screenplay."

"I'm making $3,500. And by the way, before we become completely absorbed in your success, I have the new draft here for you to read. I have to give it to Carmen on Thursday, so I'd love it if you could read it by tomorrow."

"*A Time for Revenge*," she said, quoting the cover page. "I'm really looking forward to it, Mitchell. I'll read it tonight when I go to bed."

"If you're not reading the look of love in Geoffrey's eyes."

"That's not going to happen," she said forcefully, which definitely meant she wanted it to.

She started straightening a shelf of hideous, half-priced coffee mugs – lingering remnants of Victor's hopeless taste.

"I think I've made some real improvements to the script," I said, feeling like a boastful parent. "It's more commercial now. Lots of dramatic action. Snappy dialogue. But I really want your honest opinion. I'd rather hear any criticisms from you than from Carmen."

"I know I'm going to love it. I love everything you write."

Just then a customer cleared her throat to get our attention.

"Excuse me, are you Ingrid Iversen?"

"Yes." Ingrid eyed the woman suspiciously.

"I saw that story about you in the paper. I came in to see your paintings. They're lovely."

"Really?" Ing looked shocked.

"Forgive her," I said to the woman, "she's not used to being a superstar."

"I'm sorry. That's so nice of you," Ingrid gushed, recovering. "Would you like a coffee? Let me give you one."

As she was pouring, I whispered in her ear, "You shouldn't be giving things away. You're supposed to capitalize on your fame. Remember your new role models: Dolly Parton and Zsa Zsa Gabor."

After the woman had gone, Ing sat down at a table with me. She shuddered. "That was weird."

"She was nice."

"Just having a complete stranger know who I am. It's creepy."

"No one's going to assassinate you just because your name was in the paper. Anyone else who notices the story is just going to be happy for you."

"I'm being an idiot, aren't I? Geoffrey keeps telling me to relax."

"So be honest, you really don't think anything's going to happen with him?"

"I don't know, Mitchell. He's always really nice to me, but I just don't think he's attracted to me."

"He thinks you're 'lovely' and 'sparkling'."

"Those are words *you'd* use. What if he's really gay after all?"

"Definitely not."

"You're sure?"

"No," I confessed.

"I just can't figure out what he really wants."

Suddenly the light in the shop dimmed. Outside the window a white CITY-TV news van had pulled up.

"I wonder if there's been an accident," Ing said. We went out the door to check the street.

Climbing from the van was a man with a camera, followed closely by a female reporter in a mini-skirt. She wielded a large microphone. They came directly towards us.

"Oh my God, Ing, I think they're going to put you on the news!"

"No, Mitchell. I don't want to be on TV. Geoffrey never told me about this."

And then there was Geoffrey, rushing along the sidewalk from around the corner.

"Ingrid, I've got a wonderful surprise."

My script delivery continued as I walked to Ramir's brownstone. I picked up my own copy of the *Globe* and splurged on a bag of his favourite cashews from the Uptown Nut House. I relished the thought of recounting Ingrid's brilliant performance in her first TV interview. Witty yet down-to-earth. Sweet yet intelligent.

I would oh-so-subtly rub in her success

I pressed the buzzer over Ramir's mailbox.

The lobby of Ramir's building is one of those tiny 1920s cubicles with elaborate woodwork that's been scratched up and revarnished annually. It always smells slightly of urine – or is that just a very sulfuric brand of cleaning fluid? I always wonder.

I waited thirty seconds, then buzzed again. Ramir had said he was going to be locked away, writing all day.

I should have known to call before coming over.

I buzzed again. And again.

Finally another tenant opened the door on his way out, and I pretended to be fumbling for my keys, so the guy let me in because I look so honest and sincere.

I figured I could slide the envelope under Ramir's door, or if it was too thick, just leave it on the floor. (Even though *that* idea started me on paranoid fantasies of some neighbour stealing the script and producing the movie without giving me credit.)

I climbed the four storeys, getting out of breath and re-membering the day I'd helped Ramir move in, struggling with his floppy lead-weight futon on a frigid February night.

I was just bending down to squeeze the envelope under Ramir's door when I heard voices inside. Ramir and Fred. They were talking loudly, but all their words weren't distinct.

"– immature selfish jerk – taking advantage –"

"– that's not –"

"– you're just too – you don't know anything about –"

"– I really –"

Suddenly the door swung open and there was Montgomery Clift towering above me.

"I – I was just dropping off my script," I said.

He gazed down as if I were a piece of shit on the sidewalk and stormed past me towards the stairwell.

I straightened up and looked inside the apartment. Ramir was sitting hunched on his futon. He was wearing only boxer shorts.

The air smelled faintly of marijuana.

"I brought you my script," I said.

"Oh right," he said lifelessly.

He didn't seem inclined to take the envelope – or the cashews – from my hand, so I set them on the dresser by the door.

"Are you okay?" I asked inanely.

He grunted a laugh.

I crouched down beside him and put my hand on his bare shoulder. "Is there anything I can do?"

"Not right now." He had dark circles under his eyes. His cheeks were damp, as if he'd been crying. "I just have to think some things over," he said. "You know, I actually thought this one could have worked."

"I'm sorry, Ramir."

"And I fucked it up."

"Do you want to talk about it?"

"I'll call you later."

"I can stay if you want."

"Not right now."

"Phone me tonight, okay? Promise?"

I backed out, shutting the door, feeling awkward and stupid for barging in on him in the middle of a fight. Stupid as well because Ramir was acting as if he really loved Fred.

How could he ever care about a guy who was so arrogant? And didn't he think it a strange coincidence that we were both always setting ourselves up with inappropriate men?

Down on the street, Fred was nowhere to be seen. He'd probably zipped away in a brand-new Ferrari.

I debated going back, but I decided it'd be better to let him settle things in his own mind first.

It made me feel sick to think how upset Ramir looked.

Maybe I should have insisted on staying to help, comforting him in his hour of need. Maybe in such a vulnerable state he'd suddenly see me in a new light and realize that we're destined to be lovers until the end of time.

It was just as well that I left.

☆

Walking home, I thought more about Ramir and my hopeless crush. Selfishly, I also realized that, after an episode like that, he wouldn't be in the most positive frame of mind to read my script.

I stewed about it all the way home.

Then, just as I was approaching my apartment, I saw Antonio Banderas. Or Carmen's ex-boyfriend, or whoever he is. His car was parked in front of Juice for Life. He was leaning on the hood, reading a newspaper.

Carmen had said she'd told him to back off. But there he was. Still as gorgeous as I remembered.

I pulled out my keys and walked quickly, hoping to get to my door before he looked up.

Carmen had warned me not to talk to him.

It was chilling, seeing him there. Was he spying on me?

Just as I was turning the lock, I checked over my shoulder. He was staring at me. Intense. Intimidating. Holding me in place.

Then I broke free of his grip and slammed the door behind me.

When I got upstairs and looked out the window, his car was gone.

I called Carmen to tell her that Antonio was back, but of course, I just got her pager. Maybe someday she'll actually call me back.

TUESDAY, JUNE 17

Waiting for people to read your work is like waiting for a firing squad.

Ingrid didn't have time to look at my script last night. After work she'd gone to Geoffrey's house to watch her début on the news. They'd edited her fifteen-minute interview down to one pithy sound bite: "I think this is a great way for new artists to get started." Not very profound. But she looked great and they showed three of her paintings.

Afterward she and Geoffrey installed the new canvases. She got home at two. And not even a glimmer of romance.

Anyway, she promised she'd definitely read my script by tomorrow.

Ramir didn't call me last night, even though he'd promised he would. And he isn't answering his phone today.

At least Ben and I are going out tonight. That should keep my mind occupied. But I have to wait four more hours until he comes over.

TV, as always, is the answer.

"So I've developed this theory," I said, idly tapping the triceps of Ben's left arm.

"Uh-huh," he said.

"I've had hours to think about this, while I've been bored out of my skull sitting in an office cubicle."

"Okay. So what's your theory?"

We were having one of those ridiculous after-sex conversations. (I think everyone else has them.)

It was eleven in the morning and Ben was lying naked on his stomach beside me in bed. Usually as soon as I wake up, I feel compelled to start accomplishing something. So it was a nice change to have some company as an excuse to be lazy.

It was also nice to gaze down at Ben's smooth bare backside. He really has an incredible body. All that pedalling.

"My theory is that bicycle couriers wear those tight Spandex shorts just to torment all the sexually repressed office workers they deal with all day."

"Is that really what you think?"

"Yeah. Is it true?"

"If you're asking me if I rub myself in the elevator to get a hard-on just to turn on the receptionist – no, I've never done that."

"But will you admit that a lot of a bicycle courier's wardrobe is meant to intimidate conservative office temps like myself?"

"First of all, you've never seen me in my working clothes – though I can tell you're dying to. Second, bicycle shorts are designed for riding bicycles. And third, if somebody's going to be scared off by the way I look, then there's no point in letting them get to know the rest of me, is there?"

"So you admit it! It *is* a strategy to intimidate people."

"You really think everything a person does is meant to make other people think about them a certain way?"

"Yes, and by saying you use your wardrobe as a screening method, you just admitted that you do the exact same thing."

"I didn't admit that at all."

Ben scratched his nose and reached across me to get a Kleenex. I grabbed his head and started raking through his hair. "What are you doing!" He laughingly tried to wrestle himself away. Buried amidst the brushcut, I could see the curved black outline of a snake.

"I just wondered if it was the kind you can wash off in the shower."

"If you'd heard me yelling in the tattoo parlour, you'd know it was real."

"So why would you put a snake on your head if you weren't trying to make people think you're some kind of tough rebel bike-courier dude."

"I put it on my head so I'd have the option of showing it when I want to."

"Except when you're fifty and you go bald legitimately."

"Who knows if I'll even live to fifty? Anyway, I was going through a fucked-up, rebellious period. I thought the snake was cool."

He went on about the other designs he'd considered and how you have to put extra sunscreen on a tattoo when you're at the beach. I wasn't paying attention. When he'd said that thing about not living to fifty, part of my mind had just stalled.

"Ben, can I ask you a personal question?"

"Best kind."

"I'm serious."

"I'm ready."

"Just what you said about not living to fifty . . . ."

"Yeah?"

"Have you ever been tested?"

"I was kidding – I hope. And yes, I get tested every six months. And so far, so good. What about you?"

"Negative," I said, obfuscating.

"So we might make it to Christmas." He kissed me hard on

the mouth, and then abruptly pulled himself away. "We'd better get moving. I have to start my shift at noon." He retrieved his underwear from the floor.

I sat there in bed a moment longer, feeling morally reprehensible.

But everything we'd done was safe.

"I have to work till eight tonight," he said, squeezing into his jeans. "So what are you up to today?"

"I'm meeting Ingrid for lunch."

"Oh right, so you can talk about your script."

"Maybe she'll give me some suggestions – help me make it better."

"You should let me read it."

"Definitely not."

"Why?"

"For one thing, I've been pledged to secrecy by Carmen. I shouldn't even be showing it to Ingrid."

"Now I want to read it even more."

"And also because this was only our second night together and if you hated it, I think that might make me feel rather awkward in the future."

"So show me one of the kids' shows you wrote."

"They're too stupid, trust me. But actually, you know, I do have something you might be interested in."

I went to the book shelf and pulled out my file folder of porn magazines. I opened a copy of *Blueboy* to page 23 and set it in front of him.

"'A Humpy Flight'," he read.

"They changed my title. I called it 'Special Passenger Service.' I think that was more tasteful."

"You wrote this?"

"Look at the byline."

"Chad Stiffman."

"You see, my name really is Chad."

He burst out laughing.

"You didn't think somebody so nervous and uptight could be a published pornographer, did you?"

"I'm impressed. What a turn-on. Millions of men jerking off to your words."

"I'd never thought about it quite like that."

"So how do you come up with them? Are they all based on real life?"

"Not *my* life."

"So you just have a fantasy and you sit down at the computer?"

"Once you get the hang of it, there's sort of a formula. You set up the situation, describe the characters, throw in some foreplay with a few double-entendres. Then you cover a good range of sexual acts. I always try to make sure every story has enough action for two Kleenexes."

"That's considerate."

"I like to think I'm giving good value to my readers. Some people express themselves on paper. I express myself on Kleenex."

Ben was leafing through another magazine, looking for another Chad Stiffman story. "Can I borrow these?"

"You actually want to read them?"

"You bet."

"Those are my only copies. But I can print them off my computer."

I went to my desk and turned on the monitor and printer.

"Did I tell you I used to work in computers?" he said. "I still do a couple of times a month, when I need extra money. Going to people's offices, debugging the software. I used to work for this company full-time. Suit and tie and everything."

"You wore a suit and tie? This was pre-tattoo?"

"It caused the tattoo."

"You got fed up?"

He nodded. "I figure if you're going to spend that much time at something you'd better love it. And I didn't love it. Life's too short, right?"

"Do you love being a bicycle courier?"

"I like riding my bike."

"So don't you ever want to do anything else?"

"I don't think about it."

"Not ever?"

"I'm taking a course in environmental studies at U of T. I love that. So do you love writing?"

"I've put my whole life on hold because of it. All I've been working towards is becoming a screenwriter."

"But do you love it?"

"I guess so, or I wouldn't keep doing it."

Ben glanced at the clock. "Shit, I'm going to be late for work." He went into the bathroom and I went back to my computer, deciding which porn stories to print for him.

I wondered some more about whether or not I love writing. It drives me crazy most of the time. But I'm certainly committed to doing it well.

I couldn't help thinking it was strange that Ben had no discernible ambition. Not that it should matter.

Last night, for our first official date, we'd met for dinner at Il Fornello, the little Italian restaurant down the block. All through our custom-designed pizzas we chatted away. No yawning pauses like I've had with most of my previous paramours. And there was so much sexual tension we didn't even bother with coffee before coming back to my apartment.

Suddenly I heard Ben gagging and spitting in the bathroom. Choking? I rushed to the door. He was bent over the sink letting the water run directly into his mouth.

"What happened?" I could smell something mediciny.

He grabbed a tube of Aquafresh and squeezed toothpaste directly into his mouth. "Nothing," he gurgled. He used his finger to scrub.

I started to laugh, "What did you do?"

"Nothing. It's okay. Just leave me alone a second." He was genuinely embarrassed, which provoked me all the more.

"What did you do? Drink the Drano?"

He shook his head, laughing.

"You have to tell me."

"No!" He tried to close the door and push me out.

I pinched his bum.

"I thought it was mouthwash," he said. He pointed to a plastic bottle filled with green Noxzema skin cleanser.

I couldn't stop laughing. He punched me in the arm to make me stop. "Now lend me your toothbrush," he said.

As he tied his shoes, I couldn't control the smile on my face. Ben had done something idiotic. Something *I* would normally do.

He pulled his bicycle out of the kitchen and carried it to the door. "So when do I get to see you again?" he asked. It was strange to have somebody ask *me* that.

"Do you want to come to Ramir's show Saturday night?"

"It'd be fun to meet him. You talk about him so much."

"Maybe you can invite me back to your loft afterwards."

"I don't know. I'm not sure if you're ready yet for The Vault."

"It's an S&M dungeon, right?"

"Could be."

"I like to save physical torture for my fifth date." I handed him a large envelope filled with my pseudonymous fiction. "You might notice that one of them is set in an office mailroom with a bicycle courier named Ben. That one's not finished yet."

"You wrote a story about me?"

"Are you flattered?"

"I don't know. I haven't read it yet."

He started to pull the pages out of the envelope.

"Don't look at it now. I'll blush."

"I think you've lost your right to blush about anything, Chad Stiffman. Next time we'll act it out."

We stood facing each other. It felt like there was something looming between us, some inclination to say "I really like you" maybe. But neither of us made any reference to it.

He kissed me good-bye. I puckered. I said, "Have you been drinking beauty products again?"

He slapped me lightly across the cheek.

From my window, I watched him push off on his bicycle and sail down the street. He looked over his shoulder and waved the envelope up at me.

He really is cute. And funny. And sensible.

Even if he doesn't have much career focus.

After he'd ridden out of sight, I kept staring down at Bloor Street. I wondered if I could actually sustain a lasting relationship.

Then my eyes refocused and I noticed that all the lampposts on the street were coated with a fresh series of Ramir's pink poster for *Eruption*. Even from three storeys up I could see there was now a big black bar across the bottom.

New posters?

I pulled on shorts and a T-shirt and rushed downstairs to the street.

There was the maniacally screaming Human Bean that Ing had drawn, accompanied by new bold type that announced: NOW AT THE DAILY GRIND!

The show was going to be at the store?

Why hadn't Ramir told me? Why hadn't Ingrid?

And obviously Ramir had been there right in front of my door without bothering to buzz me. Maybe he thought this was an acceptable alternative to returning my phone calls. Or maybe he didn't want to talk to me. Maybe he still felt uncomfortable because I'd seen what had happened with Fred.

I tore down the poster and ran back upstairs to call the Good Karma. One of the serious granola heads answered. "No, Ray's not here," he said, sounding totally spaced-out. "He's taken the rest of the week off to work on his show."

Now Ramir's taking vacations and not informing me. With no salary, how's he going to pay his rent? And how's he ever going to pay me back the hundred dollars he's owed me for six months?

I called his home number and got his answering machine. I hung up.

I stared at the ripped pink poster lying on the kitchen table. Resentment burst and I stretched my mouth into a big mocking scream. Part of me wanted to scrunch up the paper and throw it in the garbage, but instead I stuck it on the fridge – holding it in place with a magnet that's an exact replica of Barbra Streisand's nose.

☆

I headed to Toronto's newest art gallery/performance venue, following Ramir's posters as though they were pieces of bread strewn by Hansel and Gretel. Or popcorn dropped by Bobby and Cindy in the Hawaiian double-episode of *The Brady Bunch*.

He must have been out all night. Or perhaps he had reacquired the experienced poster-hanging assistance of Fred.

My annoyance almost made me forget the real reason I was going to Ingrid's. I was hit with a moment of fear, wondering if she'd liked my script. But I soothed myself with the fact that she's liked everything else I've written. Why wouldn't she like this?

When I got to The Daily Grind I nearly bumped into a man exiting with a cardboard tray of four coffee cups. The place was packed again. At this rate, I'll have to phone for reservations if I ever want to sit in my favourite spot.

Even Frances Farmer looked encroached upon. In her brown Pucci pantsuit, she was hunched on her stool by the window – possessively reserving her section of the counter with a huge Harrod's shopping bag.

People were bustling about the shop, staring at the new collection of twelve paintings that overwhelmed the left wall.

Ingrid was serving the line-up of customers, so I just joined the queue. She raised her eyebrows pitifully to apologize as I waited. She looked exhausted.

When it was my turn, I said, "I'd like a mocha latte and two tickets to *Eruption*, please."

"Don't even joke about it," she said. "Kinita, I'll be back in twenty minutes."

Kinita sneered at me resentfully – "Have a nice lunch" – as Ingrid grabbed her bag from the back room.

"Let's go to the Little Buda," she said.

I could see my envelope sticking out the top of Ing's red canvas sack and it put me on edge. Her first words hadn't been that she'd adored the script. Of course she hadn't really had a chance to say anything yet. But she knew what it was like to be an insecure artist. Or maybe she'd already forgotten that desperate condition.

"So Ramir told you about the show?" she said as we walked, retracing the trail of posters.

"I was informed by the lamppost under my window."

"He called me last night to ask if he could do it at the store."

"Why would he change the location when it opens on Saturday?"

"He couldn't get the money together to pay for the theatre. He kept stalling them, but his time ran out."

"He had $1,500. He never could stick to a budget."

"All the audio-visual equipment and the posters were more expensive than he expected."

"So you're letting him take over your store for a week?"

"He needed help."

"What else is new?"

"You're being too hard on him, Mitchell. If I didn't let him, he'd have had to cancel the whole thing."

We arrived at the Little Buda. Ing seemed to drag her feet as we headed to our customary booth at the back. Magda the Waitress followed us and we ordered two raspberry sodas.

This was clearly Ing's moment to let loose a deluge of compliments.

Ing rubbed her forehead. "Of course, once Kinita heard about Ramir's show, she asked if her band could perform at the store the week after."

"What did you say?"

"I said I'd think about it. She really has helped me a lot."

"She's not *helping* you. She's *working* for you."

"I'm just so tired already. And Geoffrey keeps pushing me. Talking about a long-term marketing program. It's like having Victor on my back all over again. I just want some time to myself so I can paint."

"So is all this a subtle way of saying you didn't have time to read my script?"

"No, I read it," she said inscrutably.

"And?"

"It was good."

"You hated it."

"I didn't hate it."

"What, then?"

"Honestly, Mitchell, I couldn't get to sleep last night after I read it and it's been driving me crazy all day wondering what to say to you. You told me you wanted my honest opinion. And the truth is, it just didn't work for me."

"No, no, I'm glad you're being honest," I said, trying to put on a brave face. Then my face crumbled. "This job is a total nightmare."

"I didn't want to hurt your feelings."

"No, if that's what you really think, I need to know. So do you have any 'constructive criticisms'?"

"Well, I kept reminding myself that you said you wrote it to be commercial. And you know I love a good trashy novel as much as you do, but some of the scenes just seemed sort of – artificial."

"It's not supposed to be realistic. I wanted it to be like an old-fashioned movie. Larger-than-life. A melodrama."

"Maybe that's it. But some parts are just *too* melodramatic."

"So you have any specific examples in mind?" I queried delicately. Even though I wanted to stop the conversation right then.

"That scene where Pandora finds the guy going through the files." Ingrid flipped through the pages to find it. "It felt over-the-top – and like I've already seen it before in a bunch of other movies. Here it is."

INTERIOR. TORNAMETTI CONSTRUCTION OFFICES. NIGHT.

It's ten p.m. and PANDORA switches off the light in her grand corner office, then confidently strides through the darkened corridors towards the exit. As she turns the corner into the unlit file storage room, she sees a MYSTERIOUS FIGURE with a flashlight looking through a drawer.

Her eyes widen with curiosity and amusement at the burglar's audacity. PANDORA calmly flicks on the light switch. RICARDO looks up from his searching.

PANDORA
What exactly are you looking for?

RICARDO
Pandora, I was just on my way to your office.

PANDORA
You said goodnight to me four hours ago.

RICARDO
I came back after dinner. I just needed some more information on Victor Felcher.

PANDORA
I gave you his file this morning. And do I need to point out that you're looking in the wrong drawer? What are you really searching for, Ricardo?

RICARDO
We need to talk.

PANDORA
No, *you* need to talk.

RICARDO puts his arm around her shoulders. PANDORA stiffens and knocks his arm away. He follows her into the open office area.

RICARDO
I didn't want to tell you this, Pandora. But I don't like keeping secrets from the woman I love.

PANDORA
And I don't like it when my men keep secrets.

CUT TO:

INTERIOR. LITTLE BUDAPEST RESTAURANT. DAY.

"They're both so smug. And they both talk in clichés, like on a soap opera. It's like they're trying to outdo each other. It's hard to believe they could really be in love."

"Well, at this point in the story they're just finding out things about each other that they weren't expecting."

"I know. I just think Pandora should be more likable."

"I tried to make her like a confident, bitchy heroine from Jacqueline Susann."

"Even in Jacqueline Susann and Jackie Collins the women have a vulnerable side."

"So you're saying it's shit."

"No, I'm not saying that. I can see it's well-written. But for my taste there's not enough sincerity. There's just not enough *you* in it."

"Carmen said there was *too much* of me in it and that's why she hated it."

"You didn't tell me she hated it." Ing looked genuinely shocked.

"She said my last draft was too wimpy and wishy-washy."

"Then she'll probably love this, Mitchell. She's the one who's paying you, so you should give her what she wants. But I'm just saying that – well, even *Hell Hole* had a nice sense of humour. Sort of a warped perspective. I could tell it was from *you*."

"You think I've sold out."

"Mitchell, you're putting words in my mouth."

"This script isn't *my* idea of good. It's *her* idea of good."

"Right. So my comments are completely out of line. I'm just saying that I like your work better when you follow your own voice."

"My own voice. Sometimes I think I have twelve of them talking at the same time." I drank some raspberry soda, hoping that swallowing would settle me down. "I don't know what I'm going to do."

"I don't think you should rewrite it or anything. Just show it to Carmen – maybe this is exactly what she wants. Who am I to judge?"

"But if my friends don't like it . . . ."

"I'm sorry, Mitchell. Do you hate me?"

"No, of course not."

"I'd understand if you did. I'm sorry. Listen, I really have to get back to the store. But I couldn't lie to you."

She reached for her wallet.

"No, it's on me." After all, she had done me a favour.

She left and I sat there by myself.

☆

I couldn't handle going up to my apartment for more solitude. So I went for a walk.

I knew what Ingrid had said was true. The script isn't some great personal work of art. But Ing's not the intended audience anyway. And how many people am I trying to please? I could be rewriting this thing until I'm ready for retirement.

Still, how could I proudly hand it over to Carmen if I knew my friends thought it wasn't any good?

I walked up Howland Avenue, gazing at the old red brick houses with their big front porches and giant trees – wondering if I'd ever be able to afford to live in one. Never, if my life stays on its current path. All the luxury I'll ever experience will have to be borrowed from hotel lobbies and cocktail lounges.

I had just crossed over a block and was heading down Brunswick Avenue when I noticed two women walking towards me – one had a strangely familiar face. Relaxed smile. Short, frosted blonde hair.

Anne Murray.

After all my pretending with Spot the Celebrity, it was jarring to be confronted with the real thing. Her hair was perfectly highlighted, perfectly styled. She was wearing tan linen pants and a simple white shirt. Crisp cotton, the collar turned up. Even her linen looked professionally creased.

Her friend was equally well-dressed, well-groomed. Rich people really do look different.

They were absorbed in conversation as they passed me.

As if hypnotized, I turned to follow them.

Here was one of the most famous people Canada has ever produced. "You Needed Me" is my mother's favourite song. A guy I'd gone on a blind date with last year had a complete collection of her albums.

And she was right there in front of me.

It really shouldn't have been such a surprise to see her – I've always heard she lives somewhere outside Toronto.

But here she was. Fame incarnate. An international star. Larger than life. And I'm taller than she is. I walked close enough behind her to hear her low throaty drawl. From this body, from this very head, emanated a sound that people around the world would recognize.

And despite this, she was walking on the same sidewalk as me. She and her friend stopped by a dark green Jeep and opened the doors.

When I passed, she glanced at me – looked into my eyes with the expression you give a stranger. A bit of questioning, a bit of reserve, but mostly blank. It was unsettling, even sort of frightening, to have someone I know so intimately look back at me completely without recognition.

I wanted to ask, "Doesn't your life feel different? Don't you know that wherever you go, whenever people see you, they know it's a special moment? Doesn't that make your life feel more potent, more real?"

I kept walking down the sidewalk and a moment later, they drove past me.

I decided to give Carmen the script the way it was.

When I got back to my apartment, there were three hang-ups on my answering machine. I wondered if the calls had been from Carmen. She'd said she'd phone me on Thursday to set up our next meeting. Or maybe it was Ramir.

I dialled *69 but the recorded voice said the last number that called my line was unavailable.

I tried Ramir, but there was no answer.

Then I sat down here and typed out my day.

The phone rang as I was washing dishes. I wiped my hands on my jeans and half-heartedly turned on my professionalism. "Hello, Mitchell Draper speaking." The person hung up. The same caller as before?

Then the phone rang again. I picked it up immediately and just said, "Hello."

A rough male voice said, "So I hear you're writing a screen-play."

I admit that at first I had a moment of hope. Maybe somebody else wanted to hire me. Then I sensed something was not quite right. I said nothing.

"I thought it'd be fair to fill you in on Carmen."

"Who is this?"

"If I were you, Mitchell Draper, living at 446 Bloor Street West, I wouldn't waste my time."

"Are you the guy who was standing across the street?"

"I might be standing there right now."

I looked out the window but I couldn't see his car.

"Carmen told me not to talk to you."

"Of course she'd tell you that. But I'm doing you a personal favour."

"I don't know what you're talking about."

"The movie's never going to get made, Mitchell Draper. Carmen's a spoiled little prima donna. The movie's just a stupid dream. If you're smart you'll drop the whole thing and never mention it to anybody ever again."

He hung up. And I sank onto the couch.

"*The movie's never going to get made.*"

Exactly what I'd feared all along. What if it were true? What if Carmen really was a total fraud? What if I'd been deluding myself every step of the way?

I called Carmen's pager. Which, of course, was pointless.

I called Ingrid, then Ramir, then Ben. Not one of them was home to help calm me down.

"*If you're smart, you'll drop the whole thing.*"

All that time and sweat. What if it really was all for nothing? I'd be thrown back into my former hopeless state, perpetually waiting for my Big Break.

All along Carmen had acted as if she were doing me a favour. What if she was just using me for her own egomaniacal Hollywood fantasy?

I was angry at her for getting me involved in this, for subjecting me to threats from a total stranger. Angry at myself for ever hoping, for ever believing.

"*Never mention it to anybody ever again.*"

The whole situation was such a movie cliché, I shouldn't even take it seriously. But at the same time I genuinely felt scared.

Maybe I was overreacting. Maybe the phone call was really just more jealousy from a bitter ex-boyfriend.

But I couldn't simply sit here in my apartment waiting for him to call again. So I went to the Bloor Cinema for both the seven and nine o'clock movies. Both of them were Japanese art films. I couldn't concentrate enough to keep up with the subtitles.

I wondered if Antonio would really come to my apartment and kill me just to shut me up. What was so important about Carmen's movie?

When I got home at eleven-thirty I approached my answering machine with trepidation. But there were no messages – neither from friend nor foe.

Maybe it was ridiculous, but the only way I could feel safe was to push the bookcase in front of my apartment door. This process involved unplugging the TV cables and taking down most of my books. Then, once the bookshelf was in place, I wondered how I'd get out in case of fire.

I turned off the ringer on my telephone, took two muscle relaxants with a mouthful of tequila, and fell into a leaden sleep.

Merciful oblivion.

The next thing to hit my consciousness was buzzing. Sharp jabs, then long hard whines. In my drugged state, I couldn't tell what it was. I looked at the clock. Eleven. Light in the window. Eleven in the morning.

More buzzing. Suddenly I realized it was the buzzer from the door downstairs. The man on the phone had come to kill me.

I leapt out of bed and shoved up the window. There was Ramir down on the sidewalk, looking up at me with hopeful, desperate charm.

"I knew you were home," he called up.

"I was asleep."

"I need your help."

"I'm still asleep."

"It's an emergency. Please. I brought breakfast." He raised a brown paper bag as bait.

I knew nothing could make him go away when he wanted something. "Just give me a minute."

I pulled on my shorts and T-shirt. There was still a heavy lump of deadness in the centre of my brain. I splashed cold water on my face. At least I'd finally be able to discuss the phone call with somebody. Enjoy the solace of human company.

I pressed the buzzer to let him in. Then I hurriedly, awkwardly, shoved the bookshelf back into its regular spot so I could open the door.

"I bought cheese danishes at the Harbord Bakery." Ramir hugged me as he handed me the bag. "Sorry to wake you up, but

I'm in a serious panic situation. There's one section of the show that I need you to help me write."

Suddenly my annoyance with Ramir returned.

"Of course."

"I can't get any of the radio dramas from the CBC, so I have to write something new. It's a background audio track. I need a really mushy love scene."

"So naturally you thought of me."

No questions about why I looked like shit. About why I was still sleeping at this hour of the morning.

"I'm going into the studio at three to edit the videotape. We're going to do the voice recording at the same time. That's why I need some dialogue right away. I've got an actress coming in to play the other part."

"Have you written *any* of it yet?"

"I'm totally stuck on this section. But the rest of the script is coming along really well. I thought maybe you could look at it to give me your opinion."

"Why don't you ask for Fred's opinion?"

He stared at me, apparently mystified. "You saw what happened."

"You haven't talked to me since," I said. "You haven't returned my calls in three days. You moved your show to Ingrid's store and you didn't even let me know."

"I put that poster in front of your door. I wanted to surprise you."

"We're supposed to be friends, Ramir. You should have told me in person."

"I thought you'd think it was funny. Anyway, Ing's been great. Things are back on track. My agent pulled in a big favour and there's going to be a story in *The Star* on Saturday. I've been so busy running all over the place, getting things together."

Running, running, running.

Listening to him, tiredness settled over me again.

"I bet you haven't even looked at my script," I said. "Not that it matters."

"I totally forgot. I haven't had time –"

"Whenever *you* want something, you find time." His eyes widened at my bluntness. "You know something else? Ingrid is actually pissed off that you asked to have the show at her place. She only agreed because you wouldn't let her say no."

"I don't manipulate everybody. I didn't have any alternative. I *had* to ask her."

"So necessity makes it okay."

"I didn't have any money for the theatre."

"You had *fifteen hundred dollars*, Ramir."

He smiled tightly, but he didn't say anything.

"What happened to it? You had the money when you booked the place."

"I broke up with Fred, remember?"

I was speechless.

Ramir turned his face to the window.

"You told me you got the money from your parents."

"*You* said that. Fred offered to loan it to me. It was his idea. Then it turns out he's just a part-time bank teller. I had to ask Ing to use the store. I was desperate."

"So Fred was just a big fake."

"He said he could afford it. He said he thought the show was a good investment."

"A good investment if he wanted you to keep fucking him."

Ramir gaped at me.

"So if *I* had the money, would you fuck me, too?"

"What's going on with you, Mitch?"

"Finally, you start to pay attention to me!"

"Is everything okay?"

"You didn't come here to hear my problems, so don't pretend you care. I just don't feel like being *nice* and *helpful* anymore. I never get anything out of it anyway."

"Did something happen to your script?"

"*Now* you think to ask. Yes Ramir, other people actually have important things happening in their lives. Not that you ever notice. You haven't noticed while I've been pining pathetically over you for the past two years."

"What are you talking about? Are you kidding?"

"Maybe you should just run off to some pick-up bar and find a fresh shoulder to cry on – somebody else who can help you."

"I don't believe this." He looked at me with shock, as though I'd betrayed him. "This is exactly what I need when my show is opening in two days. Thank you, Mitch. Thanks a lot." He stormed down the stairs.

"Don't worry," I yelled after him. "Everything always works out fine for you. The show must go on!"

I was shaking. I'd never talked to anybody that way in my whole life.

I had to speak to Ingrid. Tell her my side of what had happened with Ramir. Tell her about the threatening phone call and Carmen's insults and lying to Ben about my stupid HIV test. I had to get everything off my chest.

The Daily Grind was full again. Kinita was alone behind the counter, serving the clot of customers. Before I could even ask, she pointed to the back room. "Ing's busy reading the paper."

Ingrid sat at her desk, elbows on the newspaper spread out before her. Her hair was loosely pulled up, but several curly tendrils had escaped. She was staring down at the paper. She looked fragile.

A giant café-au-lait bowl filled with hot chocolate sat on the desk beside her.

"You always say hot chocolate's too fattening," I said, hoping to sound lighthearted.

"I needed something comforting."

"What happened?"

She gestured to the paper. "My first bad review."

"That's impossible." I twisted my head to see the column. She covered it with her hand.

"He calls my work 'derivative'."

"Your paintings aren't derivative. That's not true."

"That's what everyone's going to read. That's what everyone's going to think."

"He's wrong. Nobody takes that guy seriously, Ingrid. He

doesn't like anything."

"I mean, every piece of art is derivative when you get right down to it," she said. "Everything in the nineties is just referring to something from the past. *Fin-de-siècle* and everything. But I've never intentionally copied anything."

"This is exactly why Stephen Sondheim says you should never read your reviews. You can't listen to that stuff. It takes your focus off your work."

"He says Geoffrey has a history of finding unknown artists, declaring they're talented, and then all his dumb clients automatically start buying. 'An exercise in star-making, Warhol-style.'"

"You're just beating yourself up, Ingrid." I pulled the paper from her and crumpled it into a giant ball. "Let's symbolically throw this in the garbage."

"He said the colours are muddy and my ideas are childish. He says everybody's already seen it. That my work is already passé."

"What does it matter what he thinks? You paint for yourself. You've always said that. And no matter what that guy wrote, you still sold them all."

"That's what Geoffrey says. 'If you've got the money, you're the one who's the winner.' But maybe people bought them because they don't know any better. They're just lemmings and they didn't really like them at all."

Just then Kinita stepped into the room. "Ingrid, some woman from a university radio station is on the phone. She wants to set up an interview."

"Tell her I'm not here," Ingrid snapped, and Kinita departed with a peeved click of her tongue.

"I'm really sorry, Ing."

"This is exactly what I was afraid of. Public humiliation."

"No one'll remember it by tomorrow. Even *you* won't."

"I'm just so tired."

I didn't know what to say.

"Ramir was here till midnight last night," she said. "He was figuring out how to set up the seating. He wanted me to paint him a special backdrop, but I said no."

"Did he talk to you yet today?"

"I don't want to get between the two of you," she said, firmly and cryptically. Then her hand fell on an envelope buried in the paper on her desk. "Damn, I promised I'd take his press release to *The Globe and Mail.*" She was suddenly on the verge of tears.

"I'll do it," I volunteered, before I realized for whom I was doing the favour. "So do you think his show will be any good?"

"Who am I to criticize?" she said, and I immediately regretted my question. "I don't really care at this point. But Geoffrey thinks Ramir's show is a great idea. It'll bring in more people to see the paintings. The thing is, Mitchell, there's one thing that's right in that review. Geoffrey's just in it for the business. He doesn't care about what's good for me – or anything about me."

Kinita interrupted again. "Brenda from my band just called. She wants to know if we can rehearse here the night before our show."

"I don't have enough energy to think about that right now."

"We need to know."

"Why don't you ask me after Ramir's finished his?"

Kinita huffed. "Brenda's going to love it when I tell her that," she said, and exited.

"Kinita's been nagging me all the time. I feel like I'm giving my whole life away. At least when Victor was here I didn't have to do everything myself."

"Ingrid, we need to talk." There was Kinita at the door again.

"About what?"

"You mean I have to explain?"

"Yes, I guess you do."

"You do favours for all your so-called friends, while I'm the one who's been working like a slave here, saving your ass. And you won't even give me a simple answer to a simple question."

"Kinita, you're fired."

"Pardon me?"

Even I was startled.

"I don't want to say it again."

"You can't fire me. Only Victor can fire me."

"Victor put me in charge. And you're fired."

"Is that so?" Kinita said, flaring her eyes.

We were all stunned into a momentary stand-off.

"I might as well tell you," Kinita said, high and mighty once again. "Our band's been invited to an experimental jazz festival in Germany. I was going to quit in two weeks anyway. So good luck in the meantime."

She turned with a belligerent shrug and walked out.

"Wow," I marvelled.

"That was really smart," Ingrid said.

"Do you think she was making that up about Germany?"

"I shouldn't have fired her."

"What do you mean? You've wanted to do that ever since she started here."

Ingrid pulled a brown apron over her head and her manner took on an eerie calmness.

"Now it just means I'll have to work twice as hard. I need to get behind the counter, Mitchell." With sunken shoulders, she went out to take her place. "I wish none of this had ever happened."

The Spadina Avenue streetcar was jammed as usual. Hot. Smelling of sweat and overripe vegetables as we picked up passengers at Kensington Market, that ramshackle jumble of open food markets and used-clothing shops. Then potent fish climbed on board as we passed through Chinatown.

I stood clinging to a handrail as we stopped and started with jolts. I held Ramir's envelope delicately, trying to protect it from my sweaty palms. Doing him yet another favour.

Maybe he'd see this as an apology. But how could I ever apologize sincerely when so much of what I'd said was so plainly true?

I got off the streetcar at Front Street and started walking west towards the *Globe and Mail* building. A national institution in the middle of nowhere. A low mass of 1960s white brick. Across the street was an open field, a wasteland beside the expressway. Gutted railway yards waiting to be transformed into a glittering urban neighbourhood.

Just a few days ago I'd imagined being interviewed by this venerable newspaper. Mitchell Draper, famous Canadian screenwriter. Maybe while I was here I could apply for a job in the mailroom. Perhaps I could work my way up.

It all happened in a blur, but my memory has divided the events into sharp freeze-frame images.

I heard a car door slam beside me. I glanced over my shoulder. A black sports car. Antonio. I started to run towards the building's front doors. Antonio grabbed me, twisting my arm up the centre of my back.

"I told you to shut up about this." He wrenched my arm.

"You're hurting –"

"I told you to forget about Carmen's fucking movie." He grabbed the envelope from my free hand.

"It's a press release. I don't – "

"You're not talking to the papers or anybody else. This is the last time I'm warning you. Serious people want this story dead."

He shoved me against the line-up of newspaper boxes on the sidewalk. Then he rushed back to his car.

Dazed, I leaned there on the boxes to catch my breath. Senselessly, all I could think about was how I'd let Ramir down by losing his press release. He'd be mad.

Then my reason was restored.

I headed to the building's entrance to call the police. But what would I tell them? That a press release had been stolen? That I'd been assaulted by Antonio Banderas. I hadn't even gotten a look at his license plate.

I realized that he must have followed me all the way here. Perhaps he'd been following me for days. Tapping my phone. Watching my friends.

As I took a taxi home I kept hearing his voice repeating that ominous statement: *"Serious people want this story dead."*

When I got back to my apartment there was a message on my machine from Carmen.

"Mitchell, you've got to change the script. Cut Aaron Vogel right out. I don't care how you do it, just make sure he's gone.

Change all the characters' names. Use whatever you want. And instead of the real estate business, make it an insurance company. You need to rewrite the treatment and all the scenes you've done so far. You got that? And I have to have it all on Saturday. I'll make it up to you, I promise. You just need to come through. For both our sakes. I'll be at your apartment at three o'clock sharp."

All the pieces suddenly fell into place.

I'd been writing an exposé of a murder.

☆

I took the subway and then the bus to Willowdale. There was no way Antonio could have followed me.

I paid a surprise visit to my parents. For about five minutes, they acted pleased to see me. Then we sank into our old routine.

My father and I sat and watched the news while my mother made a tuna casserole.

None of us said very much.

After dinner, we all went back into the living room and watched TV – exchanging words only to decide what show to watch next.

I spent the night in my old bedroom and vividly remembered my claustrophobic adolescence – feeling like an alien at school, figuring out I was gay, watching TV every night and going to Saturday matinées at Fairview Mall – believing that becoming famous was the only way I'd ever get out of there.

In the morning I took the bus from my parents' house – after waiting half an hour at the desolate bus stop where I'd spent huge chunks of my teenage life.

When I got to Finch subway station I called Ben from a pay phone and asked him to meet me at three inside the front entrance of the Metro Reference Library. He was puzzled by my choice of location, but I promised to explain everything in person.

I couldn't ask Ingrid or Ramir – not after what had happened yesterday. I couldn't help but feel distanced from both of them.

Out of necessity I went back to my apartment, taking back streets, then rushing around the corner to my front door. Once I was inside everything appeared perfectly normal. Peaceful and undisturbed. Probably there'd been no reason to go to my parents'.

From the stack of paper on my desk I retrieved my file of notes for the screenplay. Then I headed to the library, once again avoiding the main thoroughfares. I was certain Antonio couldn't be following me, but still my eyes darted at the sight of every black car.

The library is a massive bland brick building with an atrium stuck in the middle. The place is so vast and busy it's not hard to feel anonymous.

I sat on a bench by the rock pool in the lobby, facing the obligatory art installation: a jungle of dangling cotton strings arranged to resemble moss hanging from trees in the Louisiana bayou.

I kept my back to the main doors.

I sorted through my notes, searching for clues and trying to piece together everything I knew. Antonio and his gang must be pressuring Carmen, or she wouldn't have asked me to make those changes in the script. She wanted me to create misleading evidence.

Maybe she'd been trying to blackmail someone. And now the people she was blackmailing think I'm one of her cohorts.

I felt a tap on my shoulder and I yelped in surprise.

"Did you think I was going to push you into the pool?" Ben asked.

"Actually that's exactly what I thought" I said, trying to regain my composure.

"I haven't gone to the library for a date since high school. What are we going to do? Neck behind the book shelves? Or do you want to find the mailroom so we can act out your story? I really liked it, by the way."

"That's good," I smiled weakly. "But right now I sort of need your help. You know the script I've been working on?"

"The one you wouldn't let me read?"

"Well, things have gotten sort of complicated."

He sat down and I told him the whole crazy tale. About Carmen's unconventional hiring methods. About the man I'd thought was cruising me who was actually following her. Then about the phone call, yesterday's attack and Carmen's instructions on my answering machine. The fact that I had no way to contact her. I even had no idea if Carmen Denver was her real name – or who any of the people mentioned in the screenplay actually were.

"It's ludicrous. I'm writing an exposé of a murder, but I have no idea what I'm exposing."

"It's amazing," Ben said, intrigued and apparently entertained. "So how does Carmen know about this murder?"

"I have no idea. She said from the very beginning that the movie was going to be controversial. I didn't know that meant it was true."

"So obviously the people she's trying to expose know what she's doing."

"And they think I know too. Yesterday that guy must have thought I was giving the story to the paper. But I don't know any-thing. All I've got is a half-finished screenplay."

"And Carmen told you everything to put in it?"

"She gave me the basic facts. I elaborated a lot and tried to turn it into something dramatic. Not that I actually succeeded."

"Can't you just tell her you quit?"

"I'm going to when I meet her tomorrow. But Carmen's been lying to me all along and she'll probably lie to me again. So I figure if I can find out the truth – if there really was a murder – then at least I'll know where I stand. You think I'm crazy, don't you?"

"It does sound pretty wild."

"I swear I'm not making it up. I know I could have come here by myself, but I just felt I should tell somebody else."

"Now they'll have to kill us both," he said absurdly. I didn't know whether to laugh or be offended. But he was still willing to help. "So where do we start?"

"Well, in Carmen's message, she told me she wanted me to change all the characters' names, so I figure that means all the names in the script are real. I've been going through my notes from the day that Carmen told me the story. You see right here, she said she wanted the murder to take place in September 1976 in New York City. So it follows that we should look through *The New York Times* from September 1976."

"Hence the library," he said. "Let's get to work!" He slapped me on the knee.

It bothered me that he was treating the whole thing as if it was a joke. But even I was beginning to see parallels to *The Hardy Boys*.

We passed through the turnstiles and descended the curving, carpeted staircase to the newspaper room.

"My big clue is that Carmen told me to put a library scene in the screenplay – the main character looking through the newspaper archives to research the murder. So maybe she did this exact same thing herself."

The archive room was wide and mauve-carpeted, scattered with pine tables where people of every nationality sat reading newspapers from around the world. Against one wall were banks of hulking filing cabinets holding microfilm of past issues. Along the back was a dimmed area with special viewing desks.

We followed the signs to the last row of filing cabinets, and Ben recited the drawer labels: "*The Times of London. The Washington*

Post. The New York Times – 1851 to 1867."

"The 1970s are over here. Right next to *The Village Voice.* That's another possibility."

Ben opened the drawer marked 1974 to 1976, revealing rows of small red and black cardboard boxes.

"You take September 1 to 17," he said. "I'll do September 18 to 30. And whoever gets through first can start on October."

"A race to find out who's stalking me. How exciting."

We took side-by-side carrels, each with a backlit display screen built into the bottom of the desk.

"When you meet Carmen again," Ben told me, "you should just lay it on the line. Tell her you need to know the whole truth or next time that guy shows up you'll tell him exactly what she's been up to."

"That'd work if he ever gave me the chance to say anything."

We each fumbled with the narrow film strips, wrapping them onto tiny take-up reels. I adjusted the focus and promptly discovered that I'd put in my film upside down.

"According to the screenplay," I said, "Nick Tornametti killed Aaron Vogel because Aaron was going to expose Nick as some kind of money launderer. So watch out for both of their names. Or anything else that's unusual about lawyers or the real estate business."

We worked silently for a few minutes, winding through the reels.

"Are you feeling sick to your stomach?" Watching all the pages fly by was making me nauseous.

And I had no idea it would be so boring. *The New York Times* didn't just include the news on microfilm. It was every single page. Grocery ads. The classifieds.

"This one section of the paper has over 70 pages," Ben said, giving me a twinge of guilt.

"I wonder if such an important paper even covers local murders. Look, here's a story about Rudolph Nureyev. 1976. Nobody'd even thought about AIDS."

"Ancient history."

Page after page.

"So do you think the guy who's following you could actually *be*

Nick Tornametti?"

"He's not old enough. Twenty years ago he would have been in public school."

"Here's a good headline," Ben said, "'Frozen Yogurt is a Hot-Selling Item'."

"The beginning of a major historical movement."

We stared on, becoming hypnotized (and increasingly queasy) as days flew by.

For a while I paused and read an interview with George Lucas, who was in the middle of shooting *Star Wars*.

"Shit, Mitchell, I found something." I leapt from my desk and leaned over Ben's shoulder. Saturday, September 25. A small story tucked at the bottom of a column. I swallowed when I read the headline. Up until now this whole situation really could have been my own hallucination.

Prominent real estate lawyer disappears

A Manhattan real-estate lawyer has been reported missing amid widespread speculation of foul play.

Aaron Vogel, 39, is a partner in Vogel, Flemming & Associates. He has recently been active in a crusade to uncover money-laundering schemes involving several shopping malls in New Jersey and Arizona. His efforts last year brought criminal charges against developers, The Baker-Hammer Group.

Mr. Vogel was last seen leaving his office at One Liberty Plaza on Thursday, September 23.

"Write down the page number. We can copy it on that other machine later. Go forward and see if there's a follow-up."

"Put the reel for the beginning of October in yours."

We both rolled forward.

"Maybe Carmen is related to Aaron Vogel," I wondered aloud.

"She could be his daughter."

"And she wants to expose his killer. The title is *A Time for Revenge*."

It all made sense.

Past pages and pages of ads. Day after day.

"Look Ben, here's another one." Thursday, October 7. In a box titled "Metropolitan Briefs" at the bottom of the page:

No leads in missing lawyer case

Police are continuing their investigation into the disappearance of Manhattan real-estate lawyer Aaron Vogel. Interviews were conducted with some of New York area's most influential real-estate developers.

Police questioned Clarence Munger of Pinnacle Developments, Nicholas Tornametti of DMI and Gino Santangelo of Broad Street Construction. No charges have been laid.

According to Sergeant Carl Borczak of the New York Police Department, "Vogel's car is still missing, and his family remains hopeful that he will be found alive and well." He admitted police have few further leads.

"So Nick Tornametti was a suspect, but he wasn't charged."

"Keep going forward," Ben urged. "Maybe there's another story."

"Obviously Carmen thinks he actually did it. That's the whole reason she's making the movie. It's her own warped way of bringing him to justice."

"It'd be easier to go to the police."

"Maybe she doesn't have any evidence. She just wants to embarrass him. Public revenge."

"He could sue her for slander," Ben said.

"Or kill her."

"So if Nick Tornametti has got somebody following you, he must have friends here in Toronto."

A sick thought dawned on me. "Or maybe he moved here himself."

We went through the rolls of microfilm for October, then part of November, but there was no further mention of the story – not even in the obituaries. The rushing pages made my mind spin faster and faster, imagining the implications.

"You can spend the night with me," Ben suggested, "if that'd make you feel any better."

"We have to go to my place first," I said. "There's something I have to check."

As soon as we stepped in the door, I went to the fridge.

"He's been here," I said.

"How can you tell?" Ben stood behind me as I peered into my freezer, neatly stacked with file folders and packages of frozen food. "Why do you keep paper in the freezer?"

"It's supposed to be fireproof. It's where I keep everything I've written. Carmen's script is still here. But I always put the bag of vegetables on top. See, somebody's moved it to the side."

Ben looked doubtful. "It could have fallen over."

"Not unless somebody shook the whole fridge. Not unless there was an earthquake. I saw Antonio Banderas across the street two days ago when I was coming home. He must have broken into the apartment and read the script. That's how he knows what it's about."

"So if he knows everything already, you're off the hook. There's nothing else you can tell him."

"They've been in my apartment, Ben. They really think I'm trying to expose them."

"How could they break in without you knowing?" Ben's expression was skeptical.

"I can tell you're not taking this seriously," I said. "You've been laughing to yourself ever since I told you."

"I believe you. I just think you may be overreacting."

"These could be genuine Godfather types, Ben. The Mafia – John Gotti, Jimmy Hoffa. Aaron Vogel was killed because he knew Nick Tornametti was involved in some kind of organized crime. Now I'm just like *The Man Who Knew Too Much*."

"If Carmen honestly knew about a murder, she'd go to the police – not make a movie about it."

"Maybe that's what *you'd* do. But you've never met Carmen. God, this is becoming just like one of those hokey thrillers where everybody thinks the hero is going insane."

"If you think something's wrong, you should go to the police yourself."

"What would I tell them? They'd never take me seriously."

"Exactly. So *you* shouldn't take it seriously either. Carmen's going to meet you tomorrow, right? So I'll stay here with you and we'll find out for sure what's going on."

"I don't want to get you involved in this. I can handle it by myself. I'll probably end up as a gangland slaying on the front page of the paper. That'd be just like me – to be famous and miss the whole thing."

"Mitchell, listen to yourself!"

"Okay, I'm rambling. I'm upset."

"Mitchell, I like you. You're bright. You've got a good sense of humour. But I think you're screwing yourself up with all these famous movie star and gangster stories."

"You don't believe me. You think I'm hysterical."

"I think you're blowing things out of proportion. Real life isn't like the movies."

"I know that all too well, thank you. It's one of my life's greatest disappointments."

"Okay, so you've got a problem. You deal with it. You don't make things worse by getting distracted by a bunch of fantasies."

"These aren't fantasies. This is my whole career I'm worried about."

"It's one job for one movie producer."

"Being a writer is what I've wanted my whole life. This is all I care about. I guess you can't understand what that's like because you don't *want* anything."

"I want plenty of things. But *real* things."

"What I want is real," I said – I practically shouted. "I'm glad you're happy being a bicycle courier. But if you don't have any ambition, how can you understand that this is serious?"

Ben regarded me coldly. He spoke softly. "If you don't understand what I want, then you really don't understand me at all."

He looked into my eyes and waited for me to respond. I didn't say anything.

"Listen, Mitchell, I know you're having a hard time. But I

don't like you very much right now. So I'm going to leave."

And he did.

I suppose it was for the best.

Wanting a boyfriend had caused me enough trouble. And I don't need any more complications in my life right now.

I moved the bookshelf back in front of the door, turned off the phone and took another dose of muscle relaxants.

INTERIOR. OFFICE BUILDING ELEVATOR. NIGHT.

Nervous, fast details of a handsome BUSINESSMAN as he rides the elevator down. Highly polished shoes. Leather briefcase. Blue blazer. Silk necktie.

CLOSE UP

The elevator button: P2.

ANGLE ON MAN

Gold-rimmed eyeglasses – his right eye, a striking light blue, tense with thought.

INTERIOR. UNDERGROUND GARAGE. NIGHT.

Almost deserted for the night. Only a few cars remain. Focus on a dark-green Jaguar parked tightly beside a black Cadillac with deeply tinted windows.

ANGLE ON DOOR TO GARAGE

The MAN enters the underground garage walking rapidly.

TIGHT SHOT

His polished shoes ringing sharp footsteps on the cement floor.

HIS POINT OF VIEW

Walking towards the Jag.

TIGHT SHOT

He pulls keys from his pocket. A silver baby rattle dangles from the key chain.

TIGHT SHOT

The front window of the Cadillac. Figures in the dark interior?

MAN

He turns sideways to squeeze between the cars.

A SERIES OF CUTS

. . . as the passenger window of the Cadillac silently, smoothly descends and a LEATHER-GLOVED HAND appears through the window. The hand holds a knife with a long slender blade.

. . . as the MAN steps into the knife's range.

. . . as the knife plunges into his back with a sound like a shovel cutting into sand.

. . . as the MAN's blue eyes grow wide in shock. A deep guttural groan.

EXTERIOR. DOWNTOWN STREETS. NIGHT.

Seen from above, the two cars exit the underground garage. Both turn in the same direction.

Pull up into the city sky, floating high above towering office buildings. Then a few blocks away, swoop down into a construction site – a wide deep pit – descending towards the newly poured foundations.

ANGLE ON CONSTRUCTION FORM

Suddenly a large black bag is dropped into a wooden construction form – a narrow trench, shaped like a coffin.

INTERIOR. WAREHOUSE. NIGHT.

The green Jaguar, now without tires. Pull back to see the car crushed flat between giant metal plates.

EXTERIOR. CONSTRUCTION SITE. DAY.

Jarring morning light. Voices of construction workers. A cement truck. The trough being guided into place. Wet cement begins to pour into the construction form.

TIGHT SHOT ON THE CONSTRUCTION FORM

A tear in the black plastic – a knife slit. We close in tight for a split-second shot of AARON VOGEL's still-open right eye – before cement fills and darkens the scene to black.

CUT TO:

INTERIOR. MITCHELL'S APARTMENT. 4 A.M.

I woke in a cold sweat, my heart pounding. It was like the scene I'd written for the opening of Carmen's script, but the nightmare was filled with different details. I couldn't tell whether I'd been dreaming or seeing the truth.

I tried to focus. Think this through.

Pandora was trying to get her father arrested for Vogel's murder. Suddenly it hit me.

I grabbed the phone book and flipped through the pages.

One Tornametti – with the initials "C.P."

Carmen Pandora.

I copied out her phone number and address.

Even though it was four in the morning, I dialled the number.

A voice-mail answering service picked up on the first ring. Carmen's throaty voice: "This is Denver Productions. I'm in L.A. right now, but I'll be back in town Saturday midday, so leave me a message."

I opened my bottle of tequila and poured myself a glass.

On Monday I'll start a new long-term temp job and maybe, in

a few months, I'll start writing again. A novel. Total fiction.
Quietly, steadily, and maybe I'll be able to accomplish *something*
before I die.

But first I have to deal with Carmen and settle this once and
for all.

I stood at the foot of Carmen's apartment building in Yorkville. Naturally she lived in one of the most expensive condominiums in the city. A tall, terraced tower of grey concrete. Neighbour to both the Park Plaza and the Four Seasons. How convenient for her. All she'd had to do was cross the street to destroy me that day at lunch.

She'd told my answering machine that she'd be at my apartment at three o'clock. I couldn't just sit at home, waiting for her as if I were waiting for an executioner. I planned to take her by surprise by arriving at her door just before two – between her return from the airport and her departure to meet me.

I gazed down the length of Cumberland Street. I reassured myself that by the time I was back on this sidewalk I'd be free again to live my life in peace – to attend Ramir's show tonight and get things settled with him and Ingrid.

As I approached the building's deep-set entrance, the oak door swung open, held by a doorman in classic uniform. The lobby was modern, though decorated to feel traditional and old-world. Polished peach marble walls. Persian carpets. Massive armchairs of intricately carved dark wood.

My scrutiny was interrupted by the white-haired concierge sitting at an antique desk.

"May I help you, sir?" An impeccable English accent.

I cleared my throat. This would be my final confirmation. "I'm here for Carmen Tornametti."

"Is she expecting you?" the man said.

I was right.

"She'll see me."

He reached for the phone. "May I give her your name?"

"Tell her it's Aaron Vogel."

He dialled. We waited. "There's an Aaron Vogel here to see you," he said.

Silence as he listened to the response.

I tried to imagine Carmen's reaction. A ghost come calling. Would she guess who it was? I liked the thought of making her panic.

The concierge looked up and smiled. "Go right up to 2619."

This was my last chance to turn back.

I walked to the rear of the lobby. Dark Renaissance paintings. Leather wing chairs. Polished brass elevator doors.

An elevator was already waiting.

I stepped inside and pressed twenty-six.

I watched as the light moved up along the numbers.

Five, six. . . .

My forehead was damp with perspiration. How could I convince Carmen that I was confident and in control?

Ten, eleven . . . .

I took a deep breath.

Fourteen, fifteen . . . .

Be aggressive.

Twenty, twenty-one . . . .

I could threaten to blackmail her, threaten to find Nick Tornametti and tell him everything.

Twenty-six.

The elevator door slid back.

CUT TO:

INTERIOR. APARTMENT HALLWAY. DAY.

Standing in front of the elevator doors is ANTONIO BANDERAS.

>   ANTONIO
> Very funny, Mitchie. So what else do you know about
> Aaron Vogel?

MITCHELL reaches for the "door close" button. In that same instant ANTONIO steps forward and blocks the elevator door with his shoulder. He grabs MITCHELL by the wrist and yanks him out of the elevator. He twists MITCHELL's arm behind his back and bashes his face against the wall.

When he jerks MITCHELL back there's a smear of blood on the creamy fabric of the wallpaper.

>   ANTONIO
> You saved us a trip. Carmen and I were just coming to get
> you.

The elevator door silently slides shut behind them.

>   MITCHELL
> I just came here to tell Carmen I quit. I don't want any-
> thing to do with this.

>   ANTONIO
> Too late, Mitchie. You're already in serious shit – you and
> Carmen both.

ANTONIO pushes MITCHELL down the hall, his arm still twisted painfully behind his back.

>   MITCHELL
> (loudly) Let – me – go!

ANTONIO shoves MITCHELL against the wall again to silence him.

ANTONIO
Don't bother trying that again.

MITCHELL
My friends know where I am. They're calling the police if
I'm not out in five minutes.

ANTONIO
Why would they need to call the police, Mitchie? I haven't
hurt you, have I? You know what else, Mitchie? You're a
lousy liar.

Halfway down the hall, ANTONIO opens a door and pushes
MITCHELL through.

FOLLOW TO:
INTERIOR. CARMEN'S APARTMENT – FOYER. DAY.

The foyer is lined with smoked mirror. Piled in the corner is a
mountain of luggage – fresh from Carmen's trip.

MITCHELL sees his reflection in the mirror. Blood is dripping
down his chin. He touches his face in astonishment.

ANTONIO
Go on in. Make yourself at home.

FOLLOW TO:
INTERIOR. CARMEN'S APARTMENT – LIVING ROOM. DAY.

The living room feels like a giant dark cave. Steel grey walls. Black
leather furniture and more mirrors. Italian Moda. A huge TV
screen and stereo look like they belong in a recording studio.

The apartment is a mess. The glass dining room table is heaped
with dirty dishes, empty cereal boxes and cookie bags. There's a
pile of laundry by the hall. Beside the couch is a collection of
empty Diet Coke bottles and potato chip bags.

ANTONIO
Nice, eh? She rented it when she moved out of the house.

As if hypnotized, MITCHELL steps to the centre of the room. Oversized sliding glass doors open to a stone-paved terrace – large as a backyard – furnished with a sleek metal table and chairs. A perfect view of the city skyline.

CARMEN enters from the hallway. Her hair is a mess, her eyes swollen, her face has pink welts as if someone has just slapped her.

> CARMEN
> You fucking idiot, Mitchell. I told you to keep this to yourself.

> MITCHELL
> I just came to talk to you – and this guy shoved me against the wall. I think he broke my nose.

> CARMEN
> Just shut up with your complaining, Mitchell.
> (loaded with secret meaning) Did you at least bring me the final draft? The one with all the changes I told you to make?

> MITCHELL
> (appalled) Why would I do any more work for you?

> CARMEN
> Great, Mitchell, just great. You are a real fuck-up. I might have been able to get us out of this.

> MITCHELL
> You've been lying to me all along. You didn't tell me I was writing a true story. Anyway, as of right now, I'm quitting.

> CARMEN
> Oh, really? Like I wasn't going to fire you? Now we just have to sit here and wait for my fucking father to come.

> MITCHELL
> Your father? You mean *Nick Tornametti*?

> CARMEN
> Yeah, Nick Tornametti. See if your whining works on *him*.

MITCHELL
Carmen, just let me out of here. I won't call the police.

CARMEN
You're the one who got us into this shit, Mitchell! You're
the one who put that story in the paper this morning.

MITCHELL
(mystified) I don't know what you're talking about.

ANTONIO
(laughing sarcastically) Sure you don't, Mitchie.

ANTONIO hands MITCHELL the *Toronto Star's* arts section. A
large photograph of Ramir, smiling seductively, wearing an unbut-
toned white shirt. The headline: "Café brewing up one-man show."

ANTONIO
(pointing to a few pertinent paragraphs) Read it.

MITCHELL
"The Daily Grind is already a popular arts hangout, featuring an exhibition of paintings . . . . Tonight's performance
was co-written by Martinez and Toronto screenwriter,
Mitchell Draper, whose screenplay *A Time for Revenge* is
going into production this fall."

CARMEN
I told you this project was secret, Mitchell.

ANTONIO
(taunting) Now the whole world knows you're making a
movie about Nick Tornametti.

MITCHELL
I didn't have anything to do with this. My friend Ramir
talked to the paper.

ANTONIO
Sounds like a great friend.

MITCHELL
I only told him the title. Honestly, he doesn't know anything else.

CARMEN
You shouldn't have told him anything, Mitchell. That was part of our deal. You knew that from day one.

MITCHELL
I didn't know your ex-boyfriend was going to spy on me and attack me.

ANTONIO
She told you I was her *boyfriend*?

MITCHELL nods.

ANTONIO
(laughing with derision) Tell me, Mitchie. Does she really look like my type?

CARMEN
Shut the fuck up.

ANTONIO
She's gone through two husbands. She doesn't need me for a boyfriend.

MITCHELL
(to CARMEN) Then who is he?

CARMEN
He's a fucking asshole.

ANTONIO
I'm her brother. Her cute little brother, Leo. There used to be a family resemblance, but you can't see it under all those layers of fat.

CARMEN slaps LEO across the face. Immediately LEO slaps her face in return. She tries to slap him again, but he grabs her hand.

CARMEN
(to LEO) You're going to pay for that, Leo.

LEO/ANTONIO
Carmen's been a fucking liar since the day she was born.
That's what Dad always says. A cokehead and a liar.

CARMEN
Obviously he thinks you're a loser, or he wouldn't give you
shit jobs like following me around for a month and a half.

MITCHELL
(awkwardly interjecting) Obviously this is a private family
matter. Why don't I just leave? I don't care if your father
killed anybody –

LEO
(Viciously) That was just a bunch of nasty rumours he
wants people to forget.

CARMEN
He's the one who says they're only rumours.

LEO
Show me some evidence. Did they ever charge him?

CARMEN
It's proof enough that he gets so freaked out any time anybody ever mentions it.

LEO
Tell him that yourself. I have to phone him – let him know
we've got Mitchie-baby here.
(gesturing at the apartment)
This place is a fucking mess. Why don't you clean up? Do
some real work for a change.

CARMEN half-heartedly picks up a William Ashley shopping bag
and fills it with strewn wrapping tissue. She shoves it in a cupboard beneath the VCR.

Through the doorway, MITCHELL watches LEO in the kitchen using the phone. MITCHELL gingerly touches his nose. It doesn't seem painful.

Apparently exhausted from all her cleaning CARMEN sinks to the floor. She leans against the bottom of the sofa.

> CARMEN
> So how did you know to come here anyway?

> MITCHELL
> When you told me to change the names in the script, I looked up Tornametti in the phone book.

> CARMEN
> Aren't you smart? And I'm the only Tornametti in Toronto. After the police investigation, when my father came up to Canada, he changed the family name because he was so ashamed of himself.

> MITCHELL
> Even though he says he didn't do it.

> CARMEN
> Doesn't that tell you something? Then last year I changed my name back to Tornametti because I didn't think we should hide our family history.

> MITCHELL
> If you're so proud of it, why did you tell me your name was Carmen Denver?

> CARMEN
> It's my married name. I didn't want the whole film business knowing who I was, what I was doing. He would have stopped me right away.

> MITCHELL
> Do you have any idea how hard I worked on that script?

> CARMEN
> I paid you.

                          MITCHELL
Underpaid me. And all along you knew the movie was
never going to get made.

                          CARMEN
I could have done it.
(she breaks for a moment and wipes her eyes)
You can't imagine what my father's like, Mitchell. He
turned my mother into an alcoholic with all his fooling
around and drugs and his so-called "business deals." He
even screwed up my brother, but he's too much of a moron
to know it. All because of his inflated ego. He tries to keep
this stupid secret that everybody already knows.

                          MITCHELL
That doesn't mean you had to make a movie about it.

                          CARMEN
I had to prove I could do it. I had to show him I'm not
some hopeless fuck-up. Anyway, I scared him. That's what
I wanted.

LEO comes back into the living room.

                          LEO
Dad's in the car. He'll be here in a few minutes. Hey look,
Carmen, it's two o'clock! We can watch your favourite show.

                          CARMEN
Just shut up and leave me alone, Leo.

LEO pick up the remote control and turns on the giant TV set.
Police Line-Up. The credits are already in progress, backed by the
show's urgent, pounding theme.

                          LEO
It's making lots of money in syndication.

                          CARMEN
It's a piece of shit.

The titles flash: EXECUTIVE PRODUCER DOMINIC MANNO.
LEO makes an exaggerated hoot and bursts into applause.

>   CARMEN
Shut up, Leo.

>   MITCHELL
(tentatively) What's going on?

>   CARMEN
You haven't figured that out, too, Mitchell? My father is
Dominic Manno.

>   MITCHELL
The Dominic Manno?

>   CARMEN
Producer of sleazy low-budget trash, watched by millions
of idiots around the world.

>   MITCHELL
You made me write a script that calls Dominic Manno a
murderer?

>   LEO
(delighted) See? You really are in deep shit.

>   MITCHELL
This could wreck my whole life. I had no idea that Nick
Tornametti was really *Dominic Manno.*

>   CARMEN
That's why I hired you. You don't have any connections.
You wouldn't go squealing back to him.

>   MITCHELL
So I just ran directly into your trap?

>   CARMEN
Stop being so dramatic.

LEO

You want to know what got Carmen started on this whole movie idea, Mitchie? She'd just gotten out of detox in L.A. and Mom didn't want her in the house anymore. So she came up here to live with Dad and me. He gave her a job as a production assistant on *Police Line-Up*. Shit job. But easy. He wanted to get her cleaned up, give her a fresh start. But she kept screwing up.

CARMEN

The production manager was incompetent.

LEO

She was late picking up the actors. Lost a truckload of props. Dad gave her a bunch of warnings. And then he had to fire her.

CARMEN

He didn't have to fire me on the set, right in front of the entire crew.

LEO

Next thing you know, she moves into this place and she's calling herself a movie producer. Sneaking around to casting companies, acting like a big shot – trying to keep the plot of her movie top-secret. Then she wonders why he's coming down so hard on her.

CARMEN

He can't stand it when everybody doesn't worship him . . . when they don't pay him all the respect he thinks he deserves.

The phone rings two short blasts. The effect is like a freeze-frame.

LEO

(with nasty glee) Zero hour.

CARMEN bites her lower lip.

> LEO
(on the phone) Of course, send him up.

Then, abruptly, there is a storm of activity.

LEO flicks off the TV, grabs up a potato chip bag and a pair of sweatpants from a chair. CARMEN goes to a mirror and claws her hair into shape.

> MITCHELL
What's your father going to do?

> CARMEN
How the fuck should I know?

Caught in the panic, MITCHELL looks in the mirror at himself. He wipes the blood off his face and touches his nose. It doesn't look swollen.

LEO opens the door even before there is a knock. A moment later, with an even stride, DOMINIC MANNO enters the apartment. Youthful, though he must be in his sixties. Trim and darkly tanned. His black hair is combed precisely back from his face. He wears a black suit and a white shirt buttoned to the top. No tie. He's carrying a very plain black briefcase.

Ignoring his children, he goes directly to MITCHELL. He shakes hands as though he is greeting a guest in his own office. There is no friendly smile. His voice is tense and controlled.

> DOMINIC
It's a pleasure to meet you, Mitchell.

> MITCHELL
(petrified) It's a pleasure to meet you.

DOMINIC surveys Carmen's apartment.

DOMINIC
(to CARMEN) Your mother must be giving you a great deal of money if you can afford a place like this.

CARMEN
It's none of your goddamn business.

DOMINIC
I know your two ex-husbands aren't paying you alimony, Carmen, so therefore the money must be coming from your mother. And since your mother's money comes directly from me, it is very much my business.

CARMEN
At least she still believes in me.

DOMINIC
You have yet to give me a reason to believe in you, Carmen. And this episode hasn't alleviated my doubts. But we'll discuss that later.
(turning back to MITCHELL)
Where should we have our talk, Mitchell? What about the terrace?

MITCHELL
The terrace would be very nice.

DOMINIC
Leo, bring us some iced tea. And Carmen, of course, I want you to join us, too.

CARMEN sneers. Then MITCHELL and CARMEN follow DOMINIC to the sliding glass doors.

FOLLOW TO:

EXTERIOR. CARMEN'S APARTMENT – TERRACE. DAY.

DOMINIC MANNO leads the way onto the open terrace – constructed on the roof of the apartment below.

DOMINIC takes the railing-side seat at the white metal table.

> DOMINIC
Carmen, I want you to sit here beside me.

> CARMEN
I'm not coming anywhere near you.

Instead, she stands against the sliding glass doors, arms folded across her chest.

> DOMINIC
It really is an exceptional view. Perhaps even finer than from the Park Plaza. The very first night I came to Toronto I was invited for cocktails at their rooftop bar. The quintessential Rob Roy. Very dry. Have you ever been to their bar, Mitchell?

> MITCHELL
I was there a few weeks ago. Actually I had the Rob Roy myself.

> DOMINIC
A connoisseur. Very good.

> CARMEN
You're both making me sick.

LEO arrives with two glasses of iced tea. He sets one in front of DOMINIC and one in front of MITCHELL.

DOMINIC raises his glass for a single-sided toast and savours the drink with closed eyes before setting down his glass.

> DOMINIC
(with a sense of suppressed anger) Mitchell, I must apologize for asking you to witness our little family drama, but obviously you know by now that you've become involved in a complicated situation.

MITCHELL nods tightly.

DOMINIC

However, I am certain that we can come to some resolution and put this incident in the past, where it belongs.

MITCHELL

That's exactly what I want, too. Totally behind us.

DOMINIC

I must admit that, when I first found out about Carmen's film project, I thought it was a sign of promise – at last she was focusing her energies. But if I had known what she was actually conspiring to do, I would have saved us all this trouble and stopped her right at the beginning.

CARMEN

That's what you tried to do! You told everybody not to work for me. You had Leo scaring Mitchell so he'd quit. All because you're terrified of what I could do to you.

DOMINIC

I was not terrified, Carmen. I simply did not want you repeating old and groundless gossip. We have discussed this on numerous occasions and you have been consistently determined to defy me.

CARMEN

You think you're so powerful that nothing can touch you. But you know I could have screwed up your whole damn business.

DOMINIC stands sharply and CARMEN is startled into silence. His face is burning with intensity. He begins to pace the terrace. MITCHELL and CARMEN watch in nervous anticipation.

DOMINIC paces, slowly, methodically. Then he stops at the edge of the twenty-sixth floor terrace. He turns to face CARMEN and leans back against the railing – a bar barely high enough to reach his hip.

DOMINIC

Tell me, Carmen, do you intend to push me off?

MITCHELL and CARMEN stare at him, speechless.

DOMINIC
Apparently this is your fantasy. To see me smashed on the pavement.

CARMEN
(to MITCHELL) You showed him the script, you two-faced –

DOMINIC
Mitchell had nothing to do with it. You should be aware by now that I can find out whatever I need to know, *Pandora*.

CARMEN
Don't call me that.

DOMINIC
From the script I presumed that was the name you preferred this week. So, *Pandora*, aren't you going to carry out your role as arbiter of justice?

DOMINIC's face is flushed and his shoulders are tensed – though he shows no other sign of stress.

DOMINIC
Don't you want to push me over the edge?

As if hypnotized by his dare, CARMEN moves towards him, one slow, resentful step at a time.

DOMINIC
From your script, it seems you imagine that I might be willing to kill you – kill you before you can hand me over to the police for a murder that happened over twenty years ago. You know, of course, that the police would laugh at you. You have no evidence. You have no credibility. I have told you since you were a child that you need to work with substance to achieve success, but you have never listened.

CARMEN
You've never listened to me.

DOMINIC
Push me off then. You can read the headlines in the paper tomorrow: "Daughter kills father and saves the world from evil."

CARMEN
(growing angrier) I don't have to put up with your mind games anymore.

DOMINIC
You want to prove to me how powerful you are? How righteous you are? That's what you want? This is your chance, Pandora – your 'time for revenge.'

DOMINIC releases his hands from the rail and raises his arms, reaching out to either side, like an eagle about to take flight.

CARMEN's eyes are bulging, her face a gargoyle of confusion. She charges at full tilt. Then stops, only an inch away.

DOMINIC grabs her by the upper arms and holds them both still. For a moment it resembles an embrace.

CARMEN
Why do you keep doing this to me?

DOMINIC
You should have learned by now.

She pulls away from him and sits roughly down at the table. DOMINIC straightens his jacket and sits down beside her.

DOMINIC
Carmen, look at me. Look at me.

Finally CARMEN obeys.

> DOMINIC

This is what you are going to do. You are going to move
back to Los Angeles. Live with your mother if she'll have
you, or rent your own apartment. If you are still interested
in working in television I can make a few phone calls and
you will start again as a production assistant, from where
you will work your way up.

> CARMEN

I'm a forty-two-year-old woman. Don't you know how
humiliating this is?

> LEO

(sniping) Why don't you just get married again? That's
how you solved all your other problems.

> CARMEN

(to DOMINIC) I don't need your help.

> DOMINIC

Then I want to see evidence of that.

CARMEN looks into her father's eyes and her hurt hardens back
into anger. She goes to the sliding-glass doors.

> CARMEN

I'll be back in an hour and I want you out of here or I'm
calling the police.

CARMEN exits, and a moment later the front door slams.

> DOMINIC

(quietly) Despite her anger, I expect she's seen my point of
view.

> MITCHELL

(pushing up from the table) Maybe I should get going,
too.

> DOMINIC

No, no, Mitchell, we need to get to know each other a
little better. Leo, would you give us some privacy?

LEO goes back into the apartment and MITCHELL is left alone
with DOMINIC MANNO.

DOMINIC reaches into his pant pocket and removes a small cylinder. He holds it to his opened mouth and gives two short sprays,
then returns it to his pocket. Medication? Breath freshener?

He holds his hands together – just the fingertips touching – and
lowers his head. He takes deep breaths as though meditating. But
the last thing he seems is relaxed.

MITCHELL sits silently, watching, waiting, growing more nervous
with each of DOMINIC's long exhalations.

Finally DOMINIC lifts his head.

                    DOMINIC
        What do you want, Mitchell?

                    MITCHELL
        Nothing. I don't want anything.

DOMINIC laughs softly, watching MITCHELL wipe perspiration
from his forehead.

                    DOMINIC
        Are you certain?

                    MITCHELL
        I didn't know why Carmen was making the movie. I'll never
        tell anyone what it was about. I promise I don't want any-
        thing.

                    DOMINIC
        I know you won't tell anyone, Mitchell. But that's not
        what I'm asking. I want you to tell me what you want.

                    MITCHELL
        I – I don't know.

                              DOMINIC
It shouldn't be hard to guess. I imagine you want to be a
famous writer.

                              MITCHELL
Yes. Yes, you could say that.

                              DOMINIC
Of course, a famous screenwriter is almost a contradiction
in terms. Perhaps there are eight or ten of them today that
people in certain circles might have heard of.

                              MITCHELL
I've always been big on deluding myself.

DOMINIC chuckles and looks at MITCHELL as though judging
him anew.

                              DOMINIC
Do you know what fame actually is, Mitchell?

                              MITCHELL
I suspect this is a trick question.

                              DOMINIC
You're right, it is. But tell me anyway.

                              MITCHELL
Respect . . . appreciation . . . immortality . . . .

                              DOMINIC
Fame is advertising.
(a pause for impact)
When you have a product to sell, you advertise its bene-
fits. With a television show you advertise the actors
because they're the special features – even though, in fact,
they do the least work. But they're often very pleasant to
look at, and that's what sells your product to the public.
Toothpaste has baking soda; a new movie has Julia
Roberts.
(smiling at his own wit)

Very occasionally a writer might have such a reputation that he or she becomes a selling point. But that doesn't happen very often.

                    MITCHELL
You're making it sound like . . . .

                    DOMINIC
No, no, speak up. I'm interested in hearing.

                    MITCHELL
What about when they write stories about Julia Roberts in the paper, in magazines?

                    DOMINIC
Advertising of a less conspicuous variety. Newspapers sell more copies by hitching onto the bandwagon of fame.

                    MITCHELL
So it's all about making money.

DOMINIC nods.

                    DOMINIC
The pitfall is when actors, with their fragile egos, begin to take the advertising personally. They think being famous means they're actually special. That being famous proves they're worth something.

                    MITCHELL
But some people are special. They're famous because they deserve to be – because they do something really well.

                    DOMINIC
Sometimes, yes. Perhaps more so in days gone by. But nowadays, that special person will quickly be bought up by a large corporation and they will become advertising, too. An athlete sells running shoes. A singer sells records. Somewhere, someone behind the scenes is making money. And that's the only reason we make people famous.

DOMINIC looks off towards the glittering downtown skyscrapers, his glance lingering on the spire of the CN Tower.

DOMINIC
I'm explaining this to you for a reason, Mitchell. I'm explaining it to you so you'll understand why I don't appreciate certain things being said about me.

MITCHELL
You want to be famous for running your production company – not for what you did before.

DOMINIC
I am not interested in being famous, Mitchell. I'm interested in power. Fame is easy to acquire with a few dollars and a few phone calls. Power takes time. Power is getting things done, making things happen. One needs skill and knowledge and patience. Power requires *substance* because it is the source of making money, and the source of making other people famous – which is a very desirable ability. But power lies to a great degree in how other people perceive you.

MITCHELL
So they keep listening to you and you keep making money.

DOMINIC
You've understood, Mitchell. I have spent a great deal of time creating what I have and I will not be controlled or diminished by an event from the distant past.
(his face is reddening again)
Some people feel that by spreading rumours such as these, they can diminish my power and thereby increase their own. You can imagine how I might feel about that.

MITCHELL
Not good.

> DOMINIC
> Now Mitchell, a man in my position could obviously be
> very helpful to an aspiring young writer. However, the
> reverse could also be true. I'm sure you've heard that old
> cliché: "I can make sure you never work in this town again."

> MITCHELL
> Yes, I've heard that expression.

> DOMINIC
> Frankly, I'm not sure if it's entirely possible. Partially
> because of what you said yourself – about someone doing
> exceptional work that draws attention. However, excep-
> tional work *is* the exception. And I do know that, under
> regular circumstances, it's possible to make things very
> difficult for someone to move ahead. Do you grasp my
> meaning?

> MITCHELL
> Yes.

> DOMINIC
> I shared this same lesson with a lawyer I once knew in
> New York City.

A meaningful pause.

> DOMINIC
> I want this entire screenplay incident with Carmen for-
> gotten. Is that understood? On Monday morning Leo will
> arrange a courier to pick up all the materials connected to
> it. Everything.

MITCHELL nods in understanding.

DOMINIC reaches into his briefcase and sets a thick document on
the table. The title page reads: *Hell Hole*.

> MITCHELL
> How did . . . .

DOMINIC
Leo tells me there's a photocopy shop quite convenient to
your apartment.

MITCHELL
(dumbfounded) Just down the street.

DOMINIC
I gave your script to my writing staff and they were very
impressed. You could have quite a career ahead of you,
Mitchell.

MITCHELL
That's what I've been hoping for.

DOMINIC
As soon as we're back at the office, I'll have Leo FedEx the
script to my associates in Hollywood.

MITCHELL
You mean you might produce it?

DOMINIC
I could arrange it. Do you like the idea? A favour for a
favour?

MITCHELL takes a moment to consider. He nods.

DOMINIC reaches into his briefcase again and pulls out an envelope – just as Carmen had done so often before.

DOMINIC
Consider this a temporary reservation on the rights. I
trust the amount is satisfactory.

MITCHELL
I'm sure it'll be perfect.

Without looking inside it, MITCHELL folds the envelope and
slips it discreetly into his pocket.

DOMINIC
I gather you're a friend of Ramir Martinez?

MITCHELL
(startled at the change of subject) We've known each other
a few years.

DOMINIC
We considered him for a role in a new series we're doing,
but the fit wasn't right. Still, he's a very handsome young
man. Very charismatic. Actually we have him in mind for
another project. Perhaps someday I'll make him famous.

MITCHELL
(raising his eyebrows, acknowledging the in-joke) I'm sure
he wouldn't mind.

DOMINIC
I noticed his picture in the paper this morning. That's why
I read the story. That's what led to our meeting today.

MITCHELL
(ironic) I'll have to thank him.

DOMINIC
(smiling) I hope you mean that kindly, Mitchell. In any
case, be sure to give Ramir my best for his show tonight.

MITCHELL
(a stroke of inspiration) Why don't you come?

DOMINIC laughs dismissively.

MITCHELL
I'll make sure you get the best seat in the house.

DOMINIC
I don't think so.

MITCHELL
It's multimedia. Very high-tech. Better special effects than
Phantom of the Opera.

> DOMINIC
(laughing to himself, pondering) What time?

> MITCHELL
Eight. At The Daily Grind, at Brunswick and Bloor.

> DOMINIC
How long?

> MITCHELL
Probably not more than an hour.

> DOMINIC
All right. It's a deal. And Mitchell, I trust you'll remember what we've discussed.

> MITCHELL
(with certainty) I won't forget.

CUT TO:

INTERIOR. CARMEN'S APARTMENT – FOYER. DAY.

LEO holds the door open for MITCHELL to leave.

> LEO
I'm going to miss following you around Mitchie-baby.

> MITCHELL
(uncomfortable) I'm sure you've got better things to do.

LEO suddenly leans in close to MITCHELL – as though about to kiss him on the mouth.

> LEO
I saw how you looked at me on the street that day, Mitchie.

He grabs MITCHELL's ass and squeezes it roughly.

> LEO
If you forget what my father said, I'll have to come talk to you myself.

CUT TO:

INTERIOR. FOUR SEASONS HOTEL – MEN'S WASHROOM.
DAY.

I left Carmen's building and rushed across the street to the Four
Seasons. I went straight to the washrooms beside the Studio Café
and locked myself in a cubicle.

My heart was still pounding. I wondered if I'd sold my soul to
the devil. But Dominic owed me, too. He wanted my silence. It
seemed like a fair bargain.

I pulled the envelope from my pocket and looked inside. A pile
of thousand-dollar bills – I'd never even seen *one* before. And I
counted ten.

But better than that was the news about *Hell Hole*. A screenplay that I'd written might actually be on its way to becoming a
major motion picture.

I might be a famous writer after all.

Well, maybe not *famous*.

SUNDAY, JUNE 22

When I got home from Carmen's apartment yesterday I was still overwhelmed with nervous energy. I could hardly wait to tell Ingrid and Ramir everything that had happened. But I decided to save my surprises to heighten their impact. Ramir would have to forgive me after I delivered Dominic Manno.

I paced my apartment.

I hid the $10,000 in the freezer. Then between the pages of *The Love Machine*. Then under a loose floorboard.

I re-ironed my shirt yet again. I realized that I could now afford to buy more good clothes. But somehow the idea of shopping didn't fill me with as much excitement as it had before.

Part of me wanted to phone Ben and tell him that my screenplay had been purchased. But I still felt too ashamed to face him. And seeing Ramir would require all my grovelling skills for one night.

Half an hour before show time, I headed to the store. As I walked down the block my stride felt longer, my head felt higher. Were these unfamiliar sensations associated with self-confidence? Tonight, finally, my life was on the right track.

In the middle of the sidewalk sat The Daily Grind sandwich board. Ingrid had replicated her drawing of Ramir as a screaming Human Bean with ERUPTION in his mouth. Underneath was written: CLOSED FOR A PRIVATE PARTY.

Ramir's show was really happening.

Madonna was at the door – clipboard in hand. She looked at me cheerfully but blankly. "Hi-eee. Tonight's by invitation only. Can I get your name please?"

"Don't you realize who I am?!" I shouted. No, I didn't. I said, "I'm Ingrid's friend, Mitchell Draper. We met this week."

"Oh, righ-eeet." Madonna checked the clipboard anyway. "You can come in."

The Grind had been transformed yet again. The windows had been draped with blackout curtains. The serving counter had been pushed against the right wall to make more room. All the tables had been moved outside to the patio, and all the chairs from outside had been brought in. Now ten rows of chairs faced the back where a stage area had been cleared.

Two stage lights mounted on poles were pointing back towards Ingrid's mural. But in front of the mural there was a large black metal stand, stacked with a stereo, VCR and a giant video monitor. So this was Ramir's idea of multimedia.

The image on the TV screen was a smiling head shot of Ramir that I've always hated – it made him look like a white-bread Sears catalogue version of himself. He looked so absurd, it was funny. I hoped it was intentional.

The only person seated so far was Frances Farmer, attired in a floor-length red velvet gown – perfect for opening night at the Metropolitan Opera. She sat erect and alert as though she was already absorbed in the performance.

"Mitchell, why haven't you called?" There was Ingrid, hugging me from the side. Tonight she was dressed elegantly but practically, wearing a form-fitting mock turtleneck and a hip-hugging knee-length skirt, both in taupe. The most figure-revealing outfit that I've ever seen her wear.

"I've been worried sick about you," she said.

"I've had a complicated day. But I need two seats, front row centre, for me and *Dominic Manno*."

"The TV producer?"

I nodded.

"We have to talk!" she said with the urgency only inspired by fabulous gossip. She grabbed my hand and pulled me out the side door to the table-jammed patio.

"Is Ramir here yet?" I asked on the way.

"He's out back, psyching himself up. He was working all afternoon with some technical person, plugging in the cables and setting up his tapes."

"So how does the show look?" I tried to sound casual.

"He didn't have time to rehearse. But he put me in charge of lighting."

"Typical," I said fondly.

"So tell me what happened!"

We sat on tabletops and I gave her a quick rundown of everything that had transpired since she'd given me the envelope with Ramir's press release. If we hadn't been eagerly awaiting Ramir's show, she probably would have been pissed off that I hadn't told her everything sooner.

"So anyway, I invited Dominic and he said yes. From the way he talked it sounds like he's planning to cast Ramir in a new TV series."

"Ramir'll be over the moon. But we shouldn't tell him right now. It'd put even more pressure on him."

"Maybe Dominic'll make the big announcement tonight."

"And he's going to produce *Hell Hole*, Mitchell! I always knew it was good."

"I'm still trying to absorb it all. But what happened with *you?* The last time I saw you, you'd just fired Kinita."

"Honestly, I didn't realize how horrible it was having her around until she was gone."

"I never understood why you were so patient with her."

"She scared me. Anyway, right after Kinita left I called Madonna and she came in and took over. And I went home and cried. And then I slept for twelve hours straight."

"You've been working so much, Ing, it's no wonder you were exhausted. I bet that's why you flipped out."

"Anyway, this afternoon in the bathtub I decided what I want to do."

"And that is?"

"I'll work out my one-year contract here. I'll delegate more, the way I should have been doing all along. That way I'll have more time off to paint. And Madonna said she has a friend who's looking for a job."

"Cher?"

"The thing is, the store's been bringing in three times as much as we did before, so I'm actually starting to make some extra money."

"And what about Geoffrey?"

"I have plans for him too," she said confidently. "After the show tonight, I'm going to invite him out for a drink and I'm going to make a deal with him – very business-like. I'll keep putting up my paintings, and if people keep buying them, I'll keep giving him his commission. But only 33 1/3 percent."

"I don't see how he could argue."

"Then in September we can try putting up some other painters to give them a break, too."

"Very philanthropic."

"And then, after we've had our drink, I'm going to make myself so sexually available, if he doesn't make a move, I'll know it's never going to happen."

"Ingrid, are you kidding?"

"Why would I kid?"

"You're going to be a shameless hussy?"

"I'm going to try."

"So you have to tell me, what exactly will you do in order to make yourself 'sexually available'?"

Madonna was at the patio door. "Ingrid, there's lots of people starting to arrive."

"I have to go in and help," Ing said, conveniently rescued from having to disclose her feminine wiles. "It's another big night at The Daily Grind."

"I should go and talk to Ramir."

"You should."

"Wish me luck."

"Wish *me* luck!"

The store was filling up. Lots of people were waiting outside on the sidewalk. Self-important media types chatting in cliques. Their eyeglasses competed to say the most about their wearers. Ramir had certainly brought out the right crowd.

I squeezed through the back room, now piled with Ramir's props: the famous Mexican sombrero, a toy machine gun, a huge plastic machete, the remote control for all the video equipment.

I slipped out the back exit and around the corner into the alley. Ramir didn't notice me right away. I watched him. He was wearing his black leather jacket, a white T-shirt and tight bleached jeans. He hammered his fist in the air, silently screaming his lines at the brick wall.

"I never liked that wall myself."

He turned with a start. "Hi," he said, trying not to seem surprised. "I'm glad you came."

"You knew I wouldn't miss it. Things look great out there. There's a crowd already."

"There is?" A moment of stage fright. "It's weird being back here by myself. No cast, no crew to help me get pumped up. So much of the show is on tape. I hope I don't screw up and confuse all my cues."

"You'll be great."

"I hope so."

"You look really good."

"Hours of make-up."

"Ramir, I have to apologize. I said some horrible things."

"Yeah," he agreed, nodding.

"When we've got more time, I'll tell you everything that's been going on – not that it justifies anything."

"I wasn't ever trying to lead you on, you know."

"I know. Anyway, I think I've got things in better perspective."

"You got me thinking, too. I was trying to figure out how to make it up to you. Did you see the story in the paper?"

"I saw it," I said. I was almost killed because of it, I thought. But we'd get into that later. "I guess we're finally famous. Do you feel like a totally different person?"

"Totally."

"So tonight's your big chance to be discovered."

"Cross your fingers," he said. "I think you'll like the show. You'll be surprised."

"Not if it's good. Actually I've got a surprise for *you*."

"What?" He was genuinely intrigued. I liked that.

"You'll see. You'll be indebted to me for the rest of your life."

"As if I'm not already."

I rolled my eyes at the sappiness.

We hugged.

I hoped so hard the show would be good I thought I might cry. Finally, though, it felt as if I'd taken Ramir off the pedestal and planted him firmly on the ground.

"Knock 'em dead," I said and I went back in to the noise and crowd.

The room had filled up even more. A few people had taken their seats. Some had squeezed out amid the tables on the patio, so they could have a cigarette. No sign yet of Dominic Manno.

Ramir's parents, dressed in their Sunday best, were sitting discreetly in the back row. His mother looks just like Lena Horne. And his father resembles Johnny Mathis.

"How is he?" Ingrid asked.

"Good. Everything's okay. I hope I didn't distract him."

"I'm sure he feels better knowing you're here."

"Did he tell you that?"

"I'm not getting involved."

"You're such a Switzerland. What time is it?"

"Quarter to eight. Fifteen more minutes."

"I feel like I should recognize all these people. Do you have any idea who they are?"

"Just from Ramir's list – the ones I checked off. That woman with the blank eyes and the really tight plastic surgery, she's a theatre reviewer for CBC Radio."

"We can rebuild her," I said, quoting *The Six Million Dollar Man*.

"And those two blonde women in black tights work for a casting agency. Do you think they're a couple?"

"I think they *were* a couple, but they worked through all the shit at a therapy weekend so they could continue to respect each other as business partners."

"And that guy in the Malcolm X T-shirt. That's Ramir's agent, Hank."

"You're kidding. I always pictured a young Henry Fonda. He looks more like Henry Winkler."

"Ramir says he can be a really tough negotiator."

"Oh my God, Ing, he's here."

Dominic Manno.

I deserted Ingrid and shoved my way to the door where Dominic, dressed in a formal black suit, was trying to bargain admittance from Madonna.

"It's okay. He's with me," I said.

"He's not on the list."

"It's okay. Ramir wants him to see the show."

"I'm just doing my job," Madonna whined.

"Dogmatic doorpeople," I apologized, and heartily shook Dominic's hand. "I'm really glad you made it."

"I don't normally attend events like this, Mitchell, but I thought a spontaneous evening might be a nice change."

With him was a voluptuous East Indian woman in a skintight red mini-dress. How could I be so stupid? Of course he'd bring a date. I needed another seat.

"Naomi, I'd like to introduce Mitchell Draper. He's a very talented young writer I've met."

Naomi smiled with just enough of a snarl to inform me that attending fringe theatre was not her preferred way of spending a romantic evening with a millionaire TV producer.

Dominic pointed appreciatively to my Calvin Klein shirt. "Already out spending your money, I see."

"This old thing? I've had it for weeks."

"I trust the show's not going to ramble on, Mitchell. We have dinner reservations for nine-thirty."

"You'll have plenty of time," I said, technically making no commitment whatsoever. "We've got the best seats in the house. Front row centre."

Ramir's geeky agent Hank butted his way between us. "Nick, great to see you!" I shouldn't have been surprised. This was a room filled with TV people – they'd all want their turn to schmooze Dominic Manno. And maybe Ramir's agent could do some good for the cause.

"I'll be back in a minute, Mr. Manno," I assured him, even though he didn't seem to care.

Somewhere over my shoulder, I heard an excited whisper: "There's Dominic Manno!" This might become a feeding frenzy.

I rushed to Ingrid's side. "Give me a Post-It note. I need to make another reserved sign for the front row."

She was staring at Dominic Manno with mystified wonder. "So that's the man who started all this."

"He's spooky-looking, don't you think? Ramir was right. He's the most intimidating person who ever walked the earth. What time is it?"

"Ten to eight."

"Go back and tell Ramir the show has to start right on the dot. Dominic has to leave by nine-fifteen. But don't mention Dominic's name."

I was about to return to Dominic's side, feeling like an anxious chaperone, when Geoffrey Abrams appeared, looking as movie-star handsome as ever.

"Mitchell, how nice to see you. How are you?"

"I'm good actually. I've had a very good day."

"Ramir's managed to assemble a very interesting group of people."

"They're all potential customers for Ingrid, too."

"That thought had crossed my mind. I see he's even managed to bring out The Killer TV Producer."

He startled me with that. "What do you mean?"

He laughed at the apparent obviousness. "Dominic Manno, the TV producer with the murderous reputation."

"Dominic Manno's not a murderer."

"No, of course not." But Geoffrey's smile was tongue-in-cheek. "One shouldn't talk that way about a man who's been a gangster in the mob."

"Where'd you hear all this?"

"Just rumours. No proof, of course. But the story goes that he murdered a lawyer in Manhattan, and then he moved to Toronto hoping no one would find out."

"So does everybody know about it?"

"Local legend. He's very sensitive about it – to say the least. Kindly don't mention that I told you, Mitchell. Forgive me, but I see an old friend."

He sailed away, eager to schmooze in less controversial pastures.

So everybody really *did* know about Dominic Manno's past.

I leaned against the counter and took a breath.

I watched Dominic hold court with a fleet of media bigwigs. They were hanging on his every word. He looked so confident, so arrogantly above it all.

A mobster and a killer. And I was indebted to him for the rest of my life . . . .

Ingrid grabbed my elbow. "I just showed Ramir the guest list. Everyone he invited is here, so he's ready. We've jammed in almost a hundred people. I just hope the fire inspector doesn't show up." Then she noticed my expression. "What's the matter? You look sick."

"Something weird."

"Are you okay?"

"I'll explain later."

"I'll go dim the lights. I guess I'll be watching from the back room." Ingrid headed off.

"Is Mitchell here? Let me talk to Mitchell."

A bellow above the din. It was Carmen's husky voice.

My stomach dropped.

There she was at the door, arguing with Madonna. I pushed her back out onto the sidewalk.

"Carmen, what are you doing here?"

"I wanted to set things straight, Mitchell."

"You didn't need to." I never wanted to see her again.

"It wasn't you I was mad at this afternoon. It was Leo and my father."

"That's okay. I understand."

"Now you see all the bullshit I've had to put up with my whole life. Anyway, after all the crap that went down, I didn't want to sit in my apartment all night by myself. I thought it might be fun to see your friend's show."

"Carmen, I don't think you should stay. Your father's here."

"What?"

"He's in the front row."

"You are such a fucking little schemer, Mitchell."

"I wouldn't scheme about your father. He told me he wants to cast Ramir in a show, so he asked if he could come."

She shook her head. "This day has just been too fucking much."

"I couldn't agree more."

"Don't worry, I won't cause some big scene. That's what *he* does. It's not what I do." She stood on her toes and looked in the door at the crowd. "Oh God, there he is. I'll just stand at the back by the window. I'm not going to talk to him."

The lights dimmed and people began to flock towards the chairs. "The show's going to start any second."

"Don't tell him I'm here," Carmen said, pushing her way through the door.

"Don't worry, I won't."

I took my seat beside Dominic and Naomi. He frightened me now more than ever.

Dominic spoke into my ear: "One of the reasons I dislike events like this, Mitchell, is the number of people who insist on pitching me their hopeless projects."

"I guess they know how powerful you are," I said.

Dominic chuckled. "You're very good at being obsequious, Mitchell."

Naomi scowled at me for making her date laugh, and then locked her face in a bored pout.

I looked over my shoulder. Carmen was standing at the back, blocked by several other guests who had lost in the game of musical chairs.

Suddenly the room went dark. The only light remaining was Ramir's Ivory-boy face on the monitor. People laughed. A good sign.

This was it. The moment of truth.

I remembered that terrible teen-suicide play, *Youth in Asia*, that Ramir had done with the theatre collective last year. I prayed this would be better.

Ramir's smiling visage disappeared. Total blackness. Then a loud blast of noise. A cops-and-robbers scene appeared on the TV. Two leather-clad figures running through a dark alley. Two policemen chasing them. Hard-pulsing music.

Dominic leaned towards me. "That's *Crime Wave*," he whispered with suppressed pleasure. I nodded like I'd known all along.

A close-up of one of the thugs, stopping, turning to point his gun. It was Ramir with greasy hair and three-day stubble – his standard method of masking his innocent, boyish looks.

Just as Ramir pointed his pistol, one of the policemen fired and Ramir was hit. He dropped to the ground. The video freeze-framed. Silence, and then a blood-curdling scream pierced the TV-lit darkness.

Everyone was taken off-guard.

The stage lights came up fully, blinding us for a moment. The live Ramir swaggered out from the back room, holding the VCR remote control like a gun.

"Good evenin', ladies and gentlemen." A tough Puerto Rican accent. "My name is Gang Member Number Two. You jus' saw my firs' and final role. I have to confess, it hurts like fuckin' hell gettin' shot. But when you're dyin' on a TV cop show, you have to go quietly. Macho death. Screamin' like that, it feels good to finally let it out."

Everyone laughed. And Dominic didn't seem to resent the poke at his own show.

I looked back at Carmen, now perched on a tall stool. She seemed genuinely intrigued.

"This whole chasin', shootin' thin' on TV, it looks like that's all me an' my buddy ever did. But actually, we were having a very nice evenin' before that. Me and Gang Member Number One – we didn't have big enough parts to get real names – anyway, me and Number One, we were sittin' in a diner, talkin' about old times. Back in San Juan, every Saturday night we'd cruise the streets and pick up *señoritas*. Then we'd go down to the beach for a stroll."

I leaned towards Dominic: "I wrote this part."

"We were missin' the old days. So we decided to get a car and drive to the beach. It's a long way from Spanish Harlem to Coney Island! But the car we were drivin', we didn't own. Details, details."

Everyone laughed.

"And then . . . *this* happens."

He rewound the tape and replayed the shooting scene.

"My final moment, recorded forever. Fuckin' lame way to be remembered. But what more can you 'spec' from life when your name is Gang Member Number Two?"

He pressed rewind and play, rewind and play, showing the death scene over and over. His morbid obsession quickly became disturbing.

He paused at the point where the gang members were just starting down the alley still vibrant and alive.

"You know, I think I'm going to stop this thing right here."

Lights out. Another blood-curdling scream.

I imagined Ingrid in the back room following Ramir's lighting instructions scribbled on a napkin.

In the total darkness a recording of Ramir with an even-paced Native Canadian accent began to play. "If you would only allow us to reclaim our ancestors' territory, all of our problems would be resolved."

Then the garble of an old radio dial changing frequencies. Ramir's voice with a British Indian accent. "May I pour madam another cup of tea?"

Another garble to a jivin' ghetto dude: "Who be the first to kiss my black ass?"

Then a hyped-up lounge-act introduction: "Ladies and gentlemen, the many voices of Ramir Martinez!"

A blast of canned applause. The lights came back on. Ramir was beaming with joy, waving down the thunderous ovation. Then he created silence with his remote control.

"Good evening, my name is Ramir Martinez." He turned on a moment more of recorded applause. "To settle the debate about my actual ethnic origin, I want to inform you that I was born in Port of Spain, Trinidad, and my parents moved to Canada when I was five years old. I grew up in the charming suburban community of Mississauga, Ontario."

The monitor showed raw amateur video of a rundown, grey-brick townhouse.

"For two years, we lived in this spacious luxury townhome with my aunt and uncle who'd come to Canada the year before. Four adults and seven children in three bedrooms. Eleven people living on top of each other. Yes, we were a classic immigrant family. But we were very happy. On that back patio right there, that's where I first saw snow."

The video cut to Ramir's television début – playing a confused, abused teenager on *Night Heat*. He was crying as he was questioned in the back seat of a police car.

I breathed a sigh of relief. At least Ramir wasn't going to embarrass himself – or me – in front of Dominic Manno. This show really could earn him a leading role.

I looked back at Carmen. She was smiling.

I noticed that Naomi had pursed her lips in a way that might indicate she was mildly entertained.

The *Night Heat* segment ended with Ramir thrown in a jail cell. Back to home video. This time showing a suburban school yard.

Ramir narrated: "This is Tomken Road Senior Public School and this is the exact spot on the wall outside the cafeteria where kids surrounded me and called me a Paki. Even though I wasn't from Pakistan. I tried to explain this fact to them, but most of the kids didn't seem to care. My favourite TV program at the time was *Saturday Night Live* and my favourite band was Supertramp."

Next was a scene from some innocuous CBC television drama of Ramir playing a good Pakistani son at the family dinner table.

I wondered if Ramir had included all this video to make up for the fact that he'd written so little.

But Dominic was watching intently, totally absorbed.

Ramir was so confident, charismatic. Building his case for non-traditional casting without being preachy. I was genuinely proud of him.

He talked about his Buddhist philosophy of peace with the background of a gang fight from *Kickers*, his kick-boxing film masterpiece.

Another scream. Then amateur video of the Good Karma: A camera placed in a grocery cart was careening up and down the natural grain aisles. Ramir read from a corporate video script designed to motivate insurance sales people to higher productivity.

The hyped-up recorded announcer again: "Now ladies and gentlemen, a word from our sponsors."

The Mexican salsa commercial in which Ramir played a Frito Bandito. The department store commercial in which there's just a flash of him trying on jeans in a fitting room. Everyone roared. A public service announcement, which never actually aired, in which he talks about HIV and safe sex.

Then back to him live: "I've only actually had one screen kiss." He showed the clip. Awkwardly embracing a pretty Pakistani girl in another scene from the sensitive CBC drama.

Then on the screen flashed stills of famous (white) film couples kissing: Vivien Leigh and Clark Gable, Anne Bancroft and Mel Brooks, Julie Andrews and Christopher Plummer, Lucille Ball and Desi Arnaz.

During this sequence Ramir pulled on a trench coat and fedora. "They just don't make love scenes like they used to."

Ramir pointed his remote control and on the screen appeared a still close-up of Ingrid Bergman from *Casablanca*. Then his own taped voice echoed through the speakers doing a perfect impersonation of Humphrey Bogart. He was lip-synching the words, speaking to Ingrid Bergman on the screen: "*I didn't want to tell you this, Pandora. But I don't like keeping secrets from the woman I love.*"

For a moment I was confused. The words were familiar, but they were completely out of context.

A woman's voice: "*And I don't like it when my men keep secrets.*"

Then I recognized it. I remembered the script I'd left for Ramir to read. And I realized what was coming next.

I looked back at Carmen. She was frozen, her mouth open, her eyes wide.

I started waving my hands back and forth, hoping Ramir would notice, shaking my head violently, mouthing "No".

Ramir was oblivious as he followed the taped script. He was caressing the TV stand as if it were a woman he was seductively reassuring.

"*I work for the police, Pandora. I'm a cop. Undercover. I'm here doing an investigation of Nick Tornametti.*"

Dominic Manno turned to me in a harsh whisper: "What the hell is this?"

Ramir continued his Humphrey Bogart imitation, mouthing the deadly recorded words: "*I know you've got some sort of sick respect for him. But Nick Tornametti is a criminal and a murderer. Two years ago he killed a lawyer named Aaron Vogel."*

People in the room tittered. Clearly they all knew the reference was to Dominic Manno. Dominic sat motionless for a minute. Then suddenly he glared over his shoulder at the crowd – at all the media people who were supposed to respect him.

Dominic was breathing heavily.

The female voice said: *"He may not be a saint, but that doesn't make him a murderer."* The audience burst out in laughter.

Dominic's face had turned bright red. He pulled the small cylinder from his pocket and sprayed it into his mouth.

I whispered loudly to Ramir, "Turn it off!" He was stunned by my interruption. But he didn't react.

The tape went relentlessly on: *"Everybody in the business knows the rumour. Everybody believes it's true. Vogel was going to expose Nick's money-laundering scheme. That's why he was killed. But no one's been able to find the proof."*

Everyone was laughing. I looked back and saw Geoffrey Abrams, smirking in amazement. Carmen was paralyzed with horror.

Dominic sniped in my ear: "We made an agreement, Mitchell. And you broke it."

The tape went on: *"Aaron Vogel knew too much so Tornametti killed him. It can't be that hard for you to believe, Pandora. Tornametti is the scum of the earth."*

Dominic leapt to his feet. "Turn that mother-fucking thing off!"

Finally Ramir noticed. Startled, he stopped his lip-synching and took a step back.

Dominic picked up his chair in both hands and lunged for the video stand, lifting the chair above his head.

"I've had enough of this shit," Dominic screamed.

Just as the chair was about to strike, his jaw clenched, his body went rigid.

There was a united gasp from the crowd.

His face had turned a shocking dark purple.

He dropped the chair. And the full weight of his body crashed against the metal stand. In slow motion all of the equipment began to topple backwards – back towards Ingrid's mural.

From the back room Ingrid herself emerged, bewildered at what was going on.

With a roaring smash, the plaster wall burst open. Ingrid's painting disintegrated in a cloud of white powder.

There was an electronic crackle, an explosion of sparks and a gun-fire bang as the TV screen exploded.

Ramir stood frozen, his mouth gaping.

Dominic Manno had landed on the floor face-up, his arms still out-stretched. Shards of glass spread like a halo around his head. His black suit was coated in white dust.

There was a moment of shocked silence.

Then Frances Farmer rose to her feet with enthusiastic applause.

"Phone 911!" I called to Ingrid, and I rushed to kneel by Dominic's side. Naomi joined me, dazed, and Geoffrey Abrams – always the gentleman – moved in swiftly to perform CPR.

Carmen's voice barked across the room. "That's my father. Let me through, let me through!"

Carmen pushed past the rows of chairs. She lifted Naomi by the straps of her dress and shoved her out of the way, then knelt by her father's side.

"Daddy, it's me. It's Carmen. I'm here."

The crowd was murmuring. "Is he all right? Is he alive?"

Geoffrey felt Dominic's neck for a pulse. "I think he's still alive."

Dominic's face was pale now. His lips were moving, trying to speak.

"What is it, Daddy? What are you trying to say?"

Some final words of apology? To Carmen? To me?

"Nobody –"

"I'm listening, Daddy. Nobody what?"

"You're going to be okay, Mr. Manno."

A circle of people had gathered around us.

"Nobody," he said, gasping, "is going to laugh at me."

He clenched his teeth. His eyes rolled back.

His body relaxed.

Those were his last words?

Carmen choked on a moan. There was a flash of pain across

her face.

"Daddy?"

He was dead.

Carmen grabbed me by the shirt front.

"You killed him, Mitchell! He's dead because of you and your lousy fucking script."

I stood up and stepped back. Ramir whispered into my ear, "What's she talking about? Why'd she say you killed him?"

I pushed Ramir through the now-shouting crowd and into the back room.

"He had that heart attack because of us," I said.

"What are you talking about?"

"You stole all that stuff from my script."

"I just borrowed a few lines. I thought you'd think it was funny."

"You always pretend you're some big film-business insider. Haven't you ever heard about Dominic Manno being a murderer?"

"Of course."

"Then how could you say those things in front of him?"

"Your script was about Dominic Manno?"

"I didn't find out until this afternoon. But everybody else here seemed to know."

"They think I was talking about *Dominic Manno*?"

"He wanted to put you in a new TV show. And now he's dead."

Ramir's expression slackened in shock. And there were his parents, hovering at the door, looking like worried parents.

I left them together in the back room.

The paramedics were pushing their way in. They inspected Dominic and then lifted him onto a stretcher. Carmen was sobbing, clutching her father's hand, holding it to her cheek.

Ingrid was speechless, distraught, standing beside her shattered mural, watching the ambulance attendants at their work. Geoffrey stood pressed behind her, his hands protectively on her shoulders.

I didn't want to interrupt.

At the door Frances Farmer was showing people out like a hostess at her own party. She nodded cordially as the stretcher was carried past.

I followed the paramedics out onto the street and respectfully observed as Dominic was installed in the rear of the ambulance. Carmen clambered in beside him.

They slammed the doors. There wouldn't be any need for a siren.

Eruption had ended with a blast.

My hopes of seeing *Hell Hole* produced had exploded as well.

I leaned against the store window, feeling alone, deserted, exhausted.

And there was Ben at the curb, astride an ancient, gigantic motorcycle.

"We had a date tonight," he said.

I just looked at him. What could I say?

"I listened to the show from outside the door. I bet you're ready to get out of here."

I nodded.

I climbed on behind him – my first time on a motorbike. I held tight to his chest as we roared through back streets. Past houses with cozy lights in the windows. Through Kensington Market. Men laughing and shouting in front of a crowded Portuguese restaurant.

The warm night breeze felt like it was erasing everything that had happened.

I was glad we weren't able to talk.

I was too worn out to think.

We stopped in front of a sooty six-storey brick building – one of the block-long line of warehouses on Wellington Street. Ben pushed his bike into the grimy, powder-blue lobby. On one wall was a faded hand-painted sign for a company called Festive Brassieres.

He unlocked a door to a storage room and rolled his motorcycle inside.

It felt good to be somewhere unfamiliar. No one could find me here.

We stepped into a beaten-up elevator and Ben pressed the button for three. The floor shook and we began a slow rise.

"So finally I get to see The Vault," I said, trying to raise my enthusiasm.

"Before you do, there's one thing I want to mention."

"It's nothing bad, is it?"

"No."

"You're not secretly the real killer of Aaron Vogel, and you're bringing me back to your apartment to kill me because I know too much?"

"No," he said, smiling. "You remember when we went out after Ingrid's opening, you said you thought people who buy art are all boring and pretentious."

"I might have said anything, I was so screwed up that night."

"It's just that I didn't think that was a good time to tell you."

"Tell me what?"

The elevator rattled to a stop and opened to an anonymous-looking white-painted hallway.

"You never did ask me what I was doing there at the party."

I realized that I hadn't. "I just presumed you wanted to see the paintings."

"I did."

"So what *were* you doing there?"

"Geoffrey invited me."

"You know Geoffrey?"

"I'm one of his clients."

"This isn't something bizarre, is it? You're not secretly some multi-billionaire, are you?"

"I wish."

"Then what?"

"You'll see."

Ben unlocked a sliding metal fire door to reveal a long narrow loft. The walls were a calming navy blue. The few pieces of furniture were draped in white sheets. Hanging on the walls were huge rich-coloured modern paintings. A barbed-wire sculpture of a naked man stood in the centre of the room. Creativity everywhere.

My jaw actually dropped. Ben grinned and gently punched my chin back up into place.

"How can you afford all this?"

"When I want to make some extra money, I work for that computer place. None of them are old masters or anything. They're not that expensive."

"They're beautiful."

"They're what I like."

"Ben, I have to apologize for the other day – what I said."

"You were upset."

"That's no excuse. I shouldn't have talked to you like I did."

"It's okay."

"Just because I don't want the same things as you – I mean, I don't even know what I want anymore. You've probably got your priorities figured out better than I do."

"You'll figure it out."

"I've just gotten totally confused today."

"We'll talk about it, Mitchell. But first I want you to see the rest of the apartment."

"There's more?"

"There are a couple of pieces in particular I want you to see." He steered me off to the right.

"Remember that night, how much I liked Ingrid's work. Remember, there was somebody there who bought a couple of pieces anonymously."

The centrepiece of Ben's dark red bedroom was a king-size bed covered with a black duvet. And on the wall above his bed hung the three serene blue paintings that were Ingrid's favourites.

POSTSCRIPT

None other than Donna Karan is sitting at a banquette table over by the wall, and from what I can overhear, she and a young gentleman from her staff are having a thank-you lunch with two department store owners from Japan.

And at a table next to the rosewood bar, Johnny Depp is lunching with a frail, long-haired blonde who fawns over his every word. Even with those sunglasses I'd recognize him. Frankly, he's even better-looking in person. Though I must say – if I may allow myself to be judgmental of a major movie star – he looks a teensy bit tired.

As I type these words on my smart new laptop computer, I am sitting at a white tableclothed table for two in "44," the famous lobby restaurant of The Royalton Hotel.

For years I've read about this place in *New York* magazine and I knew I had to stay here on this special trip. It's worth every cent of the $330 per night. Moody avant-garde interiors by Philippe Starck. A decadent Eurotrash guest roster, plus a regular parade of New York's publishing elite. It makes people-watching absolutely hypnotic.

I am drinking iced tea and, since I was half an hour early for my appointment, I ordered an appetizer to placate my severely handsome fashion-model waiter.

I am nibbling on a wilted spinach salad which, despite its name, is delicious.

Johnny Depp laughs very loudly. I seem to recall reading somewhere that it was in this very restaurant that Johnny once had a yelling match with his former girlfriend, Kate Moss. Now he's leaning towards his new companion, and with his thumb he wipes a dribble of wine from her lower lip. Only Johnny Depp could get away with ruining a woman's lipstick in public.

So here I sit, awaiting my first meeting with a woman who may (or may not) change my life. And this seems like the perfect time to add a coda to my tale. There's so much to tell. So much has happened – to so many people – since that cataclysmic night nearly six months ago.

Where to begin?

Perhaps best at the end.

Dominic Manno. Pronounced dead on arrival at the hospital. Apparently he'd been plagued by heart problems for years. So my initial fears of a murder charge were quickly laid to rest.

The newspapers the next day were filled with obituaries. He was at once celebrated for his career as Dominic Manno, internationally successful television producer, and reviled for his past as Nick Tornametti, notorious mobster and developer of minimalls in Arizona. The stories dredged up the twenty-year-old murder investigation and the rumours of his involvement. But they added no more hard facts about his history than I'd been able to find out myself.

It was strange to read all this casual gossip – libel that Dominic Manno would never have let pass unchallenged had he been alive. But in the end, defending the fragility of his power was the very thing that killed him.

I sound like a cheap 1940s detective movie.

But he still haunts me. Almost every day I get a flashback of that scene on the terrace. His advice to me on fame. His thoughts on the substance of power. Had he lived, I wonder what kind of role he would have played in my life.

A few weeks after Dominic's death, the papers were filled once again with stories about Manno Productions. This time with the announcement that Dominic's beloved son and protégé, Leonardo Manno, would be taking over. His first new project would be a TV drama series called *Red Light Blues* – revolving around pretty teen prostitutes struggling to reform their lives.

Carrying on the family tradition of art that ennobles.

For a while I wondered if I'd hear from Leo. I wondered if he'd hold me responsible for his father's death, the way Carmen had. Would he issue some old-fashioned Mafia vendetta? *A Time for Revenge?*

Fortunately, I haven't heard from him since.

The day of Dominic's funeral I sent flowers to Carmen's apartment, along with a note offering my condolences and a very sincere apology. That night I found the flowers pitched on the sidewalk in front of my building.

Looking back at my first meeting with Carmen, it's like a far-away dream. How quickly I'd been caught up. How unquestioning and willing I'd been. The pedestal on which I'd been so eager to place this sad fucked-up woman – the rich L.A. jet-setter.

In retrospect our relationship seems mutually parasitic. Two desperate wanna-bes. By hiring me she'd made us both feel legitimate.

When I look at the script now, with the cold objectivity of distance, I can read my desperation in every word. Desperate to please Carmen, to please my friends, to please Jodie Foster.

Out of the blue last month I got a message on my answering machine from Carmen:

"Voice from the past! Things have been going really well for me out here. And I've got a new project. I'm making a movie of my father's life. Sort of a tribute. The good, the bad. The whole thing. And looking back at everything, Mitchell, I realize that we worked together really well. So I want you to write it. It's the real thing this time. Serious interest from a major studio. It's going to be really great. So call me as soon as you can. *Ciao* for now."

I wrote down her Los Angeles phone number. And then I crumpled up the note and threw it away. *Ciao.*

In fact, I'd already heard from another L.A. production company.

Though Dominic Manno may have been a criminal and a murderer, he was also a man of his word. Apparently, the very afternoon of our meeting at Carmen's apartment, he had shipped off *Hell Hole* to his producer friends in Hollywood.

With all that had transpired I'd given up on that part of our bargain. But a few weeks later, after the dust had settled (both literally and figuratively), I received a phone call from a gentleman named Peter Bertolini of Lamott Productions. He gushed with praise. Apparently his script readers had pronounced my humble little horror film "a cathartic work of modern art with great profit potential." And they bought an option to produce it for $50,000. (This was in addition to Dominic's $10,000 – which they didn't seem to know anything about, and I didn't see why I should tell them.)

It was quite a moment. My name actually appeared in *Variety*. That blurb was blown up and framed on my bathroom wall by sundown. Even my parents were impressed.

But I haven't heard a word from the producers since. Maybe they've forgotten all about my screenplay.

Johnny Depp is now standing at Donna Karan's table – helping her charm her distinguished Japanese customers. She and Johnny seem to know each other. Or perhaps it's just that old game in which all celebrities pretend to be lifelong chums – just to make the rest of us believe they inhabit a special, separate universe, a place where everything is connected and everything turns out perfectly.

Where was I?

Ramir's show. Of course, with all the fuss around Dominic Manno's death *Eruption* also made the front page of the papers. And my name was mentioned as well – as more details came out about the scintillating dialogue which had provoked Dominic's heart attack.

More clippings for my scrapbook.

Eruption only had that single performance. Partially because to stage it again *without* the scene from my script would make it incomplete, and to perform it again *with* the scene would be grotesque. But the invitation-only audience that night gave it a special cachet, and *Eruption* immediately became an infamous event in Toronto theatre history. As a result, Ramir Martinez has become a very popular actor-about-town. Which was the whole point of the show after all.

Ramir's still dating at a furious pace. And finally, I'm not jealous.

But we've heard some interesting news about Fred – my once-and-forever Montgomery Clift, and the man who broke Ramir's heart. After a fortuitous meeting at a film festival party, Fred is now dating David Geffen.

"Isn't she here yet?"

"Any minute now."

"You left your key in the room." Ben set it on the table. "I'm on my way to the Guggenheim. You're still not nervous?"

"No, I'm great."

"Totally jaded and blasé."

"That's me."

"I'll be back around three-thirty."

"Before you leave, make sure you use the washroom in the lobby."

"Did a cute guy just go in?"

"You can wait for Johnny Depp."

"Shit, that's really him?"

"Uh-huh. But you have to use the washroom because the urinal is famous. You pee against a stainless-steel wall and suddenly it turns into a waterfall. Sophisticated men from all over the world discuss peeing at The Royalton. It's like a postmodern male-bonding ritual."

"Sounds exciting. Good luck with the meeting."

As may be gathered, Ben and I are still seeing each other. I'm more amazed than anyone. I've gone through occasional panic attacks when I feared that our relationship wasn't romantic enough, or passionate enough, or glamorous enough. But I've managed to be mature enough to stick with it.

On our one-month anniversary we went to the clinic together and had fresh HIV tests. Ben convinced me that dealing with reality might be good for my long-term health. I suffered through a sleepless two weeks. But – cliché-happy-ending as it sounds – I am virus-free.

Perhaps there's a connection, but I haven't written a line of pornography since that last story I wrote about Ben. Which we now re-enact in faithful detail on a weekly basis.

Every once in a while Ben talks about the possibility of me moving into The Vault. But for some reason I am now quite content in my humble apartment.

Tomorrow Ben and I are going on a morbid sightseeing trip to the financial district to find the office building and parking garage where Aaron Vogel was kidnapped and murdered. I want to find out how accurate that psychic dream of mine actually was.

And Ben wants to visit some galleries in SoHo. He's still collecting paintings. But he always claims that his favourites are Ingrid's because they helped him to meet me.

I always slap him for being sentimental.

Ingrid.

She was rendered catatonic in those first few moments after Dominic Manno's crashing demise. But Geoffrey stood by her side while they waited for everyone to leave. Then they simply locked the door and walked back to Geoffrey's house a few blocks away.

On his massive black leather sofa, Geoffrey soothed her with a snifter of cognac. Ingrid literally cried on his shoulder. She squeezed his muscular arm and rested a delicate hand on his powerful thigh. She kissed his cheek with a gentle thank-you and let her face linger near his. She pulled out all her feminine wiles.

And nothing happened.

Geoffrey remains as elusive as ever. But since then he's launched three other new artists: in a hardware store, a Grade 2 classroom and a public swimming pool.

On Sunday morning Ingrid and Madonna came into the store and cleaned up. Everything back to normal. Ingrid opened as usual on Monday morning, expecting to carry on comfortably working at The Daily Grind for another year.

But there was more trauma to come. At nine a.m., Victor Fellner phoned from Florida to announce that he'd sold the store to a new coffee chain from Seattle. He gave Ingrid one month's notice and bought out the rest of her year's contract.

The Daily Grind closed at the beginning of August.

The end of an era.

I've never felt comfortable entering its new incarnation.

It was a wild surprise the day that Frances Farmer was featured in a giant colour photograph in *The Star* – with an accompanying article on Toronto's favourite streetpeople.

Some dogged reporter had uncovered the fact that Frances Farmer's real name was Estelle Blythe, and that she had actually been a Broadway chorus girl and character actress.

So she didn't have delusions of grandeur after all.

Last week, for the first time since the store closed, I saw her in the window of the Future Bakery. She was wearing a floppy-brimmed hat *à la* Greta Garbo. Excited to see her again, I knocked on the glass and vigorously waved hello. But she didn't choose to acknowledge me.

I carried on walking home.

Business stays steady at the Little Buda. Just before I came to New York, the three of us gathered there for one of our traditional dinners.

As usual, Ing and I arrived first and we placed our standard order for schnitzel. Ingrid spread the table with a map of Paris and a stack of travel guides.

"I'm staying at the Hotel LeDuc for the first week – which is right here." She landed her finger somewhere in Montmartre. "Two stars, so it's probably a dump."

"You know I'm going to be miserable without you," I said.

"It's only five months. The money from Victor and the paintings should hold out that long."

"Paris in January. Isn't there a song about that?"

"'I love Paris in the winter.' Anyway, that's the only time the school had an opening."

"Did you get hold of your ex yet?"

She shook her head and smiled softly. "I decided I'm not going to tell Pierre I'm there. Going to Paris was my dream, too. He doesn't own the whole city."

"What if you run into him?"

She shrugged. "I've been waiting nearly a year for a man decent enough to date. I'm not going to rush back to him. By the way, I phoned Geoffrey today and told him what I'm doing."

"What did he say?"

"He thinks the school's really good. But he warned me not to let them 'alter my inner vision'. And he promised I could have a show in his main gallery next summer."

"The Big Time."

Just then Ramir rushed in, looking fabulous in a brand-new Versace leather jacket. He's just about to begin production on a new science-fiction TV series, *Station Centauri*. High quality. Big budget. And his name will be the third from the top in the credits.

He kissed us both with dramatic panache.

"Sorry I'm late. We did our first make-up tests to see how we'd look. It took longer than I expected."

Ramir pulled a Polaroid photograph out of his jacket pocket and set it on the table.

Ingrid and I stared.

"That's you?"

"I play an alien."

"I know. But – is your whole face covered with that brown rubber stuff?"

"That's my nose. And that's my mouth."

"And those are his ears."

"Actually those are fake."

"Oh."

"Well, at least you won't have to worry about getting mobbed by groupies."

"I can concentrate on the subtleties of my performance."

"And, of course, it's the artistry that matters most," I said, dripping with sincerity.

Ramir nodded in agreement. "Of course."

The giant schnitzels arrived.

We raised our glasses of raspberry soda and I proposed a toast. "No matter how rich, famous and glamorous we become, may we always remember the simple pleasures of good friends and big schnitzel."

I have now finished my plate of wilted spinach salad.

And the waiter just brought me a message from Lauren Lembeck. She's going to be another ten minutes late, but she apologizes and says I should have another drink on her. Now that's class. The considerate professionalism you'd expect from a top New York literary agent.

Yes, I wrote a book. In fact, it's the very thing you're holding in your hands.

The money from *Hell Hole* has enabled me live quite comfortably without the need for office temping. (It also financed my new computer and my luxury room here at The Royalton.) I spent three intense months pruning and polishing my diaries into the shape of a novel.

Naturally, I changed all the names to protect the innocent – and to save myself from lawsuits. Though frankly, I'm not revealing anything here that hasn't been written up elsewhere. And anyone who's read the papers in the past year will be able to guess exactly who I've been talking about.

I must say that those three months I spent writing were a truly beneficial learning experience. Doing it for *me*, creativity for creativity's sake, the thrilling satisfaction of self-expression. All those clichés felt real.

Finally I bundled off the pages to a small Canadian publisher. My *magnum opus* was described as "quirky" and "unlikely". But they decided to publish it nevertheless.

And here I am, about to discuss the book with my New York agent. She says she's already found interest from a few U.S. publishing houses. There's even a film company that wants to turn it into a major motion picture.

Donna Karan just got up from her table in a whirl of handshakes and bows. As she passed, I called out, "Bye for now, Donna," and she smiled and nodded at me as if she thought we were old friends.

There's some kind of lesson in that.

I think I'll turn off my computer now and sit quietly for a few minutes. Relax. Soak in the atmosphere. Enjoy myself a while.

Lauren shouldn't be much longer.

Photo: Peter H. Stranks

Warren Dunford has worked as a freelance copywriter in
Toronto for thirteen years. This is his first novel.